Designing Stella

Designing Stella

Margaret P. Cunningham

Black Lyon Publishing, LLC

DESIGNING STELLA

Copyright © 2014 by Margaret P. Cunningham

Our books may be ordered through your local bookstore or by
visiting the publisher:

www.BlackLyonPublishing.com

Black Lyon Publishing, LLC
PO Box 567
Baker City, OR 97814

This is a work of fiction. All of the characters, names, events,
organizations and conversations in this novel are either the products
of the author's vivid imagination or are used in a fictitious way for the
purposes of this story.

ISBN-10:   1-934912-67-0
ISBN-13:   978-1-934912-67-6
Library of Congress Control Number: 2014938395

Published and printed in the United States of America.

Black Lyon Contemporary Romance

For Emma.

1.

Shirking the Burka

"Kid, you give them what they didn't know they wanted," Gris told her. "That's the key to your success."

Proud words from mentor to protégé. For over a decade, Brian Grissom and Stella Gray shared the title of partner in the D.C. interior design firm of Grissom & Gray. Yet Gris remained the doting grandfather figure to his gorgeous, gifted, endearingly flawed understudy. Stella, known for blending southern sensibilities with uptown flair, remained "the talented kid from Alabama."

Stella isn't easily forgotten—by men or women. She is naturally slender with auburn hair and lush, mink-brown eyes. Her smile is slightly, disarmingly crooked, but due to its ease and sincerity, it is beyond pretty. According to her mother, Tutta Gray, Stella also possesses pretty feet and great eyebrows.

It is Stella's demeanor that sets her apart, however. In spite of her good looks she's remarkably unassuming. And refreshingly citified, retaining the warmth of her home town down south—a place where folks prefer hugs to handshakes. As Stella charmed one intimidating client after another, Brian Grissom remarked, "You haven't lost the magnolia, kiddo!"

Gris often wondered if Stella's indifference to her physical attributes was a consequence of the facial scars (and their psychological counterparts), though the blemishes—now mere shadows of their former fierceness—are barely noticeable. Even Stella has learned to look past them.

Who looks back at you from your mirror? Gris was tempted to ask his partner. But he never got around to it.

The basis for his quandary was that Stella's affable layer of unflappability was ... well, it was what Gris thought of as outerwear, like some lovely cashmere sweater that Stella had donned somewhere along the line. It felt so right and looked so good that she'd never taken it off. Over the years Gris had enjoyed glimpses of another Stella beneath the protective outer layer. Vulnerability and insecurity nested there. He couldn't tell you which Stella he loved more.

The aforementioned traits—approachability as well as the trace of mystery—are what got their clients' attention. What kept them writing the big checks was Stella's ability to give them what they didn't know they wanted.

"But what is it that I don't know I want?"

Stella posed the question to a caricature of Gris hanging on a sliver of lacquered wall beside her. The charcoal drawing was long and lean—like the subject himself—and portrayed the old man with his signature cigarette and cocktail.

Gris's mentoring days were behind him, however. Due to a mercifully brief bout of pancreatic cancer, he was now enjoying a heavenly vodka tonic and celestial ciggy while replacing the pearly gates with something a bit more contemporary. That's how Stella envisioned her partner's afterlife, anyway.

The thought made her smile, and she relaxed a little on Gris's lemony linen banquette. Her banquette, now, she reminded herself. It was all hers now. With nary a Grissom relative in sight, Gris had left the kit and caboodle of his life - the firm, the fabulous Georgetown house in which she now sat and a sizable life insurance policy—to his beloved Stella.

"So you'll find some whiz kid to take over the boring stuff," Gris had said when Stella reminded him that she knew next to nothing about the business end of Grissom and Gray.

She was considering his suggestion when an associate of Gris's made her an offer for the firm along with the house in Georgetown, and she began to entertain one thing she hadn't known she wanted. Out. Her life was beginning to feel like one big burka! Still, she wondered if grief was clouding her judgment. So she made a stab at practicality and attempted to catalog the reasons like so many fabric samples:

A. The sour economy had an alarming number of their clients rethinking frivolous re-dos. This had led to …

B. Accepting as a client the sinister Gilberto de Campos (he paid Stella with a suitcase full of cash) who possessed the deadly combination of bad taste and obstinacy. She'd dealt with this personality type (sans the aura of criminality, of course) on occasion, but at this stage of her life, it was one more back-breaking straw.

C. Stella's mom, who retained the ability to influence her daughter's life from her back porch in the depths of Alabama, tossed the catnip of a new, solo project Stella's way. She reminded her daughter that her Granny's little house—a contentious subject between Stella's parents since Granny's death—was sitting empty and unloved in her hometown of Bayview.

"My childhood home is so neglected even the college students won't rent it," she'd sniffed into the iPhone Stella had given her for Christmas.

D. Stella's few close friends had married and/or had children and/or moved away from Washington. As of late, communication had dwindled to harried texts between office and carpools. Stella could hardly remember their voices!

While pondering the whopping ramifications of continuing on in Grissom & Gray without Gris versus leaving the world she'd known for the majority of her adult life, reason E. reared its ugly head.

Stella received a call from Andrew, her marriage-phobic, decade-younger (I know, she should've known better) lover of the past twelve years with the news that he'd gotten himself engaged to a Lufthansa flight attendant. By the time Anika had served him his third glass of cabernet, they had chosen names for their first two children. Yes, he actually told Stella this. But who can argue with love (or insanity) at first flight?

And what else can a girl do under such devastating circumstances but run home to mama? So as our story begins, Stella has accepted an offer—which was, after all, too good to refuse—to buy her out, rented her own lovely Arlington condominium to a couple of movers-and-shakers-to-be, and for better or worse, is heading to Bayview, Alabama, the land of magnolias, alligators and relatives.

2.

Friends in Need

"Stell, I can't believe you would turn your back on your career. Any woman would kill for it," said Helen.

Stella sighed. "Too many unhappy memories. I've got to take a break … maybe a permanent one."

"Won't you miss working the Gray magic?"

Helen was referring to a recent magazine article celebrating the life of Brian Grissom. It had also praised Grissom's partner. "Stella Gray's innovative use of color and texture is pure magic," it gushed.

"That was certainly nice to hear," Stella admitted. "But choosing color and fabric? That's the easy part."

"So what's the hard part? Working with demanding clients?"

"Not really. They should be demanding when they're paying the kind of fees we charged at Grissom & Gray. Keeping it fresh is tough. Each project has to reflect the client's personality and at the same time give it the old Grissom & Gray flair. Otherwise every job looks the same."

Stella used complementary hues of the client's favored colors and always integrated their favorite pieces into her designs. (This presented a challenge when these beloved items consisted of a daughter-in-law's bad art, the extensive figurine collection handed down for generations or that wine cask bought on a honeymoon in Belize.)

The client's things were then jazzed with pops of the

latest "in" color (think yellow, persimmon or pistachio), contemporary pieces and contemporary paintings. Stella loved using very large mirrors and groupings of architectural or unusual botanical prints.

"But yes, I'll miss the magical part. I won't miss last minute changes, mismatched dye lots, price increases and double and triple-checking every fabric order and measurement. I'm tired. And pretty much burned out. It's time to take a break."

"In that case, what you need is something to take your mind in a completely different direction."

Stella cradled the phone between chin and shoulder while piling soon-to-be-useless woolens on the bed. "Now why do I think you have something specific in mind?"

"Oh, forget I said anything. You're probably waaay too busy with the move and everything."

Stella rolled her eyes but had to smile. Helen was one of those friends unparalleled in crisis handling. Not only was she a godsend to the newly dumped, but when not managing Bayview Botanical Gardens, she could be found soothing hysterical children, resurrecting fallen soufflés or resuscitating deadly dull parties. She'd even performed CPR in the middle of a garden soiree.

She could almost make you believe she didn't see the ugliness boiling out of your skin, thought Stella, remembering their teen years when the older, very popular Helen Dudley had befriended Stella.

Anyway, you know the type. If you're lucky. No one has all the answers, however and Helen was no exception. There was one plus-sized area that she could not get a handle on—her weight. Helen Dudley had maintained a healthy 125 pounds until her mid-thirties. That's when her love affair with carbs and distain for exercise caught up with her. She disguised the extra pounds with voluminous tops—usually something turquoisey to set off her own sea blue eyes and fabulous silver hair. And really, this achieved the desired effect. She was so pretty that you almost didn't notice that she was seriously overweight. But Stella knew how it bothered her.

Experimentation with dozens of weight loss gimmicks (except a balanced diet and exercise) had become an addiction in itself. In spite of this, Helen was losing a decades-long battle with the bulge. As her cousin, Marilee put it, Helen was a serial Diet of the Month Club drop-out. Helen, in an attempt to make light of these dietary downturns, employed an endless supply of self-deprecating jokes about her figure, food intake, clothes size, etc.

Stella turned her attention back to the conversation at hand and asked, "Too busy for what?"

"Well," said Helen, "Too busy to get involved with our favorite entrepreneur. I'm afraid she's had another setback."

"Marilee? What happened to the real estate career?"

"I'll let her tell you. It's quite a story."

Helen's cousin and Stella's oldest friend, Marilee, was every southern mama's dream daughter. A petite, book-smart, blonde beauty, she'd been the belle of every ball, yet maintained the sweetest of dispositions. And all without pharmaceuticals. She had married well, had a lovely family and the sense to appreciate her good fortune. The only fly in this pie of perfection was Marilee's misguided determination to achieve success in the business world. I say misguided because in spite of Helen's assertion that Marilee could sell dope to the Pope, one endeavor after another had failed — quite spectacularly in some cases.

These ventures were financed by Marilee's husband, Jack, who adored his wife and could well afford the losses. Stella suspected that guilt also played a part in his over-indulgence. He and their two college-aged boys were obsessively sporty, spending scads on everything from boats to box seats at sporting events. Marilee, whose tastes leaned more to flower shows and the ballet, was left alone quite a bit.

"Anyway," Helen continued. "It's the first time I've seen Marilee so glum about one of her failures … even though she's already into something new."

"What now?"

"According to her, with these depressed times, increasingly casual dress codes and global warming, what the world needs is dressy T-shirt dresses."

"You're kidding."

"Nope. And what Marilee needs is a business partner."

"No way. As much as I love her, I'm not going into business with Marilee."

"I know what you're thinking. But the dresses are great. And comfortable. I'm wearing one right now—even the extra-large size is cute, believe it or not. Marilee has them in all the boutiques around here, and I swear they're selling like tassels at a stripper convention. That's the good news."

"And the bad news?"

"It's growing so fast she can't keep up. She needs help."

"Ohhh, no."

"She is family."

"Your family."

"Right." Helen sighed. "I just hate to see her fail again so soon. And once you get Granny's house going, you're going to be looking for something to do."

"Well, that's true …"

"I'm sending you some pictures of the dresses. Just take a look."

This was vintage Helen—two friends in need, one solution.

When the heavy sweaters had been boxed and labeled, Stella fixed herself a bowl of chocolate chip ice cream and fired up the laptop. Photos of Marilee modeling her creations filled the screen.

"Good grief," Stella moaned through a mouthful of ice cream. "They really are cute."

The dresses were made from what seemed to be two tee shirts sewn together. Shrimp, crab and fish shapes cut from high-end fabric were appliqued on the front. Sequins and pearls ornamented the creatures and finished off mesmerizing underwater scenes. It was garish, but good; just short of tacky, but fun.

Like wearing art, thought Stella.

Closing the laptop, she realized that an entire half-hour had passed without her thinking of sweet, wonderful Gris or Andrew the wayward lover or even Anika, Stella's Swedish replacement (and a safe bet for queen of the mile high club).

3.

Hello, Dixie

By the time Stella's SUV pulled into her granny's crumbling driveway, she had run through every pro and con of a business partnership with Marilee. There were lots of cons. But Helen was right. She would need something creative to occupy herself. And it could be fun.

How long has it been since I've done something solely for the fun of it?

Stella decided to actually consider it.

She eased herself out of the car and into humid air at number two Whimsy Court. *Lord, it's hot*, she thought, brushing waves of auburn hair from her face and turning toward the hint of a breeze. Though she'd been home a mere six months prior, it had been a couple of years since she'd been back to her grandmother's house on the corner of LeMoyne Avenue and Whimsy Court. She shook her head at the change and rightly blamed her daddy for the deplorable condition of the place.

Stella's father, Bo Gray, was above all, a practical man—practical to a fault some men and all women would agree. He'd actually suggested selling the house while traveling with his wife, Tutta, from Granny's service at St. James Church to the cemetery. Tutta had answered him with the stink eye and not spoken to him for two days, and then it was to inform him that she would never sell "her historically significant, childhood home."

Bo's typically passive-aggressive response was to act as if number two Whimsy Court didn't exist. And he wasn't about to sink money into anything that didn't exist.

When questioned about this parental impasse, Tutta's response was, "What is my wound is my salve."

This was said with a sniff and a shrug. Stella and her sisters agreed that their mother didn't wear melodrama well, and knew that once it got started, it was impossible to deactivate.

They'd dropped the subject like a hot biscuit.

Approaching Bo Gray with a plea for rationality was also futile. Their father's obstinacy was renowned and could not be overcome—even by Stella, who was his favorite. And so, once again, everyone let the matter drop.

Stella looked at the house. Really looked at it. Slate shingles were missing from its pitched roof, faded paint curled along the eaves and ivy grew into cracked panes in the mullioned bay window. Stella's gaze followed a slate path that meandered from the sidewalk across the lawn to a small front porch. From there, the walkway wove its way around the ragged front beds and down the side of the house continuing through happily neglected hydrangeas. It ended just beyond a rattling, rusted air-conditioner hanging on for dear life in the dining room window. The AC dripped into a weedy mint bed below, releasing scent into the air.

Along the rest of the street sat the other twelve Whimsies with their steeply angled roofs, herringbone brickwork and high chimneys. Each had a small, recessed front porch. Shallow but lush front yards flowed into one another and followed the gentle curve of the street. Century-old palms and oaks heavy with Spanish moss filtered sunlight everywhere, giving the scene a deceptively cool appearance. It was both a relief and an embarrassment to see that the other homes and their gardens were well-tended. But then Stella remembered that the residents of Whimsy Court took the stewardship of their street and its history quite seriously.

A century or so earlier, an English architect named Archibald Green found himself in south Alabama. He made the acquaintance of a young debutante named Lydia LeMoyne and fell in love. Though he missed his homeland, the lovely Lydia and suitable climate turned Archie's head. He decided to make Bayview his home.

He bought a piece of land shaded by oaks and high enough to catch bay breezes. To assuage his nostalgia, he named it Whimsy Court and began building the Tudors—thirteen in all—thereby bringing a lasting touch of merry, old England to Bayview, Alabama.

Stella looked back at her own little piece of Whimsy, determined to honor Archibald and her granny by restoring it to its former loveliness.

She approached the porch and found the house key where her mother had left it—stashed in a fake rock that couldn't fool a two year-old burglar. It was at this moment that a man came jogging around the corner. He was tall and athletic-looking. As a matter of fact, he looked like he'd jogged right out of an ad for athletic gear—especially shorts. As he approached, he smiled and waved. Stella caught a flash of white teeth and strong jaw beneath the baseball cap. She gave him her sweetest smile in return and fluttered her fingers at him. *What a cutie!* she thought as she turned toward her front door.

That's when the cutie gave a sharp whistle and called, "Hey, Babe!"

Her positive feelings for the man evaporated like a popped soap bubble. She whirled around, furious with herself that an adorable pair of manly legs could turn her head so soon after she'd sworn off the whole worthless gender.

"I seriously hope you are not addressing me," she said.

The man stared at her. He looked confused.

Stella pushed open the front door to her new home and peeked inside.

•

Outside, an English spaniel named Babe bounded up to her owner, sat on the sidewalk and followed her master's gaze to the front door of number two Whimsy.

"Don't worry," mumbled the man, "I'm not getting involved with another one of those." He shook his head as if to dislodge the woman from his brain. "C'mon, girl," he said, and he and Babe trotted off.

Yet the glimpse he'd had of Stella Gray stayed with him. A pretty, unaffected woman is what the man had seen at first glance, when Stella flashed the guileless smile and waved at

him like a kid eager to make a new friend. That was before she'd
shown him the uptight, all-men-are-after-me attitude inherent
to good-looking members of that unfathomable gender.

No, he wouldn't let himself be swayed by that type again.
Look how much trouble it had gotten him into already.

•

As Stella entered her front door, she expected to be
assaulted by the odor of must and dust. But it was the smell
of her mother's house—Windex, Murphy's oil soap and fresh
flowers—that greeted her.

"Surprise!"

An assortment of friends and relatives, and a few strangers
stood or sat in lawn chairs in the empty living and dining
rooms. A card table covered with Granny's good linen cloth
held assorted munchies surrounding a silver trumpet vase of
Tropicana roses. An ice chest sat on the floor barely concealed
by Granny's tablecloth. Next to this lay her father's two golden
retrievers, Sunny and Dixie. A *Welcome Home!* banner stretched
across the arched opening to the dining room. Her parents,
Bo and Tutta Gray beamed at their eldest daughter before
smothering her with parental affection.

"The roses are from Helen and Marilee," said Tutta. "They
said to call when you're settled. And your sisters couldn't get
away, of course. But they'll catch up with you tomorrow."

The little group of well-wishers meandered through the
house and yard while inhaling chicken salad sandwiches,
swigging soft drinks and assuring Stella how glad they were
to have her back where she belonged. There were plenty of
raised eyebrows and low whistles at the amount of work to
be done. But, yep, they knew if anyone could pull it off, it was
their talented Stella. They hung around until Tutta's renowned
shrimp dip was gone, which took a little over an hour. Then
they began looking at their watches and heading for the door.

Tutta turned to her daughter. "Wasn't it good to see
everyone?" she asked. "Your daddy and I are picking up the
carpool for Alice, so we need to run. I've got your room at
home all ready for you. The key is hidden under the fern if you
get there before us."

Her dad, a pock-marked bear of a man, kissed his daughter's

cheek as if it were a newborn's. His eyes narrowed as he said, "Sorry about Gris and that son-of-a—"

"Now, Bo ..." Tutta interrupted.

Bo Gray got that "you're not the boss of me look" on his face and added, "I never could understand how a man could sit through a whole football game with his legs crossed."

"We don't want to hear about all that," said Tutta.

Bo ignored his wife, but said to Stella, "Well, sorry about Andrew. But I sure am glad to have you home."

"Thanks, Daddy. I've missed you, too."

Tutta and Bo gathered up the party fixings in a matter of minutes, and left. Then it was just Stella and the hum of the air-conditioner and the dust motes floating in shards of sunlight coming through the mullioned windows. Stella felt every one of the thousand miles separating granny's living room from Washington, D.C.

Outside a dog barked twice. The impertinent stranger with the approachable grin (that had held no suggestion of a leer, after all) popped into her brain. Then there was that shadow of confusion (and an innocent confusion, at that) supplanting the smile when she had called him out. Had she misunderstood the tacky come-on, the *Hey, Babe?*

No, she definitely had not. But what should have been a minor disappointment had her feeling gloomy and ... isolated. Attributing this to fatigue and the enormity of having flipped her life upside down, she turned her attention back to the house.

So this is home, Stella thought, trying to decide how she felt about the idea.

She'd been mentally revamping her mama's childhood home since first entertaining the idea of moving back to Bayview, so she had a pretty good idea of what needed to be done to ratchet the place up to Grissom & Gray standards. She walked the rooms several more times, mentally moving walls, placing furniture and hanging art.

As was her routine, Stella would draw up preliminary sketches for number two Whimsy. These would be turned over to an architect and/or draftsman who would come up with the final drawings. Per the Brian Grissom process, each room would eventually have its own "plan board" to which fabric samples and paint chips would be attached. The plan boards weren't really necessary for a personal project, but it was her habit. And it reminded her of Gris.

She remembered him looking over her shoulder once she'd compiled her project boards.

"All this powder room needs is a dash of fuchsia," he might say, or, "When in doubt, go bold. Whadaya say we silver the mantle and hang that lime patent leather mirror over it?" But generally it was, "You've done it again, kiddo! How about I fix us a toddy to celebrate?"

She could almost feel Gris walking beside her as she made a final tour of the house.

The four bedrooms were small, the closets and baths tiny, the kitchen cavernous. The living and dining rooms were the same size—too small for a living room and too large for a dining room. The iron railing on the stairs was wobbly, the pine floors a mess.

But the ceilings were high. There was lovely molding everywhere. And those arched doorways and the bay window curving out into the garden? Fabulous! Stella headed outside. The slate walkway that flowed around the house spilled into a patio off the kitchen. The yard seemed smaller than Stella remembered—possibly because everything from palms to camellias to honeysuckle fought for space and sun. Along the LeMoyne Street side, limbs from one of the original moss-draped Whimsy oaks shaded a high brick wall fringed with a hedge of sasanquas. A wooden fence softened by a nice row of variegated pittosporum ran down the other side making the garden private and cozy.

"Ma'am, ith there any more thrimp dip?"

Stella gave a tiny shriek and turned to find a red-headed boy four or five years-old standing in the kitchen door. He wore faded shorts and a pair of Harry Potter glasses. No shirt. No shoes. No front teeth. He held a half-empty coke bottle in one hand and a chicken finger in the other.

Good Lord, somebody left one of their kids!

But his skinny chest and direct gaze softened something in Stella. She smiled and said, "Uh, no, I'm afraid the shrimp dip's all gone."

"Thorry to hear that."

He walked past her, across the driveway to the far side of the yard where he turned and said, "Nithe party. God bleth you, thither," before disappearing into the pittosporum.

God bless you, sister? Odd farewell for a four-year-old. Sweet. But definitely odd.

Worried that she was hallucinating in the Alabama heat, Stella crossed over to the hedge to investigate. Behind the bushes there was a good-sized hole in the fence. She squatted down and peeked through.

A tall black woman in tight jeans and a tank top stood facing the child with her fists on her hips.

"Boy, where you been?"

"To a party."

"Well, I ain't seen no invitation."

"Me neither."

The woman smiled at the boy. A gold frame around one of her front teeth glinted in the sun.

"Don't be slipping off without telling Kitty. You hear me, Elliot? I don't want to have to tell your daddy."

"Tell him what?"

It was the cute—no, make that adorable—jogging man!

He had changed into a golf shirt and khaki pants. The hat was gone. His brown hair was streaked with gray, curling around the tops of his ears, damp from the shower. Now that Stella could see his face, she supposed him to be about her age. He walked over to the boy and ruffled his hair.

"Hey, buddy. What's this about a party?" His voice was a comfortable, southern rumble.

"Yeth, thir," said Elliot. "I went to a party."

"Crashed a party," said the black woman.

"What's going on?" Another female voice, very southern.

"Hey, Mommy," said the boy.

Ms. Jogging Man—her husband's female counterpart—came into view. Attired in a suit sans jacket, she looked like a Mississippi beauty queen. In other words, perfection on a stick. (If pageants aren't your thing, you might not be aware that, for some unknown reason, the state of Mississippi produces the most beautiful girls in the country, most of whom are statuesque brunettes with dazzling, dimpled smiles.)

Ms. Jogging Man was tall, of course. Endless dark waves of lustrous, mahogany hair. Light eyes catching the sun. Teeth like a breath mint commercial. Dimples so deep she didn't have to smile to showcase them. And her figure? I'm sure you've heard the expression, brick house.

"Sorry I'm late, Kitty," she said. "I was held up in court ... the Vega trial."

Court? She's a lawyer? Gorgeous and brainy?

"Mommy, I went to a party with a nithe lady and thrimp dip!"

Stella was not the envious type, but the whole too-good-to-be-true scene was a bit much for someone who'd recently lost her lover to a knock-out blonde flight attendant, so she decided to stop punishing herself, crept back across the driveway and slipped into the house. She locked up, placed the key back in the fake rock and sighed. Because after all this time and all her big dreams, she was headed back to her parents' house on Pine Street. Right where she'd started forty-six years ago.

4.

Impressions

Thanks to the long drive and her mother's cooking (fried speckled trout, jalapeño grits and a green salad brimming with feta and avocado followed by Tutta's renowned banana pudding made with fresh whipped cream), Stella slept like the proverbial log. When she awoke at dawn, she felt like a log. Resisting the urge to sleep another hour or three, she dug out her running shoes, determined to run off the calories. She was aware that the image of her shapely neighbor had something to do with this. But hey, whatever gets you going.

Stella kept a slow but steady pace down Pine Street and took a left onto Dauphine where the town's oldest, prettiest neighborhood lay beneath oaks and palms twisted by storm after storm after storm. Generations of Bayview's finest, from the city founders to present day leaders of the community had grown up behind the storied facades of the Dauphine Street homes with their imposing columns, wide porches and clipped hedges.

As Stella passed Marilee's childhood home, she imagined Marilee's brother and his wife who now resided there, waking their children. The girls would slip out of expensive PJs into private school uniforms, rush through breakfasts in a magazine-worthy kitchen and join their carpools. It wasn't difficult to imagine since Stella and Helen had spent many a night in that house.

She glanced up into the oak next door and had to laugh. They had all three had a crush on Martin "Passion Pit" Putnam, the teen heart-throb who lived there. To get his attention, the girls had rolled that very oak tree with twenty rolls of toilet paper swiped from the Bayview Country Club's storage room. Passion Pit's dad had caught Stella in his headlights as she sailed a final roll into the tree's upper branches. Luckily, the senior Putnam had a sense of humor (augmented by several scotches at the club) and congratulated the rollers on a masterful job. As long as they were back by seven AM to clean it up, he said with a wink, their parents need never know.

Though it had taken most of their Saturday to clean it up, Stella was thrilled when Martin and his friends rolled Marilee's yard the next weekend. Unfortunately, the girls had to clean up Marilee's yard, too, since tattling on Martin would have been extremely uncool.

As Stella continued the jog down memory lane, her side began to pinch, and she slowed to a half-trot. Thoughts of first-crush Martin Putnam sprinted ahead to first-really-serious-relationship Andrew. But since she had followed Tutta's advice and "washed that man right out of her hair," she forced all thoughts of her philandering ex from her mind.

This vacancy was immediately filled with alternating images of her handsome (and married! she reminded herself) neighbor's face—first smiling then perplexed, then affectionately ruffling his son's hair. The images swept through her damaged psyche like spring breezes. She was still smiling as she approached Tutta's back door where the smell of frying bacon got her complete attention.

"I knew you'd be hungry with all that jogging," said Tutta.

"Thanks, Mom, but I can't keep eating like this."

"Why not? You could stand to gain a few pounds."

Stella listened to her mother (who was a size eight, never mind that if she wasn't cooking she was eating) and cleaned her plate of bacon, blueberry waffles (with homemade fig preserves, no less), omelet, coffee and juice.

"Delicious. But tomorrow, a protein shake."

"Protein shake it is." Tutta smiled at her daughter. "It's so good to have you home. What are you going to do today?"

Stella rattled off a list of relocation priorities. "Oh, and I'm meeting Helen and Marilee for lunch at the new place around the corner from Granny's … or I should say… my house. I'm giving them a tour of the place. By the way, is George Murphy still in the painting business?"

"Yes, and he's expecting your call along with Virginia Myerson's daughter, Katie. She's a wonderful architect—just graduated and needs the work. Oh, and call Eddie Edmonds, the contractor. He's your daddy's second cousin, you know, and he's worked with Katie and George. Besides being family, he's the best in town. But with this economy, he can hardly keep his people busy. Be home by six. Your sisters are coming to dinner."

Another big meal! I've got to get out of here, thought Stella, *or I won't be able to fit in my new house.*

Laughter and hugs filled the parking lot in front of what had been the Rebel Queen drive-in back in the day. It was now called the Lemoyne Locavore and Bodega, but was known to regulars simply as the Locavore. Inside, the hospital-green formica counter of Stella's youth had been transformed into a sleek bar of black granite. The walls were silvery with deco sconces everywhere. A jazzy playlist floated from unseen speakers. Several tables were sectioned off with burlap drapes, turning them into cozy cubicles for intimate candlelit suppers.

"I can't believe you're home for good!" squealed Marilee. "And I'm sooo excited that you're considering going into business with me!"

"Ohhh … uh, me, too," said Stella, trying to match her buddy's enthusiasm. "But I'm just thinking about it, remember. So what happened to the real estate thing?"

"I'll tell you the gory details later." Marilee made a face. "Not exactly dinner conversation."

"I can't wait," said Stella.

"You're gonna looove it," said Helen in a little sing-song voice.

As they entered the restaurant a dark green pick-up truck eased out of a parking space in front of Meacham's, the men's clothing store adjacent to the Locavore. The driver of the truck had only glimpsed the back of the tall woman with the shining auburn hair, but there was something … the way the woman moved and greeted her friends, arms outstretched, the tilt of her head … body language, he supposed you'd call it. Whatever it was, it gave him a good feeling, a desire to know what it was she was saying. Her voice, the words not quite distinguishable, floated over to his open window. It was warm and light… inviting. And familiar. As she went into the Locavore, he realized it was the woman he'd seen next door, the one who'd accused him of—what? Calling his dog? He shook his head as he reversed the truck then sat still as a stone for a moment before turning toward Whimsy Court.

When the women were seated, Marilee sighed. "It's just as well," she said. "That I'm out of real estate, I mean. Y'all know my first love is fashion." At this point she morphed into a one-woman commercial for her latest brainstorm. "And why not combine flair and style with comfort?" She stopped abruptly, smiling, eyes wide with excitement and expectation, the question dancing in the air. Finally, she continued. "And what, I ask you, is more comfortable than a T-shirt? Nothing! So that's when I came up with …" She paused again for maximum effect. "… dressy tees!

"I have a seamstress—a very sweet Hispanic woman named Shirley Esposito, and I have a possible rep. I found him on the internet. He reps some fabulous designers. But I need a partner or two," said Marilee.

"I don't have the time and don't care a thing about clothes," said Helen, "But Stella …"

"Let me think about it a little longer," said Stella. "I'll let you know in a few days.

"Okay," said Marilee as their server approached the table. "Let's order." She looked over the menu. "I'll have the squash soup and salad. Would someone like to split the sweet potato fries? It's a huge platter."

"Do I look like I share my food?" asked Helen.

Stella laughed. "I'll split the fries with you, Marilee." She turned to the server. "I'll have the soup also."

Helen ordered a burger along with the platter of fries, but made certain Stella and Marilee noticed that she asked for unsweetened tea. "This new diet I'm on doesn't allow a speck of sugar!" she said.

"So," said Marilee, turning to Stella and leaving the touchy subject of Helen's nutrition behind, "What do you think of all the improvements to your new neighborhood?"

"I love it! I can't believe I'm sitting in the old Rebel Queen. With the boutiques and the gourmet grocery and locally grown organics just a few blocks away … if I didn't know better, I'd think I was in California!"

"Wow, you are glad to be home," said Helen.

"I am. Very glad. And also about to explode from Mama's meals. I can use some light cooking."

Marilee shrugged. "Tutta lives to feed," she said and finished off her spinach salad.

"That she does," agreed Stella, grabbing the check. "My treat. I'll just pay this … a bargain compared to D.C. lunches, by the way, and we'll check out the new digs. But be prepared. It's pretty rough."

"Well, you weren't kidding," said Marilee when they'd made their way through the house. It's going to be quite a job!"

"By the way, I hear your neighbor has done amazing things with his house," said Helen.

"Really?" said Stella. "Which neighbor?"

"Why, as luck would have it, he's right next door. Number four."

"Oh, that's right," said Marilee. Her brow furrowed in concentration. "Let's see. His name is Sam. Sam Poole. He moved here a few years ago, I think. I've seen him at the Locavore. Drives a big, green pickup with one of those Wildlife Federation tags. He's one of those sweet, down-home types. And cute. Extreeemely cute."

As it turned out, Marilee had quite a bit of info on Sam Poole. He owned a commercial construction company, but with the crummy economy, wasn't doing much business. Fortunately, he also owned acres and acres of timber "up the country" and several saw mills. The income from the timber and the mills had enabled him to buy foreclosures in town, fix them up (which kept his employees employed) and rent them to all those ineligible or uninterested in obtaining home mortgages.

"The man owes his life to the southern pine," said Marilee.

Stella told them about meeting Elliot the day before. She also told them about his father's whistling and calling her babe. "I was embarrassed for him!"

"Oh, that reminds me...," said Helen, as they headed outside, "Marilee, you haven't told Stella about your little misadventure in the real estate game."

Marilee had taken a crash course in real estate and of course, gotten the highest score possible on the exam. She made her first sale shortly thereafter—a hundred-year-old raised cottage. The buyer? A bear of a guy who was a bit sweet on the lovely Marilee.

Being late for a hair color appointment, the novice realtor had rushed through the house's final check-through, making it to the salon with seconds to spare. Once her hair was in foils, she'd received an urgent call from the burly home owner. He had decided to use his new toilet, he told her.

"You really don't need my permission to do that," Marilee informed him, trying her darndest to be polite while not dislodging any of the foils in her hair. "You just go ahead and enjoy your new powder room."

"I'm on the damn commode," he snarled.

"Well, I can't imagine why you called to tell me this," said Marilee sweetly but firmly.

"Because I am sitting on the freaking commode under the freaking house."

"I don't underst—"

"The freaking commode fell through the freaking floor. I liked to kill myself, lady. You get over here right now, or I'm calling TV 5's citizen hotline. I don't think you or Bay Real Estate want this on the freaking six o'clock news."

"Except he didn't say 'freaking'," said Marilee. "You know I don't use the F-word."

Stella was laughing so hard she could hardly speak. Finally, she said, "How horrible! Did you go over there? Your hair looks great, so I'm guessing you didn't."

"Of course I didn't! I called my broker, who called 911. When they all got there, the guy had a few scratches and bruises and was still picking spiders out of his hair, but all that was really needed was a roll of TP."

"And a new toilet," giggled Helen.

"Well, that, too," said Marilee. "Anyway, the man threatened to sue, and I offered to turn in my license if he wouldn't, and he agreed, and that was the end of that."

"You have to admit it was a pretty traumatic experience," said Stella.

Marilee frowned and gave a shiver. "Tell me about it," she said. "For weeks, every time I closed my eyes I would see that man, sitting there under the house."

"I meant for him!" said Stella starting them laughing again.

It was then that Stella realized that there were three people laughing with Marilee. A masculine chuckle was coming from the direction of the pittosporum. Stella made a face and pointed toward the fence. It was the same spot that Elliot, the miniature party crasher, had disappeared into.

5.

Greasing the Grapevine

Marilee marched over to the opening and crouched down to peer through. "Are you Mr. Poole?" she called.

"Yes," he said. "Sorry." Another manly chuckle. "I couldn't help but hear. You must be my new neighbor."

"No, I'm Marilee. But I know Stella would just love to meet you. If you have a minute?"

"Well… uh, okay. I'll walk over. Let me put the dog inside." Stella heard a familiar whistle, then "C'mere, Babe. That's a good girl."

Marilee got that *omigod!* look on her face. Helen tried not to laugh and it came out anyway, like a snort. Seconds later the jogging cutie came around the fence and down the driveway.

"Sam Poole," he said, extending a hand first to Marilee who was looking from Sam to Stella with a weird, expectant expression on her face. He grinned at Marilee which amplified the man's handsome, somewhat rugged features. Laugh lines deepened, setting a twinkle in his hazel eyes. At once, his whole countenance was filled with a sense of fun. "You're the killer realtor, right?"

"Former killer realtor," said Marilee, smiling good-naturedly.

But Stella's eyes were on Sam Poole. She noticed that his lips were just shy of pretty as he said the word realtor. He was tall and broad-shouldered with a runner's build. His gaze was direct as he joked with Marilee. He focused on what she was saying and laughed easily with her.

Then he turned his attention to Helen who was turning pink from the exertion of holding her stomach in. She self-consciously tucked a silver curl behind her ear before taking Sam's hand. In spite of herself, Stella was also reacting quite positively to her neighbor. Besides the good looks there was something else. She felt a connection, as she had when she'd first seen him.

Was it possible that Sam Poole was more than just a pretty boy?

Stella remembered a conversation with Helen and Marilee on a recent visit to D.C.

"Unlike men, beautiful women are a dime a dozen," Helen had pointed out. "And today women are valued for more than beauty, their ability to pick up a carpool on time and cook a decent roast."

"I think good-looking men are on the increase," said Marilee. "I mean look at how many of them are working out and eating right and getting their eyes done."

"Well, maybe," said Helen, "But they are still a fairly rare commodity, and therefore they find it difficult to keep the hunk factor from inflating their egos."

Stella admitted it was an interesting hypothesis. At the time she was involved in what she perceived as a secure, long-term relationship with Andrew. She was a mature woman. Stella Gray didn't concern herself with frivolous theories on datable men. That was the domain of twenty-year olds. But now, of course, things were different.

Sam Poole appeared to be one of those good-looking guys who is authentically charming. The all-important authenticity component combined with a disregard (bordering on annoyance) of his own good looks knocked the man's likability factor over the fence and out of the park. He also sounded intelligent. According to Helen, intelligence was another element often lacking in the physically superior male. As far as Stella was concerned, a good brain was even sexier than a good pair of legs. Even ones like Sam Poole's.

Finally Sam looked at Stella. Really looked at her face. His smile dimmed a bit, and though she was accustomed to this reaction when people noticed the scars, she was surprised at how dismayed it left her when it came from Sam.

So was her first impression the right one? Was Sam Poole just one more good-looking guy, no deeper than Andrew … her two-timing, flight-attendant-chasing ex?

More importantly, she wondered, *why do I care?*

"Welcome to the neighborhood," said Sam, shaking her hand.

"Thank you, Mr. Poole," she said with a tight smile of her own. "I'm Stella Gray."

"Speaking of embarrassing situations …" He smiled at Marilee. "Ms. Gray, I've had a talk with my son, Elliot, about party crashing. Sorry about that."

Stella smiled, remembering the funny, little boy. "That's okay. I'm glad he came. And, uh, I have an apology of my own," she said. "When I first got here, and you were calling your dog and I thought …"

"It's okay," he said coolly, and Stella reminded herself that you only get one chance to make a first impression.

"Why don't you give Sam a tour of the place?" said Marilee, sounding as chirpy as a newbie Brownie troop leader. "He might have some ideas."

Sam did, indeed, have a few ideas, which he shared as they went from room to room. None of them were very good, Stella decided. This made her feel slightly less foolish about their first meeting. By the time he took his leave, she was at least calling her neighbor Sam instead of Mr. Poole.

In spite of his coolness toward Stella, Sam Poole had an easy way about him that was awfully hard to resist. He joked with Helen and Marilee, and in minutes it was if the three of them were best buddies instead of recent acquaintances.

Comfortable in his own skin, is how Stella's daddy referred to such men. She'd gotten so used to self-absorbed, uptight Andrew, she had forgotten what it was like to be around a man like Sam. She had to keep reminding herself that he was married.

"No, he's not married," said Marilee when Sam had headed back next door.

"But I saw his wife," Stella reminded her.

"Ex-wife."

It turned out that the former Mrs. Poole had not been Miss Mississippi, but as first alternate had come close.

"If she was runner-up, can you imagine what the winner looks like?" said Stella.

Marilee explained. "Jennifer … that's her name. Jennifer Poole is an exercise fanatic."

"No surprise there," said Stella.

"Unfortunately, her talent in the pageant was a Zumba routine," Marilee continued.

"With a baton," added Helen. "Which sounds kind of dangerous, when you think about it," she added.

Marilee giggled and continued. "I don't think anyone got hurt, but from what I heard, it was grim. What's worse, the winner supposedly had a voice like Celine Dion. Anyway, that's the reason Jennifer didn't go home with the big tiara."

"She did get a bunch of scholarships," said Helen, "Which she put to good use. She's a partner at Piper, Craven and Fox. As to why the marriage didn't work out, I have no idea."

"I do," said Marilee. "I got this from Georgiana McCall, who works at Piper, Craven and Fox. Georgiana says that though Jennifer is gorgeous and smart and flashes her pageant smile at the drop of a paperclip, no one at the office has ever heard the woman laugh. Not once. Not a chuckle, not a giggle. Georgiana says that when Mother Nature was doling out the goodies to Jennifer, she must've run out of personality and a sense of humor."

"Sounds like a cold fish," said Helen. "Probably wears her second-place crown to bed."

"Who knows?" asked Marilee. "But Georgiana also told me that Sam and Jennifer got married in a fever. You know, a whirlwind courtship, as Mama used to say. Anyway, when the smoke cleared, they realized they didn't have much in common, except Elliot, of course. Jennifer, ever the shrewd solicitor, got a very nice raised cottage on Dogwood Avenue. And custody of Elliot, though he's at his dad's most of the time. Sam got the dog." She smirked at Stella. "I believe you met Babe. And Sam moved to Whimsy Court."

"Wow," said Stella, trying to process the information overload.

"And you know what? I think Sam likes you," said Marilee. "In spite of your first meeting. You know, when you ..." She made a face.

"Can we just forget about that?" asked Stella. "Because it's obvious that within five minutes of my arrival and without even trying, I repelled the only attractive, eligible man around."

"I wouldn't count Sam Poole out," said Helen. "As a matter of fact, I agree with Marilee. I saw him checking you out when we were going through the house. Keep showing him your good side. He'll come around. He's just gun shy like you."

She turned to Marilee. "What else do you know, Mare?"

"Well, here's the bad news. Every female within dating distance is after him." Marilee put a hand over her heart and rolled her eyes. "Which is not surprising. Sam Poole is quite the hottie!"

"That he is," said Helen. "Just remember. You're married. "What's the story on Kitty?"

"Kitty Petite is the housekeeper slash nanny," said Marilee. "She's real big in her church, Big Welcome Baptist down by the bay and takes the little boy to Wednesday evening services every week. Georgiana says that Jennifer isn't happy about it because she's expecting Elliot, who is extremely gifted, to be the next Clarence Darrow, and Elliot tells everyone he's going to be a preacher like Reverend Jenkins at Big Welcome." Anyway, Jennifer works all the time and knows she's lucky to have Kitty, so she's decided to take her therapist's advice and ignore all of Elliot's preacher-talk and hope it's just a phase." Marilee took a breath and rolled her eyes. "I mean he is only four. Or maybe five."

"One thing hasn't changed around here," said Stella. The old grapevine is still smokin'. Is there anything you don't know about these people?"

"Not much," said Marilee proudly.

Now that the subject of the Pooles was exhausted, the conversation turned back to T-shirt dresses. Besides getting her mind off her grief, seeing Marilee's designs had Stella's creative juices percolating. They agreed to meet at Marilee's soon, so Stella could see actual samples of the comfy/dressy creations.

Stella finished her errands and pulled up to her parents' rambling two-story house at ten minutes after six. As usual, there were cars crowded in the driveway and out front. Though she was running late, she gave herself a few minutes before facing siblings, in-laws and assorted nieces, nephews, cousins and pets.

She loved her family more than anything, but they were part of the reason she'd left Bayview. As the oldest child and grandchild, she'd practically raised her younger siblings and most of her cousins. As a teenager she began to dream of life in an adult world with white furniture free of juice stains and crayon that didn't smell like a dog.

She'd had other dreams, too. Like having a bathroom to herself. Like looking in the mirror and having a healthy face smile back at her. Like opening a medicine cabinet not filled with pills and washes and salves that were little more than prescriptions for disappointment.

That was when the cysts and lesions were at their peak. But Tutta found women who talked to Stella about their own battles with disfiguring acne. They showed her pictures of themselves as teens, suffering through the worst of it. When it cleared, they'd had laser therapies and dermabrasion and had become adept at applying make-up. Their scarring was barely noticeable. And when the self-pity party went on a bit too long, a weary Tutta admonished her daughter with, "Anybody who expects perfection in this life is bound to be disappointed. Happiness isn't a gift, it's a choice."

Stella looked back at the house, full of kids and cheery chaos. Children were wonderful, all right, but any void Stella felt by not having any of her own was easily filled. Rarely was an invitation to visit Aunt Stella in D.C. declined.

As Tutta, who had been raising children since her teens, often remarked to her eldest daughter, "There's a lot to be said for being a beloved aunt."

6.

Settling into Whimsy

The following weeks were a blur of activity. Stella met with Katie the architect and "the best contractor in town" who had modernized at least three of the other Whimsy Tudors without compromising their charm or historical significance. Katie's familiarity with the latter point was very important due to the Bayview Historical Society's insistence on rigorous adherence to original hundred and fifty-year-old paint colors, building materials and even century old landscape design and plants. Bo Gray referred to this dedicated group of preservationists as the hysterical society. But they were instrumental in procuring grants and saving many of Bayview's wonderful buildings.

It was apparent that Sam Poole was familiar with the society's stringent standards. When comparing options and cost, it turned out that a few of his suggestions were actually more practical than Stella's ideas. It was a small thing, but gave our seasoned decorator pause.

Glad to have a paycheck, workers arrived early and stayed late. The four bedrooms were reduced to three, making space for a new master bath and closets. Stella's grandmother had been content to house her clothes in wardrobes and chests of drawers. Stella remembered her grandmother getting dressed during Bayview's insufferable summer days. She'd ignored the terminal humidity, dancing with intermittent gusts of an oscillating fan while clouds of talcum powder floated from between filmy layers of linen.

The kitchen was completely reworked and would soon

have an improved butler's pantry, as well as desk space and a large island. Marble counter tops and glass-fronted cabinets would meld with the character of the house, yet look bright and modern and inviting.

Slate was ordered to replace missing roof tiles. The stairway's iron banister was tightened up and painted. It took days, but cracked, beveled panes in the house's fabulous bay window were replaced so that the old and new panes were indistinguishable. Floors were stripped of layers of stain and paint and wax in preparation for refinishing. The installation of central heat and air-conditioning was the biggest challenge, but work had finally begun on that, too.

•

When Sam Poole opened the shutters of his upstairs bathroom window (and leaned to the right), he was afforded a pretty good view of the industrious doings at number two. He told himself his was merely a professional interest. But in the process he couldn't help but observe a mutual respect between the workers and Ms. Gray. They consulted with her. They listened to her. They liked her! Which did not correlate with his initial assessment of the woman.

Maybe I just have a knack for bringing out the worst in women, he thought and closed the shutters with a snap.

•

Over the past few years, Bo Gray had slowly relinquished the management of Gray Equipment to his son-in-law, Dave. Now that his daughter owned the Whimsy house, and he had some time on his hands, he decided to get involved. To help Stella with garden chores, he showed up most mornings with a truck load of too-heavy equipment and went straight to work. Once the beds were reworked and weeded and walkways neatened up, he built an arch over the walkway to the back garden.

Besides the aesthetics of the thing, it was sturdy enough to withstand a category five hurricane. Stella oohed and aahed over it and hoped it would never have to be moved.

One dazzling sunny morning, Bo showed up with a pale pink climbing rose. "Just looked like something you might like," he said. He and Stella planted it by the back door where it would get plenty of sun and eventually soften the little overhang.

Sam Poole repaired the fence between numbers two and four, and Elliot did not reappear. Stella caught herself watching the street where her neighbors jogged or strolled and often stopped to chat. Whimsy Court was that kind of a street—a friendly street. So Stella wandered out front often, hoping for an excuse to "bump into" Sam Poole and repair that unfortunate first impression.

Every day Ruth and Al Brinkly who lived at number thirteen, meandered by. They were in their eighties, yet toiled in their yard most mornings. This was no small feat. Number thirteen was the largest of the Tudors and likewise possessed the largest garden. Not surprisingly, the elderly couple napped after lunch every day. Weather permitting, they enjoyed drinks on their side porch each day at five. Shortly after she'd moved in, Stella was invited to join the Brinklys for a glass of wine.

"I invited your neighbor, Sam Poole, to join us," said Ruth. She winked at Stella. "He's awfully cute," she added.

"Now, Ruth …" said Al.

Ruth ignored Al and continued. "But he was busy."

"I don't wonder," said Al, smiling wistfully. "What a guy."

Ruth rolled her eyes. "Don't be silly, Al. The poor man is probably exhausted. All those women pestering him day and night."

"Yep. We should all be so exhausted," said Al. He winked at Stella.

Ruth rolled her eyes again. "You know, Stella, I can't help but see them coming and going," she said. "I'm out here so much. And I've got an eye for these things. Back me up here, Al. I have an eye, don't I?"

Al shrugged. "What can I say? She's telling the truth. She's got an eye. Always has."

"None of those women are right for him," said Ruth. "But you …" She punctuated the unfinished thought with a suggestive smile.

"Eye or no eye," said Al. "Don't start match-making, Ruth. Leads to trouble. Remember the Heblemeyers?"

Stella didn't get to hear the story of the unfortunate

Heblemeyers because Al changed the subject by pointing out his runaway wisteria vine. "Been fighting that thing for thirty years. Wisteria, thirty; Al, nothing."

The mom with the blonde, bouncing ponytail pushed her twins in an oversized stroller every morning at ten. One morning she knocked on Stella's door, introduced herself as Maggie Post and while jogging in place, handed Stella a plate of carob brownies.

"I've noticed you running," she said. "If you'd ever like to join me and the twins?"

Before Stella could answer, the twins started squirming and squealing. Maggie let out an exasperated sigh. "Sorry," she said. "Gotta run. My number's in with the brownies. Call me!"

And she was off. Stella laughed and waved good-naturedly. The multi-tasking Maggie reminded her of friends she'd left behind in D.C. As she watched Maggie's amazingly toned, new-mommy body disappear down the street, she decided she would definitely take her up on her offer. Whatever Maggie was doing was working.

The gay couple who threw cocktail parties at least twice a week raced by in sleek, matching exercise gear early in the mornings. They waved, but Stella could see they were too intent on their workout to stop and chat.

A couple of times Sam and Babe trotted by as Stella was coming or going. Stella put on her warmest smile and adopted her friendliest demeanor whenever this happened. Sam returned her wave or hello, but they were indifferent gestures, and though he seemed inclined a time or two, he never stopped to talk.

In addition to the several guys who regularly stopped by, Stella noticed an assortment of what Bo referred to as "girl" cars visiting number four Whimsy. Indeed, each was driven by an attractive female. As a matter of fact, the stream of women stopping by Sam Poole's house was nothing short of remarkable. They varied in age and appearance, mostly young and all attractive in one way or another. But none seemed to meet with enough encouragement to visit more than a few times.

There were a few exceptions, however. Like the nubile

Bethany who couldn't have been more than twenty-five years old. Stella noticed her hopping out of a baby blue Mazda four times in one week! She knew Bethany's name because she had literally bumped into her.

Stella had been forced to jump the curb to keep from falling in the street. It happened as she jogged around the huge Formosa azalea that punctuated her driveway and separated numbers two and four. Sam was walking the youngster to her car, so he had no choice but to introduce the two women.

"Stella is my neighbor," he explained.

"Gosh, you're very spry," Bethany said with an enthusiastic smile on her face.

The worst thing about the remark was that the girl appeared to be sincere.

Though Bethany visited often, there was no way for Stella to know whether this was due to any encouragement from Sam.

Out of the sea of female admirers, there was one other woman who got Stella's attention. A tiny blonde. With a very good, tiny figure. She was not only pretty with her pale, flawless skin, but vivacious. That was apparent even from a distance, the way she hopped out of her little Mercedes, those platinum waves gleaming in the sunlight, laughing and calling Sam's name before she even got to the door. Stella could hear her all the way from the back garden of number two! She soon decided that the woman's effervescence bordered on the obnoxious. And that laugh!

"Lord, a hyena would kill for it," she muttered unkindly as the woman dropped by for the second time in a week.

But for all she knew, a hyena hoot was music to the ears of a man who'd been married to a woman whose only expression of mirth was the plastic rictus of a bored beauty pageant contestant.

In the evenings when the dusk was studded with lightning bugs and scented with ginger, loquat and mint, Stella stopped her house-related doings long enough to sit on the back step. Sometimes, as she sat sipping the surprisingly tasty chardonnay sold at the Locavore, she would hear the hyena giggles. Stella would sigh, take her wine back inside and crank up Pandora.

More often, Sam Poole sat in his backyard playing a guitar. He was pretty good. Occasionally he sang along with his strumming. The voice didn't match his prowess with the strings, but it had a mellow sound that was peaceful and went well with the night air and Stella's wine.

Other times she heard him playing silly tunes for Elliot, who would attempt to sing along. One favorite was *Old McDonald*. Sam would play and sing, "And on this farm he had a …" at which point he would stop. Elliot finished the refrain with cow or horth or gooth. On several of these sing-alongs, Sam stopped playing and said, "Elliot, can you say horse? Like this. Horse." And he hissed out the final "s" sound. Elliot responded, "Thure. Horth!"

Stella would smile to herself in the dark.

And then she'd hear hyena woman back there. Sam's half of their exchange was spoken in normal conversational tones so Stella couldn't make out his words. But they must've been side-splitters because every other comment was followed by a hysterical guffaw, which trailed off to, "That is hilarious!"

The woman's inane comments, which Stella was certain could be heard two blocks over, centered on gossip, reality TV shows and bad—no, make that horrendous—suggestions as to what Sam should do with his house and yard. And yet, it dawned on Stella that Sam must be partial to this woman. Because as far as Stella could tell, out the bevy of admirers dropping by number four, hyena woman alone had been invited into the inner sanctum of Sam's backyard.

7.

The Big Easy

As Stella sat alone, sipping chardonnay and eavesdropping on Sam, she realized that her fear of being inundated by Bayview relatives was completely unfounded. Like her friends in D.C. her sisters were busy women with families and/or jobs to tend. And when she wasn't cooking or babysitting, mama Tutta busied herself at the bridge table and tennis court.

Alice and her husband, Peter (known to all as Doc) were doctors—she a dermatologist and he a pediatrician—with four children of their own. Stella's other sister, Ann Olive, was the alpha sibling. She didn't have a paying job, but was the mother of two, ran every committee in town and socialized with everybody. It was acknowledged by most Bayviewers that she had more influence than the mayor. Her husband, Dave helped his father-in-law run Gray Farm Equipment.

It became apparent that once the house was finished, Stella was going to need something to do. Helen's advice—*Honey, it's time to get back in the saddle*—had more than a ring of truth, so in the end Stella agreed to go into business with Marilee, who had named her company Two-A-Tee Casuals, established a web site and had business cards printed up (the capital A was wearing a little dress, and yes, it was just too precious) with Stella's name on them. As Helen had pointed out, Marilee's enthusiasm (while it lasted) knew no bounds.

Once she got involved, Stella found that playing with the designs and fabrics was a great outlet for her pent-up creative energy. She even brought her twin six-year-old nieces over to Marilee's to model the new kiddie versions of Two-A-Tee dresses. Marilee, who has a thing for little girls, having none of her own and who was immensely grateful to have Stella's assistance, let the children help her with the latest design and paint their own dresses.

As they were leaving, Marilee informed Stella that she had made reservations for the two of them at the Sequester Royale Hotel in New Orleans. A clothing market was coming to the Big Easy and so was Mr. Floyd Finger, a man who knew the dress business inside and out, so to speak. Everything market-related was happening in and around the Sequester, according to Marilee.

Mr. Finger, who was extremely impressed by the pictures of Marilee modeling her wares, had agreed to take a look at actual Two-A-Tee dresses, and "if he likes what he sees, he'll take us on!" said Marilee, who was practically delirious with anticipation.

Two weeks later the partners in Two-A-Tee, LLC pulled up in front of the hotel.

"This couldn't be right," said Marilee.

But of course, it was. To say the Sequester Royale had seen better days would be generous. Located on the far edge of the French Quarter, it was an over-the-hill harlot of a place, full of peeling, flocked wallpaper, threadbare brocade and dusty chandeliers—the kind of place Bo Gray referred to as a "ho-tel, full of tightwads and loose hangers."

Was it possible that the savvy organizers of the clothing market saw some kind of French Quarter ambience in this decaying dump? Could they have all been out of town or been laid low by the flu and turned the reservation suggestions over to an intern? Could it be that Marilee, in her good-hearted exuberance, had screwed up once again?

When Stella gently but firmly put the question to her, Marilee pressed her lips together and thought about it. She had been in a hurry when booking the reservations, and it was possible she'd gotten hotel names mixed up. Or the conventions.

As it turned out, the Sequester was hosting a convention, all right, though it seemed more like a coven to Stella. The "International Sisterhood of the Priestess" was composed of women from far and wide who claimed kinship with Marie Laveau, the voodoo queen of New Orleans. They were a predictably spooky bunch, lurking in the shadowy corners of the Sequester and chanting way past the witching hour, keeping Stella and Marilee awake.

As far as Stella could tell, the other vendors and buyers in town for the clothing market were staying elsewhere. The clothing market itself was actually happening in a converted warehouse across the street from the Sequester.

Stella and Marilee inquired at the front desk as to Floyd Finger's whereabouts.

The receptionist looked them up and down, snorted and said, "Seriously? You two are looking for Floyd Finger?"

She then directed them to a parking lot behind the warehouse. Lugging armloads of their amazing T-shirt dresses, the women staggered past the building, hopped a curb and ducked under a clump of straggly banana trees. They stopped dead still.

Basking in the shade of the warehouse was a rusted, dented, road-weary RV. And next to it, snoozing in a plastic chair was a skinny, middle-aged dude dressed in black from the doo rag on his head to his snakeskin boots. Presumably Floyd Finger.

Stella spoke first.

"Marilee, I'm gonna kill you."

"Now, let's not judge a book by its cover," said Marilee, fixing her features into a faux smile of optimism.

God bless her, she approached the reclining figure as if she were encountering Ralph Lauren in the lobby of the Ritz.

"Excuse me, are you Mr. Finger?" she said pleasantly.

Stella prayed for a negative response, but it was not to be.

Floyd had the decency to rise in the presence of the ladies, as Marilee introduced herself and Stella.

"An honor to meet you ladies," he said. "I hope we can do business."

His voice was deep, not unlike Sam Poole's, and this had Stella actually softening toward the man. But unlike Sam's, Floyd's longish hair and eyes were as black as his clothes. His nose was also overly long above what Stella's mother referred to as a dime-slot mouth. He looked like the devil. And smelled like bourbon.

But his smile was surprisingly engaging so when he flashed it at Marilee, bowed with a flourish and said, "Please step into my office," Marilee climbed into the RV. When Stella hesitated, Floyd turned the smile up a few notches and said, "I don't bite. I promise."

Inside the rolling Finger domicile, things were spare but ship-shape. A near-empty bottle of Jim Beam sat on the few inches of counter space next to several drying melamine dishes in an all-over sunflower design. If it weren't for the whiskey bottle, the place could've belonged to a little, old lady.

The biggest surprise sat on the floor near the door. It was a cardboard box containing a straggly orange mama cat and a litter of mewling kittens. The mama hissed at Stella as she entered. Floyd reached over and stroked the cat.

"Now, now. Settle down," he said. "These ladies don't want your babies." He straightened up with some effort and explained. "Found that kitty in the rain. Soon as I brought her in, she started popping out kittens. Lucky I found her when I did."

He unfolded a table, piled the dresses on top and flipped through the stack.

After a quick look at all twenty sample dresses, Floyd said, "Ladies, I think I can sell the heck out of these. I work on straight commission. Twenty-five percent. You pay shipping. I take on the headaches."

"Oh, that sounds fair to me," said Marilee.

"There's just one question," said Floyd. "Will you be able to fill orders for dozens of these? Stores will be ordering for summer, you know."

"Well, we'll do our best," said Marilee who was honest to a fault.

"Here's my card," said Floyd. "You'll be hearing from me." Marilee was frowning at the card which read, *Floyd Finger, Assistant funeral director—Ascension Funeral Home—Because I Care.*

Floyd smiled self-consciously. "Sorry, wrong card. I help my brother-in-law out sometimes," he explained.

He took the card with a shaky hand and replaced it with

another which read *Floyd Finger—Fine Clothing Representative*. His phone number and email address were printed beneath his name.

Stella decided then and there that she wasn't about to turn over twenty of their best dresses to the likes of Floyd Finger, so she assumed her most businesslike demeanor and said, "I'm afraid we'll only be able to leave ten dresses with you, Mr. Finger. I just remembered that I've promised the others to a store in town."

Marilee opened her mouth to object but wisely reconsidered, fake coughed and smiled innocently at Floyd.

"You'll be hearing from me soon," said Floyd, and he punctuated that unexpected smile of his with a wink.

Like the Avon lady calling at the convent, Stella's expectations were low. Floyd Finger was no big-time rep. Small-time rogue was more like it. She sighed and told herself things could be worse. At least the man was kind to animals. And he did keep a clean camper.

As they headed back through the banana trees, Stella decided not to say one negative word to Marilee. Her buddy had worked hard on her latest enterprise, and Stella had to admire her composure in the face of Floyd Finger. Besides, the Bayview boutiques were indeed selling Two-A-Tee designs "like tassels at a stripper convention." If Floyd hadn't come up with some orders in a few weeks, they would simply find another rep.

After all, what's the worst that could happen?

Marilee, buoyed by Stella's lack of recriminations, suggested they have a celebratory lunch before heading home. Stella agreed. As you know, there is an embarrassment of fine dining in New Orleans, but after ten minutes of discussion they decided on Commander's Palace out in the Garden District. They were soon driving down St. Charles Avenue with its fabulous mansions and gently rocking streetcars rumbling down the boulevard. Before long they came to Washington Avenue, home of Commander's Palace.

Two hours later, stuffed with turtle soup, flounder and bread pudding, Stella and Marilee stepped out onto the sidewalk. Across the street, sunshine reflected on the white mausoleums of the famous Lafayette Cemetery where a familiar-looking group was entering the iron gates.

"Look," said Marilee. "It's the voodoo girls from the hotel. I hope they're not looking for Marie Laveau's tomb. Everybody knows she's buried in the St. Louis Cemetery."

"They probably hit all the graveyards," said Stella.

"Omigod! Look who's here," said Marilee.

"Is that Kitty Petite? Elliot Poole's nanny?"

"I believe it is," said Marilee. "And, you know, she looks kind of regal in that voodoo get-up … in a high priestess sort of way, of course."

"She really does," agreed Stella.

Marilee slipped her phone out of her purse. "I love her scarf. The pattern might be good on one of our dresses."

Marilee snapped a few photos of voodoo Kitty, who was all got up in scarves and bracelets and things one would assume to be voodoo priestess attire.

"I wonder if Sam Poole knows his son's nanny is into voodoo?" said Stella. The thought of Kitty taking advantage of sweet, little Elliot and his nice dad had Stella glaring at the woman. "I thought she was so big in her church," she said. "It doesn't really jive with the voodoo thing, does it?"

"No, it doesn't." Marilee smiled. "But if Floyd doesn't do us right, maybe we can get her to put a hex on him."

Stella smiled back at her old friend, but something about this other side of Elliot Poole's nanny was disturbing. Maybe even more disturbing than going into business with a tipsy clothing rep working out a battered camper in a parking lot.

8.

No Place like Home

Stella and Marilee quickly formed a work routine. Unless Stella was otherwise engaged in the doings at number two Whimsy, they met several days a week in Marilee's converted playroom to paint, paste and sew basic beach creatures and scenes such as seahorses, coral, shells, and crabs onto tropical-colored dresses. These outlines were filled in with wonderful designer fabrics and outlined with acrylic paint. Sequins and metallic trim were either glued or sewn to finish the dresses.

The hours flew by as the friends worked, stopping only for a salad by Marilee's pool or a glass of wine at the end of the day if they ran late. They laughed and chatted while they worked, covering everything from good books to local gossip. From time to time Marilee mentioned Sam Poole. Stella usually dismissed the subject with a flutter of her hand. This was often followed by a funny, little smile or even a dreamy sigh, neither of which went unnoticed by Marilee.

In spite of the pleasant working conditions, the dresses were so labor-intensive and time-consuming that Stella was relieved when by mid-October, T-shirt sales slowed down locally, and the dozens of orders from Floyd Finger had not materialized. As a matter of fact, Floyd, himself, seemed to have dematerialized into thin air. All of Marilee's calls to him had gone straight to voicemail and remained unanswered. Likewise, emails.

And then one day, number two Whimsy was done. The pale, watery wall paints had dried to scrumptious hues.

Reupholstered and slip-covered furniture was in place. Sunshine tumbled onto newly stained floors. The windows were completed with bleached shutters and pale, fluttering linen and when she saw it, Stella felt just like Nick Carraway entering the breezy, white living room of Daisy Buchanan in *The Great Gatsby*.

The day of official completion was one of those surprising fall days in south Alabama that almost feels like actual autumn. Eddie, the contractor and several of the workers were wrapping things up at number two. Stella couldn't wait to have the house to herself, but she would miss the camaraderie she'd developed with the workmen. She'd grown so fond of them that she regretted not doing something special on this last day at her house.

As if reading Stella's mind, a little before noon, Tutta Gray pulled up and popped the back of her SUV. She was accompanied by her twin granddaughters and their younger brother, Thomas, all of whom had the afternoon off from school. The children helped their grandmother spread a blanket on the ground beneath Stella's oak. Tutta placed baskets and her battered ice chest beside it.

Soon the workmen and Stella and Tutta and the six-year-old girls and Thomas were enjoying apples, po-boy sandwiches, Tutta's home made fig bars and lemonade right there in the front yard. Tutta always made extra, so when Kitty Petite and Elliot Poole strolled by, they were invited to join the lawn party. And when Sam Poole drove by, he was surprised to see the assortment of folks partying there with his son under the oak.

He was especially surprised to see Stella Gray, whom he'd chalked up as being another good-looking but humorless woman who took herself far too seriously, sitting cross-legged in the grass in a pair of dusty jeans. Not only that, she was laughing and sharing a sandwich with old George Murphy, the painter. So Sam parked his truck and walked over to see what was going on.

"Hey, Dad," said Elliot. "We got invited thith time, didn't we, Kitty?"

"Sure did."

Sam ran a hand over his son's head, ruffling his hair. "Glad to hear it, buddy." He turned to Stella. "What's the occasion?"

"The workmen have been so good to Stella," said Tutta, "I decided to bring lunch. Here, have a sandwich."

So Sam took off his jacket and sat down on the grass next to Stella. She smiled at Sam, oblivious to a spot of Cajun mustard on her chin. And just like that, Stella Gray got a second chance at a first impression.

Thomas made Elliot's acquaintance by showing him a gross scab on his elbow. Elliot was dutifully impressed and showed Thomas how he could stick his entire tongue out through the space formerly occupied by his two front teeth.

"Wow," said Thomas, who had been wiggling his own teeth for months in the hopes of losing them.

When Thomas scrambled up a low limb of the oak, Elliot followed. They climbed around like "secret army guys," pretended to be invisible and tried to attract lizards with sandwich crusts.

When the last fig bar had been consumed, Tutta and the children gathered up the picnic supplies. She kissed Stella goodbye, hustled the kids into the car and hurried off to a tennis lesson. Stella took Sam, Elliot and Kitty on a tour of the house.

"Wow, it's really beautiful," said Sam, taking in the bleached woods and sea of serene neutrals. "So light and clean."

"When I was in D.C., I worked with color and pattern all day, every day. I like coming home to a calming palette."

"Praith the Lord," said Elliot over and over as they went from room to room. "Thith ith a plumb miracle!"

Sam looked a bit uncomfortable, but said nothing. Kitty beamed her approval at Elliot's pronouncements and agreed, saying it was "just like a piece of heaven."

Stella remembered Kitty in New Orleans all got up like a voodoo queen, and once again, thought how the two faces of Kitty Petite just didn't gee-haw. Was some split-personality in charge of Elliot? Should she tell Sam? Would he think she was over-reacting? Or worse, think she was a busy body trying to insinuate herself into his family life? It was definitely worrisome.

Finally, Kitty said, "Elliot, they's a redfish got Elliot Poole name on it. It's time we get ourselves down to the pier." She turned to Stella. "Thank you for having us to lunch and showing us around."

Elliot started toward the door, then ran back and threw his arms around Stella's waist.

"Thank you, Mith Thella. I had tho much fun today!"

When he and Kitty were gone, Stella said, "Kitty takes Elliot fishing?"

"Every Thursday afternoon. It was part of the deal from the beginning. She has dozens of relatives and evidently they all get together down at the pier and fish. It's a little unorthodox." He grinned at Stella. "But we have fresh fish at least once a week."

"My daddy taught my sisters and me to fish off that pier when we were about Elliot's age. Those are some of my happiest childhood memories."

"Yeah, Elliot and I go most Saturdays. I keep a boat at the marina. It's good father-son time, but … well, Elliot needs friends."

"I'm surprised at that. He's such a sweet kid."

"Thanks. He's had some adjustment problems, I guess you'd say. But he had a great time playing with your nephew today."

"I'm glad they hit it off. Thomas is quite the character."

The conversation turned to their respective houses. Sam was explaining changes he'd made to his kitchen when he stopped and said, "Why don't I just show you? Can you walk over later? Say around five?" He smiled and added—as if she needed an incentive. "I've got cold beer."

Stella agreed, and though Sam seemed to approve of her in dusty jeans, she headed for the shower where she washed her hair. She also did her nails, added the minimum amount of make-up and wore a blouse of peachy pink, which she had been told was her best color.

By five o'clock she and Sam were sipping very cold beers in the kitchen of number four Whimsy. The room reminded Stella of an English pub, with dark-stained woods and beams on the ceiling. Not her taste, but she had to admit it suited the house.

And its owner.

Stella and Sam swapped renovation horror stories, and it turned out that Sam not only possessed an easy smile, but had no trouble laughing at himself. After years of the ego-driven Andrew, Stella found this trait positively captivating.

When Sam asked her why she'd moved back to sleepy Bayview from the big city, she told him an abridged version of losing Gris to cancer and Andrew to the flight attendant.

Sam shook his head. "That's rough." Then he smiled at her. "It's no wonder you were a little touchy that day we first met. I apologize for assuming the worst."

Stella laughed. "The worst? What would that be, exactly?"

"Oh, that maybe you took yourself too seriously. It's a common affliction with good-looking women … if you don't mind me saying so."

She did mind. It appeared that Mr. Poole had a few touchy areas of his own. But like her, he'd earned his prejudices, so she smiled and said, "No, I believe I'll take that as a compliment."

"Good, because that's how it was meant." He smiled at her again. And he did have the most disarming smile. "Even if it wasn't very well said," he added.

Sam told Stella how he and Jennifer and Elliot had moved to Bayview when Jennifer was offered her present job. Between the move and subsequent divorce, Jennifer's recent engagement and her long hours at work, Elliot had become withdrawn and easily upset.

"She's engaged?" asked Stella, trying not to sound overly interested (or euphoric) at this development.

"Yeah. To another lawyer. He seems like an okay guy, but …" He shook his head.

"Another adjustment."

"Right. Elliot was already crying every time he went to day care. We finally hired Kitty as a nanny. It's strange, him talking like a preacher and everything, but Kitty and her church are bringing Elliot out of himself. He started kindergarten at LeMoyne Day School this fall. According to Miss Liza, his teacher, he hasn't made many friends. But at least he's going without all the tears."

"LeMoyne Day School is where my nephew, Thomas is

going. I bet he and Elliot are in the same class."

"I hope so. They seemed to hit it off, and like I said, Elliot needs friends in the worst way. Maybe it will keep his mom from obsessing over everything."

"What else?" asked Stella before she could stop herself.

"I guess you noticed his lisp. Jennifer is freaking out about the lisp. And then there's the preacher-speak, as she refers to it."

"One of my nephews had that problem … the lisp, I mean. He couldn't pronounce his Ss and Zs. Once his permanent teeth grew in, the problem solved itself. I bet the same thing will happen with Elliot. If not, don't all schools have speech therapists? I mean, how many adults do you know with lisps?"

"None. Gosh, I never thought of that."

"Besides, losing baby teeth is kind of a badge of honor in some kiddie circles, and Elliot's lost his early. It may actually help him to fit in."

"I hope you're right," said Sam. "But there's still the preacher talk."

"It is a bit unusual," agreed Stella.

"Yeah, definitely unusual. I've got nothing against the preacher or Kitty's church … or Elliot going into the ministry one day. And the counselor we took him to said not to worry about it. It's strange, though."

The poor guy was obviously in over his head in the child-rearing department.

"Have you ever thought about going to church with him?"

"You mean to Big Welcome Baptist? I'm not sure I'd fit in. It's an all-black congregation, mostly older folks. I don't want to cause a problem."

"Well, they do call themselves Big Welcome. I bet they'd be happy to have you. You could ask Kitty about it."

"Maybe I will. Thanks."

"And I wouldn't worry so much," said Stella. "It sounds to me like you're doing all the right things, and that he's through the worst of … of an awkward time."

Actually, Stella didn't know what to think of Sam's story, but in her hours of baby-sitting (not to mention her own traumatic teen years), she'd seen a bunch of kids do a bunch of weird things. What about her cousin's child? You couldn't get a spoonful of pureed carrots past his lips. Yet the boy turned around and drank an entire bottle of nail polish remover! (He's fine, in case you're wondering.) Stella had come to believe that as long as the parents hung in there with them, the children (and their parents) would make it through the traumas of childhood intact.

She thanked Sam for the beer and the tour of number four and headed back home. When she walked into her own kitchen her cell was ringing on the counter where she'd left it. It was Marilee. And she was upset.

9.

Fireworks on the Coast

"Remember the pin Jack gave me for our anniversary?" Marilee's voice was dancing along the edge of frantic.

"The starfish with the emeralds and diamonds?" asked Stella. "How could I forget?"

"Well, it's lost! I've been looking everywhere for it, and I just remembered where it is."

"Which should be a good thing."

"It's not. One of the twins put it on a dress … the one with the singing mermaids on it. I remember because it really did look great with the dress." Marilee stopped, getting herself back on track. "Anyway, it was one of the samples we took to Floyd Finger! Jack is away on business, but if I don't have that pin by the time he gets back, I just don't know what I'll do!"

"You still haven't gotten in touch with Floyd?"

"No. So I called Hazel Mills who was in charge of the market in New Orleans. It seems that Floyd has a bit of a drinking problem. Hazel says when he falls off the wagon he disappears for weeks, even months at a time. The last time he was AWOL for a year with Patsy Parker's money and all her bustier samples."

"Good grief. What can we do?"

"Hazel says Floyd has been known to unload old samples at a clothing outlet when he's low on funds. It's in Biloxi on the highway near the Beau Rivage Casino."

"Can you be ready in twenty minutes?"

An hour and a half hour later, with dusk settling over

the Gulf of Mexico, Stella and Marilee cruised up and down Highway 90 looking for the Biloxi Fashion Emporium. They finally spied it in the far corner of a strip mall not far from the fabulous Beau Rivage Resort and Casino. It was closed.

"Oh, no," said Marilee. But the woman can find a silver lining in a tornado, so she smiled and added, "I booked us rooms at the hotel. You know, just in case. We might as well get a good dinner and see a show. We'll come back in the morning."

As Stella turned the car back onto the highway, her headlights danced across a familiar rusty RV parked in a vacant lot next to the strip mall.

"I think we just hit the jackpot," she said.

They decided to park at the hotel and walk to the RV. The element of surprise seemed best when dealing with the elusive Mr. Finger. Once they got to the lot, they kept to the shadows, hurrying along a drainage ditch until they were next to the RV. When Stella tapped on the door, it swung open.

"Hellooo," called Marilee.

No answer.

"Should we go in?" whispered Stella.

"Hell, yes," Marilee whispered back.

The place was a disaster—clothing samples and papers and broken dishes everywhere. No sign of the cats.

"You think Floyd has a teenager?" asked Marilee.

"I think someone has been here before us. And Marilee, do you smell gas?"

Marilee wrinkled her nose. "I think that's how RVs smell. Oh, look! There are the dresses!"

Stella recognized her personal favorite—a pale green done up in bejeweled orange coral—tossed with some others onto a folding chair by the door. Marilee began flipping through her creations. The third one was the mermaid dress. Pinned in the maiden's flowing hair was the diamond and emerald starfish pin. Mixed in with the sequins and beads, it must have escaped Floyd's notice. Marilee quickly undid the clasp, stuffed the fabulous pin in her bra and grabbed the whole stack of garments in her arms.

"Let's get out of here," said Stella. "The gas smell is making me woozy."

"Right," said Marilee, staggering under the pile of dresses. "You don't look so good."

But as they turned, Stella caught sight of Floyd's black boots beneath a broken table. And Floyd was still in them!

"Oh, my God! Look!" she cried.

"What should we do?" squealed Marilee.

"We'll call 911. But from outside. I'm about to be sick!"

Once they were clear of the trailer, Stella took a quick, deep breath of sea air and said, "Okay, give me your phone."

"I left it in the car. Where's yours?"

"In the car!"

Keeping to the shadows next to the drainage ditch, they hurried toward the parking lot to retrieve their phones and save Floyd from asphyxiation. But that's when Marilee's strappy sandal caught on the hem of a straggling T-shirt dress sending her headfirst into the ditch. Of course, Stella climbed in after her to help.

And that's when the RV blew.

The women peered over the edge like a couple of shell-shocked prairie dogs. The RV was now a giant bonfire—with Floyd, the disreputable rep in it!

Almost immediately, they heard sirens. People came running toward them. Intent on the fire, none of them noticed two disheveled women climbing out of a ditch clutching glittering T-shirt dresses.

"Oh, poor Floyd," wailed Marilee. "It *was* gas you smelled!"

"Marilee, get a hold of yourself. There's nothing we can do for Floyd now."

"Right," sniffed Marilee, wiping her nose on a lavender and aqua seahorse dress.

Stella took the dresses from Marilee who was limping and covered with scrapes. The sidewalk was now crowded with people trying to get a look at the fire. Police cars pulled up and began turning everyone back. The two women slipped into the crowd and headed for the entrance to the hotel.

Ahead of them, hurrying away from the scene was a tall man and a red-headed woman in very high heels and a very short skirt. Why were they in such a hurry to get away from the scene of everyone else's curiosity?

The man turned to say something to his date, and Stella saw that it was none other than Sam Poole—Sam Poole, who she'd left sitting in his kitchen only a few hours ago! The woman—girl, really—looked to be half his age and was almost as beautiful as his ex-wife. Stella groaned. Because it was beginning to look like Sam was one of those guys who had to have a gorgeous woman on his arm to feel adequate.

This unattractive trait was an absolute deal-breaker as far as Stella was concerned. She'd been pursued by enough of them to know the type—the kind who would have walked across the street to avoid speaking to her when she sported a face full of zits. Oddly enough, the sophisticated Andrew had made fun of such men. Insecure losers, he called them. But that was before Anika, the overly attentive flight attendant landed in his life.

As much as Stella hated to admit it, Sam and his date made an attractive pair. There was an air of familiarity between them. Their body language told her that this was no first date.

She watched as her neighbor and the redhead passed the entrance to the Beau Rivage. They continued down the street, still hurrying and dodging people going the other way. Sam hailed a cab, and as it pulled to the curb they hopped in and sped away.

Marilee showered and changed, and except for half a box of band-aids stuck here and there, she looked pretty good. Ironically, her right breast had incurred the worst injury. The object of their quest had made a nasty scrape as Marilee tumbled into the ditch.

"I'm gonna have a heck of a time explaining this to Jack," she said.

She gave Stella a little smile, but her hand was shaking as she sipped her second glass of Sauvignon Blanc.

"You know alcohol intensifies the effect of ibuprofen," warned Stella.

"Thank God," said Marilee, as she sucked down the wine. She leaned back in her chair and said, "Are you sure it was Sam Poole you saw?"

"It was him, all right. First we see Kitty in New Orleans and now Sam in Biloxi."

"They sure get around, don't they?"

Stella noticed Marilee was slurring her words a bit. Whether this was due to trauma, the bruise on her chin or the wine, she couldn't tell.

"Yes, they certainly do get around," said Stella. "And it's very suspicious."

"So he had a date." Marilee shrugged and waved a bandaged hand. Stella noticed that three of her silk nails had cracked off in the plunge into the ditch. "There would be no reason to tell you he was coming over here," she continued. "And everyone came to see what the commotion was about. I really don't see …" Marilee sat up very straight in her chair and smirked at Stella. "You know what? I think somebody's jealous."

"That's ridiculous." Stella snorted indignantly. "I hardly know the man!"

But she realized that jealousy was indeed one of the many feelings (along with elation, shock, sadness, exhaustion, frustration and terror) that she had experienced that evening.

"So what are we going to do about poor Floyd?" Marilee was saying. She dabbed at a tear with her napkin.

"What can we do? We had nothing to do with his … his demise. And we don't know anything that would help."

"But what if we become suspects?" Marilee looked guiltily over one shoulder and then the other. "What if someone saw us leaving the RV? And you know what? I left a bunch of angry messages on his voice mail, and I sent him a bunch of mean emails, threatening to sic lawyers on him if he didn't return our dresses!"

"Marilee, nobody saw us. I think his phone and everything else is up in smoke … if you know what I mean. You didn't ask Kitty to put a hex on him, or anything did you?"

"This isn't funny, Stella."

"I know—just trying to cheer you up."

"We should have dragged him out." She closed her eyes and shook her head. "Was I more interested in saving my dresses and my pin than in saving Floyd Finger?"

"Listen, none of this is our fault. I think Floyd was a goner before we ever went in there." She gave a little shudder. "We could have just missed a murderer."

She refused to consider the possibility that said murderer, who was obviously looking for something, might have witnessed the two women entering and exiting the RV and might think they had whatever it was he—or she (Stella remembered Patsy Parker's missing money and bustier samples) was looking for.

Marilee groaned as the waiter approached. Unable to speak, she simply held up her empty glass. Stella ordered steaks for them both. Marilee was going to be one big bruise in the morning. She didn't need a hangover on top of it.

10.
A Thickening Plot

Marilee was indeed sore (and yes, a bit hung over) the next morning. She looked totally put-together as usual, but every time she moved, she winced. By the time they turned into her winding drive, she'd popped four Advil.

As Stella pulled up to the Georgian pile that was Marilee's house, she said, "You go on in. I'll get your stuff and the samples."

While Marilee eased herself out of the front seat and crept across the big front porch Stella began hauling the Two-A-Tee samples from the back seat of her car. When Stella reached for Marilee's overnight bag, she noticed a football betting sheet on the floor. Marilee must've grabbed it up with the dresses, thought Stella. She started to crumple it up when she noticed writing on the back.

It was a mixture of hastily scrawled English and Spanish. It was not signed, and the scribbling was difficult to read, but the last line clearly said, *my money or your heart, yu s o b.*

Your heart? Visions of vicious Mexican drug lords filled her brain. An actual shiver ran through her. Did vicious drug lords write mean notes on the back of betting sheets? She had no idea.

Marilee had endured enough distress, so Stella stuffed the threatening note in her pocket. She would show it to her later. She also decided it was time to get Helen, the solution guru, involved.

Stella took the dresses to Marilee's playroom/dress-making

studio and hung them up. They were in much better shape than Marilee. Stella looked around her. Portable racks held dozens of finished dresses. Boxes of T-shirts in every color were stacked in the corner. Next to these was an enormous box of shirt pieces—the sleeves and tops of tees that had been cut off and discarded when two shirts were sewn together to make the dresses.

One of the many principles Gris had taught his protégé was a zero tolerance for waste. His smoke-laced voice echoed in her ears even now.

"Whether our clients care how much money they throw away or not, it's the principle of the thing! Now fix us a drink, kiddo, and let's rethink this wallpaper."

Stella took a couple of the T-shirt pieces into Marilee's kitchen—a fabulous room filled with marble and chrome and sunlight. Her business partner was making tea and searching her iPad for news of Floyd's fiery launch into eternity.

"I don't get it. There's nothing here about the explosion … or poor Floyd."

"We'll keep checking, Mare. There's bound to be something. I'll check the obituaries, too."

At the mention of the obits, Marilee's lip began to quiver a little so Stella said, "Now, to change the subject …" She held the tee tops out. "There has got to be a use for these."

"Umm, dust rags?"

"I'm serious. It's such a waste!"

"Well, if you can come up with something, we'll put Shirley Esposito on it. Her sewing is great, but remember, her English is almost non-existent. It's hard to explain to her just what you want."

Stella fingered the betting form in her pocket and decided that even if she didn't come up with a use for the leftover T-tops, she would be speaking to Shirley Esposito. Hopefully, Shirley would be able to decipher and translate the Spanish words in the note.

After getting Marilee settled, Stella took the pieces and headed home, determined to find a practical use for the dress leftovers. Though she'd put up a nonchalant front for Marilee's sake, she kept seeing that burning RV.

There's nothing like a new project to get one's mind out of the gloom, she could hear Gris saying. Stella agreed.

Finding a use for the mountain of T-shirt tops was Stella's project of choice for avoiding that gloomiest of subjects, the spectacular demise of Floyd Finger.

She mulled the dilemma over in the morning's coolness as she filled her kitchen window box with maidenhair ferns, variegated ivy and pansies. Besides tee shirts, the hint of long-awaited fall had her thinking of autumn foliage and bowls of soup in front of the fireplace. Stella tried (in vain) not to think how it would be a fall Floyd Finger wouldn't see.

Determined to leave all morbid thoughts behind, she fixed a pot of chili, left it to cool and headed to her mother's. She was still pondering the T-top conundrum when she blew the horn in front of her childhood home.

She'd asked Tutta to go to Bingham's Statuary to help her pick out a fountain—and get a good price. Everybody knew that Herbert Bingham and Tutta had been an item back in the day. When questioned, Tutta would wink mischievously and admit that Mr. B was still sweet on her. He always paid homage to the fact with a hefty discount.

Sometimes, when Stella's daddy had gotten especially unmanageable, Tutta would smile wistfully at the mention of Herbert Bingham and say something like, "Oh, well. He who lives in the past dies a little each day." These statements were usually punctuated with a sigh.

When a sickly sasanqua required banishment from the otherwise healthy hedge in Stella's back garden, Tutta said it was nothing but a good excuse to install a water feature in the bare space along the wall. And she knew just the place to find said feature.

As Tutta slid into the front seat, Stella looked at her mother and said, "That's it!"

"What?" Tutta looked down at herself.

Like many older people, especially those who had acclimated themselves to the deep south's heat and humidity, Tutta was seriously cold-natured. At the first hint of cool air, she pulled out the sweaters. Today, she wore a long-sleeved, denim shirt. And under that she had added a dickey—you know, one of those fake turtle-neck things.

"Dickeys! That's it!" cried Stella, and she explained her plan to Tutta.

"Oooh, I don't know, Stella. I'm no fashion maven, but I don't think they're exactly in style." She fingered the dickey. "I just found this in the back of my underwear drawer and decided it might keep the chill off."

But Stella would not be dissuaded. "We could make cowl-neck dickeys ... something a little more updated, maybe. It's worth a try. I'll have Shirley, the seamstress make up some and see how they do."

Tutta figured there was as much chance of dickeys making a comeback as the return of the flip phone. Of course she'd thought the same thing about girdles and here all these young women were stuffing themselves into Spanx. What must the bra-burners of the sixties think of this turn of events? Besides, Tutta was nothing if not a supportive parent, so she reached over and gave her daughter's knee an encouraging pat.

"If anybody can bring the dickey back, I'm sure it's you and Marilee," she said. "And I'll buy some. I'll give them to everybody for Christmas!"

"You don't have to do that. But thanks."

Tutta didn't insist. Several years prior, after a decade of spousal nagging, Stella's father decided to clean out his closet. (He was actually looking for his favorite pocket knife which never surfaced.)

In the mountain of outdated masculine apparel there was a foothill of ties dating back to his post-grad days. Tutta, another anti-waste advocate who was also deep into an arts and crafts phase, made Christmas wreaths for her children out of her husband's discarded ties. "An heirloom remembrance of your daddy after he's gone," she'd explained.

All but Ann Olive, who is a chronic snob and rebels at anything that isn't her idea, dutifully placed them on their doors for the season. There was much snickering and complaining, however, and after that one Christmas, the wreaths were never seen again.

Tutta's feelings were hurt, but she'd learned her lesson. From then on the Gray children and grandchildren received cash for Christmas. Tutta admitted to the crassness of her decision, but it saved weeks of shopping and made for smiles and good behavior on the big day. She was too old to argue with success.

In Bingham's Statuary, filtered sunlight played on water lilies and turned every drop of the splashing, dripping, gurgling water into shards of sparkling light.

"How could anyone come here and not leave with a fountain?" asked Tutta.

"And how can I choose? I love them all!" said Stella.

After much discussion they decided on a wall fountain with a ram's head that would dribble or spew (depending on the pump setting) water out of its pursed lips.

Herbert flirted with Tutta and gave them a very good price. Stella and Tutta were so carried away with the ambience of Bingham's splashing water features and Herb's doting attentions that they included a cement trough below the ram where, according to Herbert, one could have fish—if the raccoons or neighborhood cats didn't get them, that is.

As they were leaving, a familiar black Mercedes pulled up and that little ball of hilarity, hyena woman, herself, hopped out.

She walked over to Stella and held out a hand.

"Hey, you're Sam's neighbor, the decorator, aren't you? My name's Lena Parks. I'm a good friend of Sam's."

Lena the hyena? I won't forget that one. "Yes, I'm Stella Gray. Nice to meet you. This is my mother, Tutta Gray."

"I wonder if I could trouble you." Excited giggle. "I'm shopping for Sam … something for his back garden." Conspiratorial giggle. "You know how these bachelors are!"

"Well, I have to get my mom back …"

"I'm in no hurry," said Tutta. "Take your time."

Stella was darned if she was going to help this woman choose something great for Sam, something that Stella herself would choose. But what if Lena bought something awful and told Sam that Stella had helped? If she'd only left five minutes sooner!

After twenty minutes of making Lena's acquaintance, she discovered another side to the woman—a funny and kind side. She liked her! Stella busied herself taking back all the mean thoughts she'd had about Lena as the woman talked and laughed and mulled over the few really bad pots and statues that Bingham's had to offer.

Stella began to hear Gris's voice. *You give them what they didn't know they wanted.*

And so she steered Lena to the best looking urn in the place—a squatty, ribbed terra-cotta delight already planted with papyrus. It would be perfect on Sam Poole's patio. She even introduced Lena to Herbert Bingham, who came off the price a bit, launching Lena into a fit of grateful chuckles.

Stella dropped her mother off sans dickey—she needed a prototype and it was possible her mother possessed the last remaining turtle neck dickey on the planet. She headed home singing along to the radio. The new fountain and the solution to the T-top problem had Stella in such a positive frame of mind that it wasn't until she was putting cooled chili into containers that thoughts of the ill-fated Floyd Finger crept into her psyche. It was a total mood buster. I mean, here she was humming around her kitchen when poor Floyd's life had literally gone up in smoke!

But people like Floyd usually came to a bad end, didn't they? He'd probably never intended to rep their wonderful dresses. He'd probably laughed at them as they left his crummy camper or RV or whatever it was. He'd stolen from them. Then almost gotten them killed along with him! And they could still be in jeopardy for all she knew. *Thanks a lot, Floyd!*

Of course, there was the remote possibility that Floyd intended to rep their dresses but found himself on the run from something—or someone. She remembered his flirty smile. And the neatness of his trailer, which was kind of endearing for some reason. Had he cleaned it up in anticipation of their visit?

And what about his soothing words to the mother cat. If Stella had saved a cat and been repaid with a litter of kittens, would she, like Floyd, have been relieved? More than likely, she'd be muttering Tutta's lament, *No good deed goes unpunished!*

Does a man (even one who slurps bourbon during the day) who saves kittens deserve to get blown to bits?

It was at that moment that she knew. She had to find out who was behind Floyd's untimely departure from a vacant lot in Biloxi, Mississippi. Yes, empathy and determination triumphed over common sense. Not knowing how else to begin, Stella grabbed one of the containers of chili and headed to Sam Poole's house.

11.

Chili and Chivalry

"Thanks. Elliot and I love chili. I just opened a beer. Would you like one? Or a glass of wine?"

It wasn't until she and Sam were seated on his kitchen barstools sipping their drinks that she realized she should have formulated a plan. Sam (in Biloxi when Floyd was killed) and Kitty (in New Orleans when she and Marilee met Floyd) were her only tenuous connections to the crime. She dared not call them clues because in all probability these events were coincidental. But it was all she had.

So how do I broach the subject in an off-hand way?

That is what she should've figured out before charging over to Sam's armed only with a freezer-ready container of chili. As it turned out, Sam, himself solved the problem.

"So, did I see you in Biloxi last night?" he said.

Stella choked a little on her chardonnay, but by sheer force of will, managed to compose herself.

"Me? In Biloxi?"

"Yeah. A camper or something exploded near the Beau Rivage. I thought I saw you and your friend, Marilee."

"As a matter of fact, we did ride over there. For dinner. Girls' night out. You know." She felt her face getting hot and took a large sip of wine. "So, do you get over there often?" *With a hot date half your age?* she was tempted to add.

"Every now and then. Did you see the explosion?"

Stella remembered scrambling around in that drainage ditch when the RV blew. She didn't actually see the explosion because she was busy pulling Marilee's skirt down over her lavender lace undies at the time.

"No, I didn't see it," she said. "Do you know what happened? Was anyone was hurt?"

"Some kind of gas leak, I heard. It's hard to believe, but no one was killed or even hurt."

"No one? I mean, no one was in the RV—or whatever it was—at the time?"

"Not according Buck Early. He's my cousin and a private investigator … of sorts. He was over there working a case when it happened and talked to his cop friends about it."

"I can't believe it," said Stella.

The shock of no one having found Floyd's body had her words coming out in whispers. She shook her head trying to settle her thoughts into place.

How can that be? I know I saw Floyd in that RV just before it exploded. How could he have gotten out of there alive? Or dead, for that matter?

Attempting the assimilation of Sam's statement with what she knew as fact sent her poor brain into a sort of overdrive. This, coupled with the intense feelings of relief flooding over her, had her so lightheaded that she had no choice but to put her head down on Sam's granite countertop. She was vaguely aware that she was sweating. Profusely.

"Hey, are you all right?"

She formed a reply, but it wouldn't come out of her throat. "Okay, you just stay right there."

Like I have a choice!

She heard water running. The next thing she knew, Sam was running his fingers through her hair, pushing it to one side of her hot, damp neck. Now he was bending over her.

Is he going to kiss my neck? At a time like this?

Instead of Sam's lips, her neck was caressed by a cold cloth. Stella came to her senses, realizing she'd been close to delirium. She was relieved and yes, a tiny bit disappointed that the inappropriate kiss hadn't taken place. But Sam's concern for her welfare, and his quick action with the wet dish towel almost made up for it.

Once Stella had more or less regained control of her

faculties, she explained. Though she hadn't seen the explosion, she had heard it. Which was very upsetting. Her wooziness had been nothing more than relief that no one was hurt.

Impressed by Stella's empathy for complete strangers (and the curve of her long neck), not to mention that like most men Sam Poole is a sucker for a delicately swooning female, he impulsively issued an invitation.

"I've got a place in the country, an old place with good hunting land. Really pretty this time of year. It's up near Scratch Ankle."

"Scratch Ankle?" Stella was still kind of light-headed and not sure she'd heard correctly.

"Right. I'm having some folks up for a dove hunt. Would you like to come?"

Two other couples were going, he said, and one was none other than Helen Dudley and her husband, Sandy. "You'll have your own room and bath. It's not fancy, but it's comfortable."

Stella could only imagine how Scratch Ankle had gotten its unfortunate name. But then she remembered her daddy's theory that some of the best places have the most uninviting names and vice versa. Besides, she was getting quite attached to the charming Sam Poole with his easy, lovely smile and laid-back ways. Truth be told, she'd have accepted his invitation to Scratch Ankle even if she was certain it meant being up to her thighs in red bugs and mosquitoes.

She also liked the fact that Sam hadn't assumed a weekend in the same house meant a weekend in the same bed. It had been a long time since she'd put herself "out there," but she'd heard the horror stories.

Though she hadn't gotten any insight as to why Kitty was in New Orleans at the priestess convention or the identity of Sam's embarrassingly young date in Biloxi, Stella felt she had accomplished quite a bit with only a whim and a quart of chili. Not wanting to make Sam suspicious or seem overly interested in his love life, she decided to let those sleeping dogs lie. For the time being anyway. She thanked Sam for the wine and the first aid, told him she was looking forward to the weekend up the country and took her leave. She couldn't wait to get home and check the Biloxi news.

When she cranked up the laptop a familiar email address had her feeling woozy all over again. It was from Gilberto de Campos, the cash-carrying South American whose condo she'd redecorated in D.C. It said, *Stella Gray, we have something interesting to discuss. I look forward to hearing from you. Soon.*

She thought, *What on earth could he want? It doesn't matter. I will not get involved with that man again!*

She deleted the email and started to call Marilee, then changed her mind. There was no sense getting Marilee's hopes up in regard to poor Floyd's possible survival. Because the more she thought about it the more she was convinced that there was no way their rep had lived through the explosion. The only thing she could figure was that poor Floyd's remains had been so completely incinerated that no one recognized them as human remains.

She found the story on her computer. An apparent malfunction in a gas line had led to a spectacular explosion in the parking lot of a strip mall near the Beau Rivage resort and casino. Miraculously, there were no reported injuries. The RV was parked illegally so there was no record of the owner.

Okay, Stella's next call should have been to the Biloxi police, but as far as anyone knew, no crime had been committed. And she wanted to know what that note on the back of the betting sheet said before she did anything further. And then there was that email from Gilberto de Campos.

It had her brain trying to make some connection. It was probably just that de Campos was an unsavory character, in Stella's opinion. And he was Spanish ... well, South American, anyway. And the note was partially in Spanish. More coincidences, but still.

Having looked up the translation for dickey, she called Shirley Esposito. After mucho bad Spanish and worse English, she gave up on the explanation for what she wanted. By the time she clicked off, she was pretty sure that Shirley planned on stopping by her house the next morning.

Finally she called Helen and filled her in on the previous night's events in Biloxi and her decision not to share the existence of the note with Marilee until she knew what exactly was in said note.

"Good Lord," Helen said. "I've never known a grown woman to get herself in as many scrapes as Marilee. Sorry I ever suggested that you go into business with her. My cousin is a disaster magnet!"

"It's not your fault. Besides, it hasn't been dull, which was my biggest worry about moving home, and it has definitely taken my mind off my troubles."

"Skydiving might have been a safer diversion," said Helen.

She agreed with Stella that there was no sense getting Marilee's hopes up about Floyd Finger. And she very reluctantly agreed that it wouldn't hurt for Stella find out what was in the note from Floyd's RV before she told Marilee or called the Biloxi police.

"Because that's who should look into the possibility of Floyd's death ... or God forbid, murder!" said Helen. "Certainly not you and Marilee! I can't even imagine what all could go wrong there!"

Helen then dismissed the idea that there was any connection between the email from Señor de Campos and ... anything.

"His yacht or plane probably needs a make-over or something," she said. "You're letting your imagination run away with you, Stella. Not that I blame you."

The subject of the weekend in Scratch Ankle finally came up. Helen's husband, Sandy, also known to many as dead-eye Dudley due to his proficiency in the dove field, was a banker by profession. He'd recently made the acquaintance of Sam Poole while handling a mortgage on one of Sam's properties. After tending to business, the conversation meandered into sports then segued into hunting and the proliferation of doves in Scratch Ankle. All this culminated in Sam extending an invitation for the weekend at his house in the country.

Stella and Helen discussed proper attire for watching other people hunt and hiking in the woods. "Jeans, jeans and jeans," said Helen. "Hiking boots, if you got 'em. And a jacket, nothing fancy. Think my kind of clothes—comfortable, only smaller," she said. She informed Stella that she would be bringing a pot of gumbo and salad fixings.

"Why don't you bring a bottle of wine and some appetizers?" she suggested. "But nothing too fattening. I'm on a new diet."

Really? Diet hors d'oeuvres? Stella wanted to ask, but didn't.

Marilee swore that Helen could convince herself that carrot cake counts as a vegetable. *Easy for Miss size-two Marilee to make fun,* thought Stella. But she worried about her friend's health. So she agreed to shake her mother down for a lo-cal appetizer. If there was such a thing.

"And don't worry about insect repellent," Helen said. "Scratch Ankle is lovely this time of year. This is going to be such fun! I just knew that you and Sam would hit it off."

In addition to running Bayview Botanical Gardens, dieting and problem-solving, Helen amused herself by match-making. This often led to more dilemmas, but being a staunch romantic, she never let this deter her. Besides, it gave her more problems to solve. And kept her mind off bread.

"Let's not get ahead of ourselves," said Stella. "I hardly know the man. I wouldn't even be going if you weren't. And he probably wouldn't have invited me if y'all weren't going."

She was speaking to herself as much as Helen.

12.

No Problemo

Shirley Esposito was a fireplug of a woman, topping off at Stella's mid-chest. And this was with a couple of inches of thick, shining hair piled on her head. But Shirley had a sweet smile and a friendly, confident way about her.

Her first words were, "My English no good. No Inglés. So sorry."

Stella smiled back at her. "Eez okay."

Why am I speaking with an accent?

She started over. "That is okay, Shirley. Mi Español es muy mal."

Shirley giggled. "Sí," she said.

Stella showed her the T-shirt pieces. Shirley nodded. Stella then showed her Tutta's dickey. Shirley, a woman of obvious good taste, reacted as if Stella had handed her a rotten tamale. Undeterred, Stella showed Shirley her own lovely, stylish cashmere sweater with the cowl neck. Shirley oohed and aahed over the sweater in Spanish while Stella attempted to explain in sign language exactly what she wanted. Finally, comprehension dawned. Shirley held up the scrap of T-shirt. Next she held up the dickey, shaking her head and frowning, then she held up the cowl-necked sweater with a smile.

"Si, Shirley," said Stella. "Gracias."

Stella got the threatening note out of her purse, but as she started to show it to Shirley, she had second thoughts. There was no telling what the Spanish words meant. She didn't want to offend this sweet woman. Besides, Shirley was probably the only person around who would attempt to create cowl-necked dickeys out of T-shirt rags. She didn't want to scare her off.

And though Marilee had warned her, Stella hadn't expected Shirley's English skills to be this limited. She might be able to decipher the Spanish words in the note, but there was no way she could translate for Stella.

So, after deciding on a week from Miércoles (Wednesday) as dickey delivery day, Stella walked Shirley to her car and bade her a reluctant adios. She was standing at the curb, lost in thought, still holding the betting form when a familiar voice got her attention. It was Sam, out for a run with his dog, Babe. The sight of his smile obliterated all thoughts of dickeys and diabolical notes. She grinned back at him. They stood smiling dementedly at one another for a few seconds before he walked over to her.

"Was that Shirley Esposito?" he asked.

"Yes. She's doing the sewing for our T-shirt business. I thought she might translate something for me, but with her English and my Spanish, it wasn't worth pursuing."

"Maybe I can help. A lot of the guys I work with are Mexican. I've gotten pretty good with the old Español if I say so myself." He nodded at the paper in her hand. "Is that what you want translated?"

"Uh, yes. But I don't want to hold you up …"

But he was already taking the paper out of her hand. He smiled. "No problema, señora. What is this, a betting sheet?"

"Yes. I found it in my car. When I was in Biloxi. I was just curious as to the message on the back."

"I hope this wasn't meant for you."

"No, I'm sure it wasn't. But I was curious."

"I'm glad you didn't show this to Shirley. All of the Spanish words are cuss words. Pretty strong stuff. The rest is incoherent English. Except for the last sentence. My money or your heart. I'd say whoever wrote this was under the influence of something and very ticked off when they wrote it. Strange that it ended up in your car. It's none of my business, but you should lock it up, especially at night."

"You're right. I will from now on," she said as another thought popped into her head.

How does Sam know Shirley Esposito?

"So has Shirley done sewing for you?" asked Stella. "I'm wondering what you thought of her work?" she added smoothly, not wanting to sound nosy—or suspicious.

"Shirley? Yeah, just alterations and stuff. She does good work."

Stella changed the subject to the upcoming weekend, telling him she had talked to Helen and was planning to bring appetizers and a bottle of wine.

"Not necessary," he said. "Buck's promised to cook all weekend, so there'll be more than enough. But all contributions are appreciated."

"Buck? Your cousin who's the detective?"

"One and the same. He's kind of a character ... just warning you. Can you be ready after lunch on Friday?"

"Sure."

"See you then," he said.

He and Babe trotted off toward LeMoyne Street, and as soon as he turned the corner, Stella's thoughts went back to the note in her hand. So it was a bunch of cussing and a threat. There was a good chance that it had absolutely nothing to do with the exploding RV or Floyd's ... Floyd's what? Stella had watched enough TV crime drama to know that if there was so much as a hair in the trailer the forensics team would have found it. Assuming Biloxi had a forensics team. Biloxi wasn't exactly Miami or New York.

She went inside, deleted yet another message from Gilberto de Campos, *It is important that I speak with you!*, looked up the number of the Biloxi police department and punched it in.

And deleted it.

Why? Because Buck Early with his Biloxi police contacts was probably in possession of some very valuable info that Stella intended to ferret out of him this very weekend. If that didn't happen, she would definitely call the Biloxi police and perhaps even Señor de Campos. And Marilee. And put all of this drama behind her.

But at that moment Marilee called her.

"Hi! I have great news. We have gotten into the Jubilee Mistletoe Marketplace on Main!"

"Which is?"

"Just the biggest Christmas shopping event in the southeast. It's put on by the Birmingham Junior League. Tiny Tots Angel Wing Hair Products dropped out and Two-A-Tee has snapped up its spot! Oh, and as a practice round, we will be appearing at the Emerald Shores Shrimp Festival weekend after next."

"Marilee, I hate to bring this up, but beach dresses in December?"

"Well, normally, I would have to say … well, no. But our one-of-a-kind, hard-to-come-by dresses are such a hit that when it comes to Two-A-Tees, I think they'll sell like—well, to quote Helen, like tassels at a stripper convention."

"In that case, do we have enough dresses?"

"I've got Shirley on time and a half, and she's sewing her little fingers off. Which reminds me, have you heard anything else about poor Floyd? I haven't been able to find anything on any news outlet."

Stella crossed her own fingers and said, "Uh, no. Nothing new. But I did meet with Shirley, and she is going to make up a batch of dickeys, but with cowl necks. We can try them at the shrimp festival."

Now that she heard the words cowl neck dickeys at the shrimp festival out loud, Stella knew it was one of the stupidest ideas she'd ever come up with. But she already had Shirley working on it, and the thought of trying to explain to the woman not to make them was exhausting. Marilee, who'd had her share of dumb ideas, bless her heart, said nothing.

13.

Doves and Grits

After crossing the Dolly Parton Bridge (so nicknamed because of its dual breast-like arches rising from the Tensaw River Delta), it wasn't long before Sam left the interstate. As the two-lane highway moseyed through woods dotted with tiny, worn-out towns, Sam and Stella entertained one another with stories about country kinfolk, life in Washington and the tribulations of the timber business. They found the same things interesting and/or amusing and laughed easily together. By the time the pick-up bumped onto a red ribbon of dirt road, Stella felt like she'd known Sam Poole forever.

They proceeded in easy silence for a while, taking in fields of cotton laced with golden rod that stretched to the earth's curving horizon. Due to a lack of frost which, aside from the infamous boll weevil, is its greatest enemy, cotton planted the previous March was still bursting from its pods. Thursday's showers had the air clean and cool. The sky dazzled blue. It was a postcard autumn day in south Alabama.

At a sign that read, *Sitaspel*, Sam turned onto a rutted drive weaving through thick woods.

"Sitaspel?" Stella asked.

"My grandmother loved to sit on the front porch and visit. So when my grandfather built the place, he named it for what he called her favorite pastime."

They emerged into a clearing. Babe, who had been snoozing in the back seat, began to bark and pace from window to window, anxious to get into the woods. Sam stopped the truck and let the dog out.

"Okay, girl," he said. "Go find Buck."

Babe sailed out of the door and headed toward a Victorian farmhouse book-ended by pines. The house was white clapboard with porches and tall, dark shutters and a sprinkling of gingerbread trim. A shell turn-around fanned out from the front.

In contrast to the pretty scene, there were several unpainted sheds and a dilapidated barn close by. Pickup trucks, an antique tractor and a barbecue grill made from an oil drum were parked beneath the nearest pecan tree.

Stella heard a screen door slam, and the tallest, skinniest man she had ever seen came out from behind the house. He had close-cropped gray hair and a wide belt with an enormous brass buckle that said Buck in what looked to be miniature brass deer antlers. Had to be the detective/cook/cousin.

Buck shook Stella's hand and said, "Welcome to Sitaspel."

"Thank you," said Stella. "I'm happy to be here."

"So you're Sam's new neighbor?"

"Yep. Back home from D.C. And I hear you are a detective."

"Well, I mostly do process-serving and hand-writing analysis. I free-lance for banks, detecting check forgeries, that kind of thing." Buck stuck his thumbs behind the belt buckle and drew his shoulders back a little. "But I get my share of undercover work, too."

"Stella was in Biloxi when that RV blew up," said Sam.

"No kidding?" said Buck, but Stella got the impression that he already knew this. "I'd like to talk to you about that. But for now, y'all go on in. I'll unload the truck while Sam gives you the nickel tour."

Inside the house there was pine paneling, sloping pine floors and heavy pine doors. The focal point of the living room was a good-sized stone fireplace with a pine mantle. A twelve-point mounted buck looked down at them benignly from above the mantle. Stella had never seen a deer that big. He was a bit moth-eaten, but still a beauty.

"My first deer," Sam said. "I was ten years-old, and I've never shot another one that big. It was just crazy luck, but my grandfather was so proud, he had it mounted."

A charming stairway made a turn and disappeared into the second floor. There was a comfortable jumble of pine furniture mixed with Victorian mahogany pieces, old photographs and threadbare oriental rugs. On the windows, crewel drapes hung from rustic iron rods.

"When my grandparents died, various relatives drew straws for the best stuff," said Sam. "Anything anybody didn't want they started bringing up here. It's gotten kind of hodge-podge."

"But it suits the house," said Stella. "I like it."

Sam smiled at her. "I like it, too. I was afraid it might be a shock, you being a famous interior designer. I didn't realize that's what you did when I was giving you suggestions on how to fix your house."

"They turned out to be good suggestions," said Stella. And I'm not famous," she added, laughing. "To be honest, I've gotten into a bit of a rut with my decorating ... everything new and white and contemporary. Lately it's all I see, and all Gris and I do ... did." Her voice caught on the word, did, but she shook off the sad feeling and continued. "I'm sure the clients are still wild for the look, but honestly, what used to give me a sense of serenity is starting to seem, well, a bit boring."

They walked through the dining area which held a round table for twelve and the biggest, bowfront sideboard Stella had ever seen. The kitchen was formica and vinyl with open shelving, a rusty refrigerator and rustier dishwasher, tin topped table and free-standing gas stove. But it smelled good, and its large windows looked out onto a wrap-around porch and the woods beyond.

The guest room that Stella was to occupy was more of the same—mismatched furniture, old quilts and lace curtains framing a view of the woods. Someone had put a mason jar of wildflowers next to the bed.

There was a miniscule bathroom with a claw-footed tub and pedestal sink. The air was a bit musty, and as she raised the window she caught a glimpse of Helen's car coming up the drive.

By the time Helen and Sandy were settled and had taken "the nickel tour," it was cocktail time. Helen put the gumbo on, and they settled in rocking chairs on the porch. Neighbors showed up, a few at a time. Most were down home Scratch Ankle natives, and a few were uptown folks getting a taste of the country one weekend at a time. More chairs were dragged onto the porch and Stella served up Tutta's crab truffles (her least fattening appetizer and an all-time favorite in Bayview).

Half the latecomers were persuaded to stay for dinner. Like Tutta, Buck always cooked for a crowd. Helen simply used mugs instead of bowls for the gumbo so that everyone got a taste. Pork tenders and sweet potatoes came off the grill. Helen and Stella arranged wildflowers and stems of berries in a crock for a centerpiece. They set the table, threw a salad together and after Buck thanked the Lord for "good friends and good cookin,'" everyone proceeded to eat entirely too much.

The neighbors kept after Sam and Buck until they took their guitar and banjo onto the porch and played mellow country songs that were totally unfamiliar to Stella. There was some impressive harmonizing with everyone joining in on the choruses.

After a few of these tunes, a pretty woman flashed a smile at the entertainment and said, "I won't be content until I hear I'll wait for you."

Sam and Buck were silent for a few seconds, as if trying to recall this piece that Stella had never heard of. Finally, Sam looked at his cousin and—like a commando asking his buddy if he was set to jump out of the plane—said, "Ready, Buck?"

Buck took a deep breath and with the same degree of gravity answered, "Yep."

Sam gave an almost imperceptible nod and the most music Stella had ever heard erupt from two instruments filled the porch. It was as if someone had switched on a radio mid-song and full volume. It wouldn't have surprised Stella to see smoke coming out of Buck's banjo. He was playing that hard, head bobbing, buzz cut catching the moonlight as he watched his fingers fly.

The music and the men's voices—Sam's gravelly but clear, Buck's a mellow twang—rose and fell like a gentle tide, then paused in delicious expectation. A smile played across their faces, Buck gave a nod and everyone came together for I will wait, I will wait for you. Stella looked at the assortment of faces and could not find a still or unsmiling one.

As we all know, as opera is dramatic, country music can be extremely heartfelt and soulful. When Sam caught Stella's eye, she knew he was singing those soul-baring words to her.

Could Juliette have felt any more moved when Romeo Montague showed up beneath her balcony? Stella didn't think so.

Stella and Helen sang along as best they could, hummed words they hadn't caught and belted out the chorus. They tapped their toes because they absolutely couldn't not.

Everyone else had heard the song before. That was obvious.

Stella, who can't carry a tune in a wash tub, was having so much fun that on the third refrain she jumped in ahead of everyone else, croaking, "I will wait ..." Sam and Buck shook their heads in mock exasperation. But Sam was smiling, and everyone else—including Stella—laughed with good nature at her musical faux pas.

They all complained when Sam put his guitar down, but he winked at Stella and said, "I learned the hard way it's better to quit too soon than too late. Besides, Buck always wears himself out on that one."

Buck raised his fingers to his thin lips and blew on them.

After everyone headed to their respective beds, Stella and Sam stayed on the porch enjoying the stars and the stillness.

"It's been a long time since I've heard quiet like this," said Stella. "It makes you realize how noisy our lives are."

"Which is why I come up here every chance I get," said Sam. "I wonder how many people live their lives never being quiet enough to hear wind in the trees."

"Too many," said Stella.

"On Whimsy Court everybody has pretty houses and pretty yards. I like that. But lawn services and air-conditioners never seem to stop. Kind of ruins it for me."

Stella thought about civilization where the drone of modern conveniences has grown more constant than the breezes that captured Archibald Whimsy's attention all those years ago. But for now she put Archibald and any other stray thought out of her mind. She listened. And there it was, like an overheard secret—the whisper of air through pine needles—and she knew exactly what Sam was talking about.

"So do you ever think about living here full time?" she asked.

A smile fluttered across his face. But it was a rueful one. "No, I've been in the city too long now. It can get a little too quiet up here. My life is in Bayview. But if I'm in one place too long—country or city—I'm itching to go to the other. Speaking of which, do you miss D.C.?"

"Yes. I really do. Sometimes I wonder if I made the right decision moving home. The longer I'm away from Washington, the more I remember the good things, and the bad memories fade."

"That's as it should be, don't you think?"

"Yes … yes, I do."

"And you'll be adding to the good times here."

"Exactly. Like tonight. Thanks for the music. That was an unexpected treat."

"Any time. Now if I remember, you volunteered us for dish duty."

They pried themselves out of the rocking chairs, took a final look at the stars and headed to the kitchen.

"So I guess Elliot loves it up here," said Stella, putting the final pot away.

"He's starting to." Sam dried his hands and leaned against the counter. "What little boy wouldn't love this place? I know I did." He shook his head as if pondering the question then continued. "My dad and I weren't close. He was always working, never had much time for me. My sister had our mom, but … well, if it hadn't been for my grandfather … my mother's father, I would have missed out on all the guy stuff. Coming up here, hunting and fishing with my cousins, those are my best childhood memories. So when I had Elliot, and I knew things weren't going to work out between his mom and me, I was determined to be a great dad." He pressed his lips together and sighed. "But Elliot's different than I was as a boy. He gets hay fever up here. Guns scare him. I think if he saw a snake, he'd pass out."

Stella remembered Elliot and Thomas climbing the oak tree

in her yard and fooling with lizards. She figured things weren't as bad as Sam feared.

"Is there anything he does like about it?" she asked.

Sam rolled his eyes. "Mostly, he likes the old books and pictures in the house."

"That's all?"

"Well, he likes to collect arrow heads and stuff. And riding in the truck." Sam smiled at this. "I let him sit in my lap and drive out in the field. And thank God, he likes to fish." He smiled. "I love fishing with the little guy."

"He's what? Four years-old?"

"Just turned five."

"Okay, five years-old. And he's had a lot of adjustments. You didn't ask for my advice, but if I were you, I'd just keep collecting arrow heads, riding in the truck and fishing. Maybe let him start his own scrapbook or picture board to hang on the wall here next to his ancestors, maybe a place for his collection of rocks and arrow heads. That's what your grandfather did for you … exposed you to the things you liked, then helped you with them."

"You know, I just assumed that my grandfather and I had everything in common. But I remember my grandmother saying that he really didn't like hunting. I thought she had it all wrong. But maybe he was just doing what I liked. I never realized … And the picture board is a great idea. It's just the kind of thing Elliot would like." He smiled at her. "You don't have a degree in child psychology, do you?"

"Not even close. But growing up, I was the only one out of a dozen cousins who didn't love all the noise and confusion," said Stella. "I know what it's like to be the odd man out."

"I appreciate your advice. And apologize for talking about my problems. It's not exactly great conversation for a first date." He grinned at her. "I'm usually a lot smoother."

Stella thought about the very smooth Andrew who had taken her on a self-promotion tour of his office building on their first date. It was impressively unromantic.

She laughed and said, "I think you're plenty smooth."

As Stella was putting a final glass into the dishwasher, Sam said, "Want to see some deer?"

"That depends. Where are they?"
"Right out back. Follow me."

14.

Like a Deer in the Moonlight

Stella followed him out of the front door. Sam put a finger to his lips and crept around the house. The moon was high and almost full, throwing lacy shadow everywhere.

When they got to the back of the house, Sam gently moved her in front of him and nodded toward the woods. Sure enough, there was a young buck and two does standing at the edge of the clearing. Soon two more does wandered out of the trees. They were beautiful. The thought of the approaching hunting season made her sad, but she knew that if the deer herds weren't thinned out, many would starve to death. She was just glad she didn't have to shoot them.

The scene was breath-taking, and she watched for a while before the damp and the cool caused her to shiver. Sam still had his hand on her shoulder, and he moved against her and rubbed her arms. The warmth of his body, his hands on her arms, his breath in her ear—it all felt so good that she relaxed into him a bit. He wrapped his arms around her. She sighed happily.

Still watching the deer, Sam nuzzled her neck. Stella, deprived of any form of male attention for probably the longest time in her adult life, just couldn't help herself. She turned to face Sam who smiled at her before bestowing one of the gentlest, most delicious kisses she'd ever tasted. When Sam slid his arms around her, kissing her more energetically this time, she became downright light-headed.

Remembering her near faint in Sam's kitchen, she got hold

of herself and gently, reluctantly ended the embrace. When she looked back, the deer were gone. The whole beautiful, romantic thing seemed like a dream. But as she looked back at Sam and he smiled at her, she knew it was wonderfully real.

The next day dawned brisk and sunny. Stella awoke to the smell of fresh coffee. She put on a pair of jeans, dusted on the minimum amount of make-up necessary to camouflage the pesky scars and smiled at herself in the mirror. She looked as relaxed as she felt.

This casual lifestyle is addictive, she thought. *Of course, I'm not doing any of the work,* she reminded herself as she headed downstairs where Buck had prepared a breakfast of pancakes and venison sausage, biscuits and just-picked figs. The two couples then piled in Sam's truck and rode out to check on timber and some leased fields. This was followed by a long hike ending at a ridge that overlooked the river. Minutes later, Buck showed up with a picnic lunch and cold beer.

There was an afternoon dove hunt with neighbors from the previous night plus a few newcomers. Helen and Stella were the only women who didn't shoot, but they went along for the ride, sitting in the bed of the pick-up watching as every shot seemed to bring down a bird.

Several boys who lived down the road were hired to pick up the doves and help Buck and a caretaker named Caesar clean them.

"Glad we got some birds," said Buck. "They're tonight's dinner."

"Do you always shoot the limit?" Stella asked Buck.

"Only when I hunt," he said.

It turned out that Buck—like Sandy—was one of the best shots in the county. "He's not exactly modest about it," said Sam.

Sitaspel's round dining table held a stone platter piled with doves smothered in gravy. There was a large crock of grits and another platter of green beans with hot bacon dressing. Helen set a basket of buttered, toasted biscuit halves on the table. Buck thanked the Lord for "the abundance of doves and straight shootin'" and they all dug in.

Since the Alabama-Arkansas game was on, and the group

consisted of Tide fans, one and all, they settled in front of the TV. After Stella commented on some questionable calls against the Tide, Sam said, "How does an interior decorator from Washington, D.C. know so much about Alabama football?"

"You can take the girl away from SEC football, but you can't take SEC football away from the girl," she explained.

"Stella's daddy, Bo, was a field goal kicker for Bear Bryant," said Sandy.

"No kidding?" said Sam. "Bo Gray is your father? I am seriously impressed. Really."

Every man she'd ever met—excluding Andrew—went all macho-swoony over the fact that her dad had been a football hero well before she was born. Spending most of one's first dates talking football grew tiresome to say the least. So at the time Andrew's disinterest in any sport except tennis had been as refreshing as D.C,'s first cherry blossoms.

But after years with her prima donna boyfriend, she was happily nostalgic watching the game and talking about the famous Bo Gray. She knew it would please her daddy. He deserved his celebrity. A slew of winning field goals, not to mention two knee replacements and a bad back had earned him that.

After the game, Sandy and Sam tackled the dirty dishes stacked in the kitchen sink, leaving Stella and Buck and Helen in front of the fireplace.

"So you were in Biloxi when the trailer exploded," said Buck. "Sam said you were pretty upset by it."

His directness threw Stella off guard.

"Well, yes," she said. "My friend, Marilee and I were fairly close to … to the scene when it happened. I was worried that someone or maybe even several people … had been hurt. And I was just so relieved when Sam said that no one had been killed or hurt or anything."

Lying was not Stella's strong suit. She looked at Helen who was wearing a pained expression as if to say, *Really? This is the best you can do?*

She looked back at Buck, and it was apparent that he didn't believe her either. They all stared at the fire and sipped their drinks.

Finally Buck said, "You know, I've been in the business of investigation and what-have-you for a long time. And I have found that folks have all kind of reasons for not being as straightforward as they might. Usually when the person is some upstanding citizen, it's as plain as my Aunt Jane that their lack of candor is due to fear."

"I really don't know what you mean," said Stella.

"Well, let's say they've gotten themselves into something they got no experience in." He raised his long hands, palms out. "Now I don't want to ruffle any feathers, but Stella, I believe you have inadvertently got yourself in a pickle. And you being a friend of the family, not to mention so darned pretty, I am offering my services free of charge. This includes complete …" He nodded toward the kitchen where Sam and Sandy were deep in conversation. "… discretion, including said family."

Stella mulled this over for all of forty seconds. What choice did she have? Buck seemed a little goofy, but how many P.I.s did she know? And according to Sam, he had buddies in the Biloxi police department. And he was free.

"Thank you, Buck. I accept your offer."

Buck handed her a card and said, "Give me a call first thing Monday. I work out of my house. On Alligator Bayou."

The card was white. Above a creepy blue eye photoshopped on its center was printed *Private Eye*. Beneath the eye it read *Ace Bobby "Buck" Early* along with an address and phone number. No email address. Scattered around the eye were the words—*process server, auto repo, undercover, handwriting analysis* and *discreet service.*

Marilee and I should have gone into business card design, thought Stella remembering Floyd Finger's equally strange business cards. But she took it from Buck, and more to stop looking at the eerie, blue eye than anything, she slid it into the pocket of her jeans.

"So Buck is your nickname," said Stella. "And your given name is?"

"Ace," answered Buck, throwing his shoulders back. "Ace Bobby, junior. Named after my daddy. Can't remember where I picked up Buck."

Helen and Buck said good night, and since Stella could

hardly keep her eyes open, she peeked into the kitchen and said, "I'm heading to bed. Sam, thanks for another wonderful day. I can't remember when I've had this much fun." She laughed and added, "Or eaten this much. Or been this sleepy."

Sam walked over to her. "We're not far behind you," he said. He hesitated just a moment, a question in those lovely hazel eyes of his. Then he kissed her lightly on the cheek. "See you in the morning," he said.

Stella snuggled into the covers remembering Sam's kisses. Especially The Kiss in the moonlight surrounded by woods and the beautiful deer. But before long other memories crawled into her reverie on ugly, little lizard feet.

She saw Sam and a sexy, young woman in Biloxi. They were hurrying away from the bonfire that had been Floyd Finger's RV. As they slipped into a cab and sped away, Sam and a tiny, chuckling blonde took center stage, laughing and dancing their way into her dreams.

15.

Back Story

A thunderstorm passed through Scratch Ankle during the night, making for excellent sleeping. The morning dawned clear, crisp and cold, and the occupants of Sitaspel were up with the sun. They pulled on jeans and vests and boots and after quick cups of coffee, headed for a last hike through the woods. Climbing ridges and dodging limbs, they trekked to a hundred year old cemetery, the final resting place of many of Sam's relatives and several beloved hunting dogs. From the graveyard Buck took them to large mounds of earth that had once been home to Native American tribes. This was one of Elliot's favorite hang-outs Sam told them. Just a month earlier, the boy had found an arrow head unearthed by some burrowing animal.

An hour later they arrived back at the house, winded and hungry. According to Sam, the hike justified a brunch of cheese omelets and fruit and grits topped with leftover dove breasts and gravy. When they were finished, not a crumb remained. Once the dishes were done, bags were tossed into vehicles, goodbyes and thanks were said and the happy campers headed back to civilization.

It was just about the time the twin peaks of the Dolly Parton Bridge came into view that the subject of Sam's recent history arose. This naturally led to the main event—his marriage and subsequent divorce from Jennifer.

"When I met Jennifer, she was studying for the bar exam. It was very intense. She was very intense. And I admired her work ethic. But I assumed it would lighten up once she'd gotten her license. Then job hunting was intense, being a first year associate was intense. When she … we, I guess I should say. When we got pregnant the intensity level just got unbearable for both of us. When Elliot was about three months-old, I realized that I couldn't remember a day that was relaxed, couldn't remember a day that we'd laughed. Or even smiled. I realized to my horror that I didn't love my wife. Except for Elliot and work, I hated my life."

"So did you go to marriage counseling?"

"Oh, yeah. For over a year. Things were better for a while, but … but then they weren't. We agreed to a trial separation for six months, and I felt like I'd been let out of a cage. There was no going back. Not even for Elliot. That's the incredible part. I'd do anything for him." He shook his head. "I was so determined to be a good father."

"There are tons of kids who survive divorce. I'm sure Elliot will, too. And Jennifer seems like a good mom. From what you've told me, maybe a bit …"

"Intense?"

"Yes."

Sam sighed. "You know, we tell ourselves the kids will be better off without the arguing and the negativity in the house, but all they really want is for their parents to figure it out, to get along and make a family again. My parents split up when I was in high school. I promised myself I would never do that to my kids. I'd marry someone responsible and good and do my part, and it would all work out." He shrugged. "I screwed it up."

"You're awfully hard on yourself, Sam. I mean, things happen. It's an imperfect world. I spent the last ten years of my life believing someone cared about me. He dumped me for someone he'd known for a few hours. But as my mother says, 'Honey, it ain't cancer'. And she's right, I guess. Things could always be worse."

Sam smiled at her. "Yes, they could. For instance, instead of your excellent company, I could be listening to Buck explain the ins and outs of the P.I. game, as he calls it."

"Sounds fairly interesting," said Stella.

"Just don't get him on the subject of handwriting analysis. It's his specialty, and he can talk for hours on it."

Stella laughed. "I'll try to remember that. And Sam, thanks for explaining what happened with your marriage. I know it's not always easy to talk about these things."

"I figured you'd be curious about what happened. And you're the first woman I've been around for more than five minutes who hasn't asked me. Or at least hinted around for the story. I appreciate that."

"Believe me, I understand. You can't imagine the questions and comments I've had since I moved back to Bayview. But I have to admit I was curious about your situation."

Sam stared out of the windshield very intently, and added, "Stella, if I ever get married again, I won't do it unless I'm sure—or as sure as I can be—that it's right. Right for me and right for the woman, of course. But it has to be right for Elliot. I thought you should know that."

"I know." Stella smiled at him. "That's exactly as it should be."

"I've never talked about it to anyone except the marriage counselor," said Sam. "And that was kind of … I don't know… clinical or something. Or maybe enough time has passed that I can be more objective. Anyway, I feel better. Thanks for listening."

"Sure. After all, I bared my soul to you."

"Do you mind if I ask you something?"

"Of course not."

"Do you miss not having kids of your own?"

"You know, I love children. I really do. But growing up, it seems all I did was baby sit. There was always so much confusion. Babies and dogs everywhere. I didn't want my life to be like that. And I've loved having my life to myself, putting my career first. Yet I have to admit, now that I'm older I think I may have missed out. You won't believe this, but I'm thinking of getting a dog."

"You're kidding!"

"Nope. Dudley and Matt, the guys at number five are expecting a litter of labradoodles in the spring. If there's a female, I get first dibs."

Sam grinned at her. "Ms. Gray, you are full of surprises."
Stella laughed. "Likewise, Mr. Poole.

16.

The Great Dickey Disaster

While Herbert Bingham and his assistant installed Stella's new wall fountain, Shirley Esposito delivered two dozen dickeys. They were neatly folded and stacked according to color. Shirley shook her head as she handed over the new line of Two-A-Tee accessories.

"I no like," she said and put her hands around her neck as if choking herself. "You no pay."

But Stella wrote her a check for more than they'd agreed on, since the dickey assignment had obviously been a challenge for sweet Shirley who, according to Marilee had been "sewing her little fingers off" getting dresses ready for the shrimp festival and the big show in Birmingham. The check put the smile back on Shirley's face, and she left, exhausted but happy once again.

Stella rang up Bitsy Van Pelt, owner of Magnolia, Bayview's primo boutique. Bitsy, who had sold the heck out of Two-A-Tee dresses and therefore felt somewhat obligated to Stella was anxiously (not in a good way) awaiting the dickey delivery.

Because Stella was in a bit of a snit—Herbert's assistant had inadvertently demolished her new planter—and in a hurry, she ignored that little voice in the back of her head and did not inspect the dickeys, but tossed the box onto the back seat of her car and dropped them off at Magnolia. She then deposited Bitsy's check at the bank.

Glowing with that mission-accomplished feeling, Stella hummed happily to herself as she left the drive-through teller. That was just about the time she got a call from Bitsy. And Bitsy was ticked.

"Stella Gray, you come get these damn dickeys right this minute."

"Wh—?"

"I'll be lucky if I don't have a lawsuit on my hands!"

"Wh—?"

"These dickeys are a disaster!"

"Wh—?"

"Ouida put one of those things on," hissed Bitsy, "And we can't get it off. How she got it over her head in the first place, I'll never know."

Stella was picturing this while visualizing Tutta easily removing her own dickey in one easy swoosh, hardly mussing her brown bob. That's when it dawned on her. Tutta's dickey was elasticized in the neck. Evidently the cowl neck part of the design had not been translated in her directions to Shirley.

Stella heard commotion in the background—women's panicky voices and some gurgling sounds interspersed with ouch! And a whole lotta cussin'.

"What on earth is going on over there, Bitsy?"

"Charlotte is trying to cut the thing off Ouida, but it's so tight, she's cut Ouida's earlobe and broken her new earring!"

Stella headed back to Magnolia. Thankfully, Ouida had gone home to rest. Stella apologized profusely, but as she was slinking toward the door, she remembered that Magnolia had a designer section for tots. The accessories that had almost strangled Ouida would probably slip right over a child-sized head.

"Bitsy, um, have you ever thought about selling children's dickeys?"

"Do you want to refund my money now or tomorrow?" was Bitsy's response.

Stella wrote her a check, made a guilt purchase of an over-priced satin boudoir pillow, and left. On her way home, she called Bayview Stems and had an arrangement sent to Ouida with a note of apology. She'd probably have to replace the earring, too.

What is happening to me? I'm turning into Marilee!

She looked at the box of neatly folded dust rags that had

so far cost her at least five hundred dollars. She wondered what on earth she had been thinking going into business with Marilee or if someone had, in fact put a hex on her. But in the immortal words of Jimmy Buffet, she knew it was her own damn fault.

As she turned onto Whimsy Court, she passed Kitty and Elliot on the sidewalk. Elliot had a tiny backpack hanging off one shoulder, and Kitty carried his SpongeBob lunchbox. Elliot waved and jumped up and down when he saw Stella, causing his owlish glasses to bobble on his face. The backpack slipped to the ground, and he tripped over it, bumping his head on the cement. Kitty rolled her eyes and helped him to his feet. Stella could see that Elliot, like her, was trying not to cry.

Stella pulled up beside them and said, "How would y'all like some of Tutta's shortbread cookies and a glass of milk?"

Herbert Bingham and his assistant and the fractured planter were gone. The fountain splashed and sparkled in the sun. Tutta was right. The tasteful water feature was just the thing against Stella's brick wall, perking up the ho-hum row of sasanquas. Kitty and Elliot oohed and aahed so extravagantly over the sight that Stella served the milk and cookies at her new iron table on the patio.

Elliot looked longingly at the fountain as they ate. Finally he drained his milk and said, "I think ThpongeBob ThquarePanth could live in there. I think he would really like it." He paused, looking at his shoes, in obvious deep deliberation over how to pose his next remark. He smiled at Stella, pushed his glasses up into place and said, "I think I thould check it out."

"Boy, you bein' rude," said Kitty.

"Actually, Kitty," said Stella, "If you don't mind, I was thinking the same thing... that SpongeBob would like it in there. But I haven't had time to see for myself."

Before Kitty could answer, Elliot had unzipped his backpack and retrieved several little rubber figures. Due to those visits from her nieces and nephews over the years, Stella recognized Patrick the starfish, Squidward, the plankton dude and S. Bob himself. Elliot rushed to the fountain, and in a grand gesture, tossed them into the water. He stood and stared into the trough for several minutes before reaching in to rearrange the figures.

While Elliot busied himself playing in the water, Stella and Kitty made idle conversation. At a semi-appropriate juncture, Stella turned the talk to travel and asked Kitty if she got to New Orleans often.

"Not if I can help it. Too much going on over there."

"You mean, uh, like in the quarter? Like bad stuff?"

"That's exactly what I mean. Some of my folk have got themselves in all kind of trouble over there."

"So you never go."

"I do my partying in the Lord's house."

The woman was not big on straight answers.

When it was time for Elliot's mom to come for him, he hugged Stella around the waist as he had before. "I like your pond, Mith Thella," he said.

"Come back any time."

"Can I bring my dad?"

Stella laughed. "That would be very nice."

Pushing his glasses back into place, he said, "Bleth you. I will."

Stella sat down and stared at the fountain. She let the rhythmic sounds of its splashes wash over her, breathed in the scent of a nearby sweet olive tree and thought about Elliot. The peculiar child was getting to her.

She knew from experience that she could help him out with his problems and that she would be good for him. But a life messy with children and their complications wasn't what she wanted, was it? Children had a way of draining the solitude, sophistication and autonomy Stella craved. Once she'd thrown in her lot with Elliot, there would be no escape. The child was too fragile. Yes, getting involved with Elliot Poole was fraught with emotional danger. And we all know that is the worst kind.

And could other dangers lurk on the far side of the pittosporum? Though the idea was crazily far-fetched, she couldn't help but wonder if some or even the entire Poole menagerie were tied to the suspicious death of Floyd Finger.

What did she know about any of them; the gorgeous, humorless mother, the untruthful—or at least very evasive— hex-throwing nanny and finally, Elliot's adorable dad—the country boy with his easy ways and difficult situation? She shook her head. If only Gris were alive.

He'd have fixed a toddy, lit a ciggy and said, "Okay, kiddo, let's get this figured out."

17.

Propositions

If someone had jinxed Stella, it was a heck of a hex. The first sign of evil in the air appeared when she checked her email only to find another missive from Gilberto de Campos.

Do not make me hunt you down in Alabama. Please get in touch.

Hunt me down? She shivered, poured a glass of wine and got in touch.

Señor de Campos, I apologize for not getting back to you sooner. I am no longer in the interior design business. Please do not contact me again. Sincerely, Stella Gray.

Her cell rang ominously. Stella looked to the heavens— *What now!*—and answered. It was Andrew, and it was obvious he'd had a few drinks.

"Hey, I know I'm the last person you want to hear from," he said.

The sound of his voice made her homesick for him, for Washington, for her old, relatively uncomplicated life.

She was too stunned to respond, however, so he continued.

"I miss you, Stella. Things ... um, things are not working out ... with Anika."

He didn't say things haven't worked out, but that they weren't working out.

Stella found her voice. "Which means you are still with her. And you have the nerve to be calling me?"

"It's so complicated," he groaned. "She got rid of her place and moved in here before I knew what was happening. I've made a huge mistake. Just hearing your voice ... you're getting your accent back, by the way. It makes me miss you even more."

Liar! After only a few dates, he'd suggested that she might want to "lose the drawl." And she had. To please him!

"I've moved on, Andrew. I'm very happy here."

But her voice caught on the word *happy*.

She clicked off, took her wine into her lovely, new bathroom where she soaked in her lovely, new tub and had a good, long cry.

Tutta Gray had taught her daughter that the way to get yourself out of a blue funk is to think about somebody else for a change. The fickle Gulf Coast weather had turned warm again so Stella picked up the phone and invited her family over for backyard drinks and appetizers the following evening.

Of course, Tutta insisted on bringing "a few bites that need to come out of the freezer." Knowing this would amount to an embarrassment of hors d'oeuvres, Stella got the drinks together, spruced up the flower beds near the new fountain with autumn ferns, lit a few candles and had herself an instant party. And sure enough, she felt the blue cloud beginning to lift from her psyche.

The guests were due after work. Bo and Tutta arrived first, of course. As Stella was answering the front door, Tutta went outside to check on things. She was rearranging the cocktail napkins when she heard the strum of a guitar. It had to be that sweet neighbor of Stella's who'd invited her up to Scratch Ankle.

It's just plain awkward having him over there strumming his lone guitar while a party's going on twenty feet away! she thought.

Just about the time Stella put platters of her mother's shrimp puffs and sausage balls on the patio table, Tutta came down the drive way with … guess who?

"Hope you don't mind," said Sam, smiling his adorable smile. "Your mom kind of insisted."

Stella had to laugh. "I'm so glad you're here!" she said, and realized that she meant every word.

After her call from Andrew, the sight of Sam Poole was like a B-12 shot to her disposition—and a reminder that she didn't have to settle for the likes of two-timing Andrew. Or the complicated but adorable Sam Poole, for that matter.

Sam chatted easily with Stella's sisters and their husbands and even the nieces and nephews who were present. He tried to leave early, explaining that he didn't want to horn in on a family gathering, but they all convinced him to stay. And after the kin folks kissed Stella goodbye and hurried off to dinner and homework and reality TV, Sam accepted another beer and sat with her on the patio.

"This fountain is great," he said. "It changes the whole space out here, gives it a focal point, I guess you'd say."

"Thanks. That was the idea. And I needed to fill the space where a sasanqua died. But mostly, I like the sound of the water … very soothing after a long day. I had a wall fountain on the patio of my condo in Arlington. I missed it."

Sam proceeded to ask all sorts of technical questions about the installation and running of the water feature.

Finally Stella laughed and said, "I don't know too much about the business end of things, I'm afraid. But you're welcome to check it out."

And so he did, taking the time to show Stella how it all worked.

"You see, it's pretty basic," he said.

"I do see. Now that you've explained it. You're very knowledgeable."

"Maybe so, but I wouldn't have thought to put it there in the first place. I'm surprised you don't miss the design business."

Stella let out a wistful little sigh. "Actually, I do. I'm starting to envision Two-A-Tee designs on furnishings. Every time we finish an especially eye-catching dress I think, wouldn't this make a great throw pillow!"

She then told him about the dickey debacle and gave him a brief run down on a few of Marilee's entrepreneurial misadventures. When they'd finished laughing at the whole ridiculous series of events, Stella added, "I can tell you it's making me wonder what I was thinking going into Mare's latest enterprise … which I know nothing about, by the way."

She was tempted to add, not to mention that our clothing rep was incinerated right before our eyes. She shivered at the memory.

"Are you okay?" asked Sam, remembering Stella's fainting spell in his kitchen.

"Oh, I'm fine," she said. "Just a little chilly. Anyway, as I was saying, it takes more than a good eye for color to run a dress business … or any business." She sighed. "I learned that the hard way when I lost Gris."

"You can acquire the left brain stuff. But the artistic side? I think you have to be born with that." He took a thoughtful sip of his beer, then said, "I'm thinking of buying a duplex not far from here. Over on Park Boulevard. It's structurally sound, but it's dated, worn out and well, it's just plain ugly. I wonder if you'd take a look at it with that designer's eye of yours and give me your opinion. If you think it's salvageable, maybe you could give me some ideas."

"Sure. I'll be happy to take a look."

"I don't know if I can afford D.C. prices, but …"

"Let me see it first. Then we can talk fees. Have you talked to an architect? I'd like to see your plans."

Sam frowned and scratched his head. "I don't exactly have a plan yet." He grinned at Stella. "Due to some pretty serious budgetary considerations, I'm my own architect and contractor. I was thinking you could help with the plans and maybe consult on the kitchen and baths. Look, I like how my house next door turned out. But yours has something extra, minor touches you've added. It's amazing what a difference they make. But then I guess that's why your work has been in all those fancy homes in Washington."

"I'm glad you like my work. And it's a compliment coming from you. You did a great job on your house. No promises, but I'd like to see your duplex. And don't worry. If I decide I can help, I'm sure we can work out a fee in line with the Bayview market."

"Great," he said. And for a second he looked a lot like Elliot when he'd seen Stella and gotten so excited that he fell down and bumped his head.

Sam stood and Stella walked him to the driveway where he turned and put his arms around her. He kissed her lightly just beneath her jaw, then at the edge of her mouth. Then, in an attempt to keep his testosterone level under control, he stopped and looked into her eyes. Gazing into those lovely eyes of Sam's on top of the tender kisses, the feel of his arms around her waist had her breathy and tingly all over.

"Stella," he said, "I know mixing a business relationship with a personal one is asking for trouble."

"Yes it is." Stella was surprised to hear her voice come out in a whisper. She cleared her throat and continued. "And on top of that we're next door neighbors," she reminded him.

"Not to mention your daddy is pretty intimidating. I mean he did play for The Bear."

She laughed. "There is that."

"But seriously, I just want you to know I'm aware of all this."

"Thanks. It's good to know," she said.

And it was. For all the reasons Sam had outlined and so many of her own, taking it slowly was a very good idea.

He kissed her lightly on the cheek and ambled off down the drive. Stella closed her eyes, reliving the sound of his voice, his arms around her, the feel and smell of him. But most of all she remembered the soft kisses and couldn't help but smile.

18.

Misnomers and Misgivings

The plan was to swing by Buck's home/office on Alligator Bayou, which sounded almost as inviting as Scratch Ankle. After her meeting with Buck, Stella would then continue on to Emerald Shores for the Shrimp Festival where she would meet up with Marilee. They were staying in Marilee's beach condo "just up the road apiece" from the park where the festival was to be held.

As Stella pulled out of Whimsy Court, she felt a prickle of unease. But why? It was a beautiful afternoon. The gas tank was full. Her suitcase filled with enough clothes for a European getaway was there on the back seat. She had directions to Buck's place plugged into her phone. Marilee had the dresses with her and was already at the condo. As far as the festival was concerned, Marilee had "taken care of everything."

What could possibly go wrong?

She shook off the prickle, put Dire Straits in the player, opened the sun roof and headed toward the bayou.

The lots on Bayou Road were deep and narrow, the houses on tall pilings. Most had decks on the top, probably built before high-rise condos impeded the view across the bayou, highway and wide, white beach to the gulf beyond. Each lot sported its own short pier and boat house jutting out into the water. Stella passed at least a dozen before she came to a weather-beaten sign with the familiar spooky blue eye that told her she'd found Buck Early.

Buck's house was as tall and skinny as its owner. His office was a converted bedroom on the first floor. It was small and sparsely furnished, but there were large windows framing a nice view of the bayou. The only personal touches were a bunch of mounted fish and an assortment of framed photos sharing a dusty bookshelf with a tattered tome entitled Hand-writing Analysis for the Amateur.

Buck pulled out a chair for Stella then folded himself into one behind the desk.

"This is a beautiful spot," said Stella. "Not at all what I expected."

Buck explained that Alligator Bayou had been named for its reptilian shape. Furthermore, it wasn't a bayou at all, but more of a coastal lagoon. Due to an influx of water from the gulf, he said, it was a bit on the salty side for gators. He then fell silent, signaling an end to the small talk.

Stella took a deep, cleansing breath and told Buck the whole (well, almost) sordid story of her involvement with the ill-fated Floyd Finger. She gave him a photocopy of the note found in Floyd's trailer and told him about the threatening emails from de Campos. She did not mention Sam's coincidental presence near the "crime scene" or Kitty's strange appearance at the Sequester Royale and Lafayette Cemetery.

When she'd finished, Buck let out a slow whistle.

"So you just found yourself standin' in a red ant bed. If it ever happens again, do yourself a favor and go to the police, okay?"

Stella nodded like a chastised child.

"First off, I doubt that Señor de Campos has anything to do with your buddy, Floyd. But again, if you think you're bein' threatened then you should notify the police."

Stella nodded again, but she wasn't sure how accepting a suitcase full of cash as payment would reflect on her.

"It might surprise you to know that I have made the acquaintance of ol' Floyd," said Buck. "He's not a bad sort in and of himself. He grew up rough, over in Farmdale." Buck shook his head. "Those Farmdale Fingers are bad news. Floyd might be the best of the whole, sorry bunch. But he's bad to hit the bottle, always got somebody wantin' to beat his— Uh, always got somebody mad at him. Folks like Floyd, they end up messing with the wrong person sooner or later."

He paused, as if unsure how much more he wanted to say or possibly just how to say it. Finally, he continued.

"Listen, I know a little bit about this … I'm pretty tight with the authorities over in Biloxi, but I'm limited as to how much I can share. Confidentiality and all that. But I'll tell you this. I don't see how Floyd was in that RV when it blew up. They'd have found something of him. In the meantime, I'll check around. I strongly advise you to get in touch with Detective Luckett of the Biloxi police department."

Well, there was no way Stella could do that until Monday, what with the Shrimp Festival and everything, so she thanked Buck, signed a very rudimentary contract for his services and headed for the door. That's when she saw it—a photo of Sam Poole and the same young woman she'd seen him with in Biloxi.

"That's a nice picture of Sam," she said nonchalantly.

"What? Oh, yeah. He and Danielle." Buck shook his head and chuckled. "What a pair."

"A pair? Really?" It was all she could think of to say.

Buck chose not to elaborate, so Stella fake-chuckled and said, "Oh, Danielle. Right."

Yes, it was lame, but how does one subtly pry information out of a private eye? PIs are pros at prying info, and Stella rightly figured Buck would be sure to spot an amateur playing at his game. But sooner rather than later, she would get the story on Danielle.

As she left the bayou that wasn't a bayou that was named for non-existent gators, she wondered if it wasn't an apropos address for Ace Bobby "Buck" Early. What was the Biloxi connection with Buck and Sam and the enigmatic Danielle? As Stella had suspected, Danielle wasn't just some random date of Sam Poole's. Was the "Biloxi Connection", as Stella now thought of it, simply one big ol' coincidence? Was it something non-coincidental but perfectly innocent like the misnomer, Alligator Bayou? Or was it as suspicious as it seemed?

19.

Snake Charming

When Stella got to Marilee's condo, her hostess was unwrapping their dinner of gourmet take-out, which they ate on the balcony. Stella waited until they'd finished their meal before she told Marilee about her conversation with Buck. She did commit a teensy white lie of omission due to the fact that Marilee was still having nightmares about drainage ditches and explosions. As a matter of fact, Stella skipped the entire part concerning Floyd Finger as well as, a. that the conversation had taken place at Buck Early's office and b. that she'd officially hired him. Marilee assumed that any discussions between the two had taken place in Scratch Ankle, and Stella didn't rectify the misunderstanding.

"A pair. Buck said Sam and Danielle … whoever she is … are quite a pair," said Stella.

"Maybe they're a pair of friends … or a pair of co-workers. I know. A pair of dance partners. Sam and Danielle are dance partners who moonlight at one of the casinos."

Stella gave her a look.

"Well, whatever. I say, let it go. We'll put Helen on it when we get back."

So Stella turned her attention to the sun which was now a slash of orange to the west, fading to pink and purple and leaving the air chilled. The gulf in front of them had gone from green to silver and was fast disappearing into the dark horizon.

They decided to ride back to the park in Emerald Shores. There they would check on preparations for the next day's festival—just to make sure they hadn't overlooked anything. But the village shops, nestled there by the marina like a flock of happy seagulls, were open. Marilee, who's never met a boutique she doesn't like, whipped into the parking lot "for a quick look."

Two pair of shoes, a scarf and a pair of jeans later they decided it was too late to visit the park and had a glass of wine at the marina bar instead. They returned to the condo and went to bed.

The next morning was chilly, but they each donned a T-shirt dress, threw on a jacket and drove to the festival. When they arrived at the sign-in booth, Marilee let down her window.

"Hello there," she chirped to the woman beneath the Vendor Admissions sign. "We are Two-A-Tee."

"Morning, ladies," the official-looking woman said. She checked her official-looking clipboard and said, "You're 3D"

"I beg your pardon?" said Marilee, her chirpiness dropping an octave.

"Row three, space D. You'd better hurry. You only have an hour to set up. Then all trucks and trailers have to be moved."

Stella started to get that little prickle of anxiety again. But Marilee looked as calm as the gulf under a north wind, so Stella gave her buddy a fake smile of encouragement and said nothing.

There were six rows of tents and booths fanned out like a rainbow beneath the trees. The only discordant note was the glaringly vacant square at, you guessed it, 3D.

"Good grief," groaned Marilee. "Somebody forgot to put up our booth!"

She hopped out of the car and smiled sweetly at an old man and woman in Birkenstocks and overalls. The man sat on a bench frowning while the woman arranged pottery on burlap-covered shelving. A large sign identified their enterprise as *Collectibles by Babs.*

The woman Stella correctly assumed to be Babs flipped a gray braid over her shoulder and stared at Marilee for a second or two. She shook her head and got back to her arranging. The old man kept right on frowning.

On the other side of Two-A-Tee's non-existent booth a man

in cowboy boots was hanging snakeskin belts from iron hooks. A rustic sign above him read, *Skins by Snake Man Conroy.* Marilee broadened her smile as he looked up. She motioned Stella over to admire the belts, then asked Snake Man Conroy who she should contact about the missing booth.

"You're new at this, ain'tcha?" he said. "You're s'posed to provide your own tent and everything."

"Well, I was not informed," said Marilee. "Whom should I speak to about this?"

"That's hard to say, ma'am. There's kind of a pecking order around here."

Marilee turned and headed in the direction of Vendor Admissions.

"Where are you going?" Stella called.

"To talk to the head pecker," Marilee yelled over her shoulder.

Snake Man grinned at the retreating Marilee with unabashed admiration. Babs shook her head again, but a little smile played at the corners of her mouth. The old man's frown grew determined, and he nodded his approval. Like Snake Man Conroy, he appreciated a spunky woman. Stella guessed rightly that he was also not a fan of the head pecker.

When Marilee returned, she broke the news that she—along with all eighty-four vendors—had indeed been notified about the booth requirements.

"They send you so much stuff. Do they really expect you to read all of it?"

Surely the question is rhetorical, thought Stella.

All sorts of mean, sarcastic remarks were trying to get out of Stella's mouth, but the vision of Bitsy Van Pelt and her employees trying to save Ouida from strangulation by dickey danced into her brain. Marilee had been such a good sport about the whole unfortunate business—accepting both the loss of face and funds with a shrug—that Stella pressed her lips over the words and remained calm.

Marilee wouldn't have noticed, anyway. She was now gushing over the snake belts, wrapping one after another around her small waist and asking Snake Man Conroy's assistance with the pesky buckles.

What is she doing? All we have is a car full of dresses and no way to display them! No place to sit, no shade, no nothing!

Stella noticed Snake Man was now helping Marilee slip her dainty foot into a snakeskin boot. He was all red in the face. If he hadn't been a guy, Stella would've sworn he was having a hot flash. It was about this time that Snake Man decided that he really didn't need to hang those belts, and Marilee was welcome to use the rack to hang her dresses.

Within an hour, Marilee (marvel of improvisation that she is) had charmed the man out of two folding chairs, an ice chest and half his change, which she had also forgotten about. So of course they felt compelled to buy something. Marilee actually bought the boots! Stella selected an expensive rattlesnake wallet. Maybe for her daddy? Tutta wouldn't approve, but Bo Gray would love it.

Though it wasn't an over-priced, dressy tee kind of crowd, by mid-afternoon they'd sold half their wares and made friends with the hippie pottery woman next door whose name was indeed Babs. She introduced her husband as "my old man, Freddie" who nodded a cold hello. Compared to Freddie, Babs was positively gregarious. And for some reason she and Stella hit it off. Stella even traded Babs a dress (for her daughter) for a set of coffee mugs.

While Marilee was modeling her Two-A-Tee dress and cowgirl boots for passersby, Stella chatted about the market circuit with Babs. It turned out that she was very well acquainted with Floyd Finger! He'd conned her out of a soup tureen and a set of coasters. Stella told Babs about Floyd making off with their dresses in New Orleans.

"Well, I wouldn't be surprised if you don't see some of them dresses on Carmen Miranda. She ended up with my coasters, you know."

"Who?"

"That's what I call her. Her first name's Carmen. Cuban woman. Does metal sculptures. Got a temper like you wouldn't believe. She's Floyd's on-and-off girlfriend."

"Really?"

"Yep. Floyd's quite the ladies' man, believe it or not."

"Whoa, that is hard to believe."

"World's full of hard-up women." She rolled her eyes in the direction of Freddie. "Anyway, the last time Carmen caught him with someone else, she 'bout killed him."

"Oh, no!"

"Yep. I heard they was going at it like two cats in a bag."

"Hush." Stella was aware that she sounded just like Tutta, but kept her focus on Babs.

"Yep. Like tomcats in a bag," she reiterated. "'Til Carmen ended it. Cleaned his clock with a piece of her artwork."

"Good grief."

Babs shook her head sadly. "And would you believe I saw him buying beers for a female taxidermist at the Destin Beaux Artistes Festival. The man likes the smell of danger, I'd say."

"When was this?"

"Month or so ago. I heard Carmen found out and threatened to … well, I won't go into details, but it concerned some of his prized body parts. If I were you, I'd forget about those dresses. It's not worth it. That Finger is bad news."

Stella shivered. *Good Lord! What am I doing mixed up with these people?*

She thanked Babs for her advice, purchased a not-half-bad turkey platter and returned to the Two-A-Tee booth. Marilee had sold three more dresses and four pairs of Snake Man's cowboy boots. She kept up this amazing sales pace until close to five o'clock when shoppers began to grow weary and children whiney. During this lull Stella filled Marilee in on the existence of Carmen Miranda, Floyd's homicidal girlfriend.

"And he cheated on her again?" asked Marilee.

"That's what Babs thinks," said Stella. "It seems that what little intellect Floyd possesses is easily suppressed by testosterone."

The sun seemed to be accelerating its descent, setting the gulf beach condos aglow and reminding folks that the day was dissolving. When things slowed to a slug's pace, Stella and her improvising partner opted to pack it in. In direct defiance of the shrimp festival rules (the head pecker would be livid), they decided to head home the next morning and skip the Sunday portion of the festival.

"After all, we want to have plenty of inventory for the

Jubilee Mistletoe Marketplace on Main," said Marilee who was so wound up over Two-A-Tee's shrimp festival success that she practically sang the words to Stella.

She retuned Snake Man Conroy's gear and change with sincere thanks.

"Hey, keep it for tomorrow. By the way," he said with a huge grin, "Do you ladies have any plans tonight?"

"We're heading home, I'm afraid," said Marilee with a sigh.

Snake Man's smile faded like cheap tie-dye. A tiny whimper escaped him.

"But don't worry," Marilee assured him. "We'll be back for SpringFest in April!"

20.

Re-evaluating (again)

Since it was Sunday morning, and everyone was in church or still snoozing, Stella had to wait to call Buck and Helen to tell them about Carmen, Floyd's fiery girlfriend who, in Stella's opinion, had risen to prime-suspect status. In addition to Helen's advice regarding Danielle, the girl/woman who obviously enjoyed a relationship with Sam Poole, Stella also needed her friend's insight into "the case."

Having been forced to watch Perry Mason reruns growing up—Bo and Tutta were fans—Stella had come to think of the events surrounding Floyd Finger as The Case of the Disreputable Rep or sometimes even The Mystery of the Missing Finger.

Any-hoo, on this fine Sunday morning, Stella switched on her new fountain and took a cup of coffee into the back garden to try and clear her mind. The splashing fountain was extremely soothing, so she concentrated on her "third eye" as instructed by Mani, her D.C. yoga instructor, and began to calm down. She was in full relaxation mode when she heard Sam's truck pull into his driveway.

Two doors slammed and she heard Elliot's voice.

"Thankth, Dad. That wath fun."

"It was different," she heard Sam say. "But hey, I really enjoyed it. It was nice of Kitty to invite me."

So Sam had taken her advice and gone to Big Welcome's service. Stella couldn't help but smile.

Oh, to have been a fly on that wall.

Stella fixed a bowl of fruit and some of Tutta's granola and returned to her meditative place in the back yard. She concentrated on her third eye. But try as she might, she could no longer empty her "monkey mind."

The sound of Elliot's and Sam's voices so close turned her heart into one big valentine. The two males' attempt at navigating the foreign territory of emotion and change was just so touching! Not to mention complicated, she reminded herself for the hundredth time. Endless problems and entanglements threatened to arise from an involvement with those two. Stella sighed. But what a sweet pair!

And then there was Two-A-Tee Casuals. In spite of the popularity of the dresses, the Two-A-Tee venture was thus far pretty much a misadventure. It did have potential, however. And it was creative. And being with the perpetually optimistic, indefatigable Marilee was always fun. Dangerous. But fun.

Yet by distancing herself from Washington and throwing herself into something fresh and different, Stella was beginning to see her old life with an increasingly balanced perspective. Interior design was what she did—her gift, according to Tutta. If the comments from her clients, peers and the prestigious Washington Home Magazine were to be believed, her "talents were exceptional in a town of exceptional talents." As Gris often pointed out, "People like to do what they're good at. Of course you love your job!"

Well, Stella Gray was starting to miss doing what she was good at. The emotional wounds inflicted by the loss of Gris and Andrew's betrayal were finally scabbing over. Though she'd been plenty busy, there was also an emptiness formerly filled with museum visits, fabulous dining, theater, the history and the aura of power and that feeling of "things happening" in D.C.

Memories of that traumatic final year were fading, illuminating the happy, good years. Recollections of the old Andrew—the one she thought she knew—were rising from the smoldering ashes of Andrew, the dirty, rotten scoundrel. It was the old Andrew—possibly the real Andrew?—who had called, pining for the old Stella.

Of course, whenever she attempted to sort out her love life, she thought about The Kiss in the moonlit woods of Scratch Ankle, Alabama. She always gave into it. Never denied herself the skin-tingling, heart-melting memory. Closing her eyes, she remembered how Sam had looked at her, like he'd never wanted anything more than her. In her mind, she breathed in the clean, masculine smell of him and felt his arms wrap her up in the cold night air. And finally, she tasted his mouth on hers. The Kiss had awakened something in her that had been lulled to sleep. Had she ever had that with Andrew?

Not even close, she had to admit. But first kisses in the moonlight are like chocolate, aren't they? Delicious! But impossible as a steady diet.

She cleared all thoughts of a romantic nature from her mind. The void was immediately filled with Floyd Finger. In regards to this category-five conundrum, Stella's own come-to-Jesus meeting was way past due. She decided to come clean. She would fess up to Marilee about the threatening note and about hiring Buck Early. And as strongly suggested by Buck, she would get in touch with that police detective in Biloxi.

Relief at having made the decision was invigorating. Stella threw on her running clothes and headed out, first making a lap around Whimsy Court. Ruth and Al Brinkly were just getting in from church, and they waved as she passed. Maggie, the young mom with the bouncing ponytail was heading out with her stroller, and Stella stopped to chat and play with the twins. Whimsy Court was starting to feel like home. She shook her head. If she were back in Washington, she would be missing Whimsy! As she picked up her pace again, Jennifer, the ex-Mrs. Poole turned into the court and stopped in front of number four, presumably to pick up Elliot. Or sent by fate as a reminder of the complications lurking next door, Stella thought. She was aware that the turmoil in her life had her lapsing uncharacteristically into melodrama.

Was she turning into her mother?

After a shower and a sandwich, she called Buck Early and relayed the gossip she'd picked up at the shrimp festival.

"It has to be Carmen who killed Floyd," she said.

"Whoa, hold up a minute, Nancy Drew. We're missing a little something known as the corpus delicti. But I'll do some digging on Senorita Carmen. See what I can come up with."

With assurances to Buck that she intended to visit the Biloxi police department the very next day, she said goodbye, wondering again what in the heck kind of private investigator she had hired.

Next she called Helen who was on her way out to pick up some lo-cal brownies she'd read about, and said she would stop by. Helen hung up the phone without saying goodbye.

What's up with that? wondered Stella.

21.

Arms are the New Legs

The afternoon turned chilly and damp, so when Helen arrived, she and Stella took mugs of tea into the living room and sat in front of the gas fire. Stella put a plate of miniature lemon macaroons—one of Helen's many favorites—on the coffee table. They were lovingly baked by Tutta, of course with the finest almond flour, butter, sugar and egg whites. The delicacies looked as if they might float right off the plate.

"Please take those away," said Helen sadly, turning from the sight of them.

"Another diet?" Stella asked with as little condescension as possible.

Helen groaned. "It's serious. Same thing happened five years ago. My cholesterol's up. Blood pressure's up. I'm back on the verge of diabetes. Marilee got me into yoga and walking and all that stuff I hate. Filled me full of fruits and steamed vegetables. Not fun at all. But I did lose weight."

"Oh, I remember. You looked great. Uh, you still do, just a bit ..." Stella cleared her throat and didn't finish the sentence. She was in dicey territory, and she knew it.

"Go ahead and say it," Helen sniffed. "I'm even getting too big for my large-n-lovely lounging pajamas. I've got to do something. But nothing works! I even hired a personal trainer—a skinny little sadist who told me arms are the new legs. And you know the best things on this body are my calves."

Helen was getting very worked up—a rare event. And the fact that she'd hired a personal trainer? Well, whoa.

"You do have great calves," agreed Stella who was feeling her own less than firm arms. "What does that mean, arms are the new legs?"

"Haven't you noticed all these women on TV are in sleeveless dresses no matter what the temperature, showing off their muscular arms?"

Now that she thought about it, it was true. Stella patted her friend's ample thigh and grabbed up the macaroons, banishing them to the kitchen. As she did so, the doorbell rang. She returned to the living room, but Helen was already at the door. Two young men, a Mutt-and-Jeff duo of evangelists in short-sleeved shirts and skinny black ties stood on the porch, benign smiles and colorful pamphlets at the ready.

"Hello, neighbor," said Mutt. "My friend and I are spreading the good word." The man's face grew serious. "I'd like to ask you a question. Do you think God is an angry God?"

Stella couldn't see Helen's face, but the way the young men drew back, she sensed it wasn't wearing an *I'm just dying to spend twenty minutes listening to a sermon* expression. At which point Helen yelled, "Look at me! What the hell do you think?" And she slammed the door in their poor, blasphemed faces.

"Oh. My. God," said Stella.

At that, Helen turned to her friend.

"I can't believe I did that," she said. "I've got to lose weight or lose my mind." She shook her head. "Those poor guys," she moaned. "Just trying to spread the good word."

When Stella could finally speak, she said, "They'll be all right. I'm sure that's not the first door ..." She decided on a different tack. "Look, you did it once before. Lose weight, that is. You can do it again. As someone very wise once advised me, "You've just got to get back in the saddle again."

Helen managed a smile.

"And we'll help," said Stella. Marilee and I will walk with you. I'll take you to my yoga class. And mama has all these healthy recipes from her nouvelle cuisine phase. They're delicious!"

Helen sighed and agreed to meet Stella in Tutta Gray's kitchen the coming week. On Tuesday and Thursday they would go to yoga class together. "It'll be fun!" Stella said.

"I appreciate it, really ..."

"But?"

"I'm feeling sort of unbalanced lately. It's like I've developed Tourette's. You know, cuss words fly out of my mouth before I can stop them. And slamming the door on a couple of innocent missionaries? You don't think I'm turning into my mother, do you?"

Helen's mother, Louise showed signs of instability as far back as Stella could remember. The woman had a nervous breakdown every three years—usually at Christmastime. Her unpredictable temper was common knowledge among her friends as well as the entire staff of the Bayview Country Club who disappeared like rats from a burning barn after Louise was served her second highball. She once threw a piece of her wedding crystal at the mailman. And this was before noon which tells you a lot.

In between hospitalizations for her nerves, Louise suffered from bouts of the "blues," which no amount of bourbon could cure.

Poor little Helen learned to make a mean Old Fashioned long before she'd mastered the times tables. Like most clouds, however, this one had a silver lining.

On her good days, Louise was a doting mother who was lots of fun. She loved to garden and Helen has actual happy memories of her mother and her tending the flowerbed Louise made for her. Also, while filling in for her mother on her blue days, Helen bloomed into the competent problem solver she is today. And Stella believed that the constant challenge of predicting Louise's moods had resulted in Helen's unparalleled judgement of human nature.

I would be remiss in not stating that much of the credit for Helen's personal success goes to Pearline Patterson, the family's long-time housekeeper and cook. Thankfully, Louise hated to cook and only wandered into the kitchen to fix a drink. This was accomplished by a split-second pass of her glass of brown liquid under the tap after which she would hurry out onto the sun porch to "sip her bourbon and water." Consequently, Pearline, who in today's vernacular would be termed morbidly obese, and Helen spent many an hour in the kitchen where Pearline showered Helen with sweetness and sweets.

In answer to Helen's question, Stella said, "No, I do not think you are turning into your mother. You're just hormonal or something … and bothered by your weight. You hardly drink and you're generally even-tempered. If you inherited anything from Louise, it would be her many good traits."

"Thanks," said Helen. "Tomorrow, I shop for walking shoes and extremely large yoga clothes." She shook her head. "God, I hate downward dog. Okay, change of subject," she said. She settled into a club chair bathed in yellow and gray linen. She looked around her. "I swear this is one of the prettiest rooms I've ever seen."

Besides a contemporary painting with slashes of aqua and yellow, the chair was the only thing of color in the room. The rest was layers of soft neutrals, just hinting at blues and grays. The antiques were predominantly French with a few English things and a lovely American pine chest. The spacious positioning of these pieces and the bare pine floor allowed the room to breathe deliciously. Each well-chosen piece made a statement, but the unobstructed focal point of the space was the wonderful mullioned window with its view of the oak and moss shaded garden.

"Thanks," said Stella. "It's one of my favorites, too."

"So what's new?" asked Helen, knowing that anyone who'd spent any time with her cousin, Marilee, had a story to tell.

Stella felt guilty discussing her troubles when Helen was in the throes of her own weighty problems. But Helen insisted that it would give her something else to think about. After hearing the latest developments, she was in complete agreement with Stella's plan to come clean to Marilee and the Biloxi police.

"It's time to remove yourself from anything to do with Floyd Finger," she advised. "Talk to the Biloxi police, tell them everything and leave it up to them." As to Stella's nostalgic feelings for her old life, including the unfaithful Andrew, she'd said, "If you didn't miss anything about D.C. or even Andrew, it would mean the last twenty years of your life were all terrible, which of course they weren't. You just needed a fresh start. Moving is like the third most traumatic event after death and divorce."

"Really?"

"Something like that. Anyway, it's not easy. Give it time. Give it all time. One project with Sam isn't much of a commitment. And at your age, you're not going to find anyone without baggage ... divorces, kids, old girlfriends. Or old boyfriends." She gave Stella a knowing look and added, "Like Andrew, for example. Besides, in spite of your misgivings, I have a good feeling about Sam. He seems to be a genuinely nice guy. With a sense of humor." She left the words, *unlike Andrew* unspoken. "And he's certainly easy on the eyes. I'd say he's definitely worth investing a little time and energy."

Helen's words sounded good and true and wise. But could the answer to Stella's problems be a simple matter of time?

22.

A Return to the Scene

By ten o'clock Monday morning, Stella and Marilee were headed back to the scene of the crime. Since Stella was on her way to fess up to the authorities, she figured she would use the time to come clean with Marilee. She told her about the note she'd found and handed her the photocopy she intended on turning over to Detective Luckett of the Biloxi Police Department. She reiterated her conviction that Floyd Finger had been murdered by exploding RV though everyone else seemed to think otherwise.

Marilee forgave her buddy for not being more forthcoming and agreed with Stella that not only Floyd's boots, but the rep himself had been in the RV when it blew up. She also agreed that the note had probably been written by Floyd's murderer. Stella then told Marilee about Helen's most recent dietary woes ending with her outburst to the stunned Jehovah's Witnesses.

"Well, I guess you don't have to worry about them coming back," said Marilee.

"I don't know. Helen feels so bad about it she's sending them a big donation."

"This is déjà vu all over again," said Marilee. "The same thing happened a few years back. Helen was overweight, out of shape, depressed and borderline diabetic."

"She said you helped her out."

"We did … my friend, Lily and I. We ate healthy with her, walked with her and exercised with her. It just about killed all of us, but she eventually lost twenty-five pounds." She sighed.

"We did it once. I guess we can do it again."

An hour later they left the interstate. Minutes later they were in Biloxi pulling up to the police station. A cold front had come through, leaving the former fishing village sunny, chilly and deserted. Detective Wayne Luckett, a paunchy man who looked to be just shy of retirement, was also a bit chilly—until Marilee warmed him up.

As you know from the Snake Man Conroy episode at the Emerald Shores Shrimp Festival, Marilee is merciless in the use of her feminine wiles. She now sat before the detective's battered desk batting her baby blues and crossing and re-crossing her lovely legs. She even dangled a dainty stiletto by her dainty toes. She smiled sweetly at Detective Wayne and hung languidly on his every word. While trying to avert his gaze from Marilee's delicate ankle, he assured the women that no one had been in the exploding RV.

"But I saw him … or someone in his boots, anyway," said Stella. "How on earth did he get out?"

"He didn't. Because he wasn't there," said Detective Luckett. "Look, you said the smell of gas was making you dizzy. You were only in there for a few minutes. I'm sorry, Ms. Gray, but if you saw boots, no one was in them."

"Well, what about this?" asked Stella, whipping the threatening note out of her purse and sliding it across the desk. He read over the note, frowning a bit at the *Your money or your heart* line.

Finally he sighed and said, "Look, Floyd Finger is a trouble magnet … involves himself with shady characters and the wrong women. This note could've been left by any one of them." He let his words hang in the air then added, "By the way, what made you ladies decide to come forward with this information now? And more to the point, what kept you from coming in immediately?"

They explained their reluctance to get involved, their fear of retribution by the perpetrators, and besides, they just needed time to think about it.

"It was Private Investigator, Buck Early, who advised us to contact you."

Detective Luckett actually laughed, which Stella and

Marilee considered unprofessional and really bad form.

When he saw the prim looks on their faces, he quickly got hold of himself. "Buck Early? Well, let's just say his methods are not always orthodox. Look, you ladies don't need to be involving yourself with amateur private detectives and what not. It could be dangerous."

He told them he'd known that Floyd, who was no stranger to the Biloxi police, was the owner of the RV. He had known it since shortly after the explosion. He appreciated them coming in, he said. Still, Stella and Marilee were remiss not to have come to the police right away, he added sternly.

"Your department is certainly on the ball," cooed Marilee.

She was laying it on pretty thick, but amazingly, it seemed to be working, so Stella gave her a supportive, little smile and hoped for the best. On the ball or not, Detective Luckett admitted that he had yet to locate Floyd, who seemed to have vanished into the salty Biloxi air.

"We'll find him," he said. "And if you hear from him, be sure and give us a call. And do not meet with him. Under any circumstances."

He gave them a short lecture on trusting the police to do their job and warned them about "doing business with folks you don't know anything about." He took down their contact information, sucked in his stomach, gave Marilee a big, lusty smile and instructed them to enjoy their day in Biloxi.

"Well, that wasn't too bad," said Marilee. "I'm just relieved to know Floyd isn't dead." She thought about this for a few seconds, then added, "Actually, I'm also a little irritated."

Stella laughed. "That he's not dead?"

"That we've been worrying about him after he stole our dresses. To tell the truth, I'm having a hard time letting this go."

"Me, too. But for other reasons. I know someone was in that RV. If Floyd wasn't blown to smithereens, how did he get out before it exploded? There was only one door… the door we came out of. I know he's a skinny dude, but could he have come to, gotten up and squeezed through the window in what, five minutes tops?"

"He must have. Or that wasn't Floyd. Maybe it was a … a

mannequin or something."

"Wearing Floyd's pointy, black snakeskin boots? I just don't think so."

"This whole thing is giving me a headache. Are you hating yourself for going into business with me?"

"Are you kidding? I never expected this much excitement in little, ol' Bayview. And you know what else? We are going to find out what happened to Floyd Finger."

Marilee smiled. "In that case I think we should drop by the Biloxi Fashion Emporium."

23.

Shopping for Answers

The Biloxi Fashion Emporium was stuffed with racks and shelves of assorted feminine apparel. Though the merchandise appeared to be new, Stella had seen better-looking stuff in Tutta's attic.

"They should rename this The Out-of-Fashion Emporium," muttered Stella.

"You're not kidding," agreed Marilee.

"Too bad they don't sell children's clothes," said Stella. "This is the kind of place that would be all over a good deal on children's dickeys."

Marilee rolled her eyes. "Let it go, Stella," she said.

An extra-large woman blossomed out of a plastic chair behind a card table in the back. A faded sign on the wall behind her read, Edna Oster, Proprietor.

"Blue dots are fifty percent off, red dots, seventy-five," said the woman with weary authority. Stella and Marilee rightly assumed her to be Edna.

A quick glance told Stella that the majority of tags had red and blue dots on them. Strangely enough, Marilee, whose tastes ran to designer apparel, was actually flipping through a rack of blouses. But if anyone could find a silver needle in a tin haystack, it was Marilee, Stella reminded herself.

Marilee pulled out a lavender silk tunic and held it up to her, then took it to Ms. Personality in the back.

"What do you think?" she asked.

Edna Oster looked her up and down. "It's your color. What

are you, size four?"

"Two," said Marilee.

"Should work, then. Those run small. Just got 'em in. I got one in cerulean."

"I bet that looks great with your eyes."

A hint of a smile played across Edna's face. "Ain't had no complaints," she said.

Marilee steered the conversation toward Biloxi's current events and segued into the explosion. Sure enough, her new fashion friend knew all about it.

"My friend, Stella and I were walking by when it exploded," said Marilee. "Just about scared us to death!"

At this point Stella put down the purse she was inspecting and meandered over to the card table.

"Do you know who that RV belonged to?" asked Marilee.

A suspicious look came into the woman's cerulean eyes. Her almost-friendly expression was shutting down, so Marilee decided to go for broke.

She looked over one shoulder and then the other. "Because we think it might have belonged to a man who stole our dresses."

The woman nodded her head knowingly. "Floyd Finger, right?"

"That's right! Did you know him?"

Edna's face crumpled. Her eyes filled with tears. She dabbed at them with the hem of her shirt, exposing a mound of pink tummy.

"Oh my gosh!" said Marilee. "Did he steal from you, too?"

"You could say that," the woman sniffed. "Stole my heart." She took a deep, heaving breath and went on. "I met Floyd when I managed Paradise RV Park over in Pascagoula. That man made me so happy I let him have a double space in the shade for free. Got me fired, that ..." She shook her head, leaving Stella and Marilee to fill in the blank. She started to cry again and added, "Then he ran off with that Cuban woman."

"Carmen?" Stella and Marilee said at once.

She nodded. "That was six months ago. I didn't even know he was in town til I saw his RV parked over there."

"He didn't even call you?" said Marilee.

"No." She released a shuddery sigh, shook her head and said to no one in particular, "Life just ain't fair, is it?"

Stella thought back on her own tribulation-filled year and though Edna's rhetorical question required no response, she said with heartfelt sincerity, "No, Edna. It sure ain't."

The three women pondered this harsh truth for a few seconds before Edna pulled herself together and continued.

"Next thing I knew, the RV blew up, and Floyd was missing in action. Well, good riddance, I say. Floyd's nothing but trouble." She sighed sadly. "But he sure was a good time. And brought me my best merchandise. Of course, I never dreamed any of it was stolen. If those dresses of yours are here, I'll sell 'em back to you for what I paid Floyd. I keep good records."

"No, they're not here," said Stella. "When was the last time you saw Carmen?"

"Only the one time, about six months ago." A look of pure hate filled Edna's unusual eyes. "Told me to stay clear of her man, Floyd." Edna shook her head. "That ho is mean as a cottonmouth. She said Floyd laughed at me behind my back. And she knows I have health issues, too. That didn't matter to her."

"Oh, no," said Marilee, who was extremely tenderhearted and so upset by this revelation that she was getting misty-eyed, herself. Marilee's commiseration did not go unnoticed by Edna, who was still sniffing back big tears of her own.

"She said Floyd called me Edna Oyster!" she bawled.

At this, Marilee rushed around the card table and put an arm around Edna until the woman composed herself yet again. When things calmed down Marilee returned to her place in front of the table.

After a decent interval and an appropriate amount of sympathetic murmurings had passed among the women, Stella asked, "Did Carmen come in here alone?"

"No, come to think of it, she did come in here one other time with her friend. Tall, black woman dressed like a gypsy. Name's Pup or something like that."

Marilee's eyes couldn't have gotten any bigger if you'd dropped ice in her undies. Stella poked her in the back and said, "Thanks, Edna. I'm really sorry Floyd did you wrong."

Stella bought the purse she was looking at, and Marilee got the lavender tunic. Though both items had dot-free tags, the Biloxi Fashion Emporium's proprietress insisted on giving them thirty percent off. She also gave them a message for Floyd in the event they ran into him, but I can't print it here.

24.
Second Thoughts

The emotional confrontation with Edna left Marilee starving and craving soft-shell crabs, so while she drove to The Crab Shack, famous for its gumbo, soft-shells and fried green tomatoes, they discussed the major news that Kitty was friends with Carmen, the Cuban spitfire, a.k.a. suspect numero uno. Stella also used this time to change all of her junk from her present purse into her new one. She was trying various things in various compartments when she decided to check her email.

"Oh, no," she moaned. "It's from Andrew. I'm just going to delete it."

"Don't you dare. No offense, Stell, but you're kind of getting in the habit of running away from things."

"Like what?"

"Like telling me the truth about Floyd. Like waiting until today to go to the police about witnessing the explosion. Like deleting messages from that de Campos man. Like leaving your career and Washington ..." She smiled. "Though I am glad you did that. Anyway, at least read the email from Andrew before you delete it. You're running away from the closure you need. In my opinion. And I hate to bring this up, but you've got another problem. Are you going to tell Sam about Kitty?"

"We don't know for sure it's Kitty."

Marilee pulled into The Crab Shack's parking lot and turned off the car. She shifted on the leather seat to face Stella.

"Really?" she said. "A tall, black, gypsy-looking woman named something like Pup? It's got to be her!"

"I swear I can't believe she would be mixed up in all this. She's so nice. And religious. I know we saw her in New Orleans with the Sisterhood of the Priestess chicks, but ... but I also know I saw Floyd Finger in the RV, and Detective Luckett says he wasn't there. I tell you, Marilee, something weird is going on."

"You think? Of all the bizarre things I've gotten myself into, this has got to be the weirdest. And thinking about it is making me hungry." She nodded toward the Crab Shack's front door. "Let's get in there before all the soft shells are gone."

After one of the best lunches ever, they headed back to Bayview. When Marilee stopped at number two Whimsy she put on her serious face and said, "Promise me you'll read Andrew's email. And if you get any even vaguely threatening messages from Gilberto de Campos you will file harassment charges. Or whatever you do when that happens. Also, you probably should tell Sam ... oh, and the PI cousin. You should tell him, too, about Kitty. I mean you can't hire a detective and then not give him all the facts."

"I don't know if I officially hired him since he's not charging me."

"There you go, ducking the issue again."

Stella sighed. "Okay. You're right. But what will you be doing while I'm getting my crazy life in order?"

"I'll be calling Helen and filling her in on the new developments in the case."

"And will you find out exactly what we are required to bring to that market in Birmingham?" said Stella.

Marilee raised her right hand. "Scout's honor. I will be prepared."

Stella sat at the desk in her kitchen and turned on her computer. She opened her email and after a short pause, clicked on Andrew's message. It began, *Dearest Stella.* She hadn't known the word dearest existed in Andrew's lexicon. She read on:

Anika has moved out. It's completely over. Stella, please forgive me. The whole thing was some kind of momentary insanity! But this terrible mistake has taught me one thing. I want to be with you. Your home is here. Your friends and clients are here. Please call me.

BTW, I heard from Gilberto de Campos. He has purchased a huge house—not sure where. He is desperate to have you do the design work—in conjunction with that big-time architect, Edgar C. Beche. You can probably name your terms including freedom from his input. I took the liberty of checking him out. He seems legit. Please call me.

"So that's why de Campos has been harassing me," Stella said to the computer. "Wow, and a chance to work with Edgar Beche ..."

Though still wary, Stella's curiosity about the "huge house" was gaining ground. In Stella's opinion, the New Orleans native, Edgar Beche was one of the finest architects in the country.

Now why is this news having a bigger impact on me than the fact that Anika and Andrew are "totally over"?

She immediately called Señor de Campos, explaining that the recent disruptions in her life were the basis for her short replies to him. The man was amazingly understanding. And persistent. He still wanted her to work on the project.

She assured him that her relocation to Alabama was permanent. He assured her that nothing in this life is permanent. She had to agree.

"Besides, the house I have purchased is not far from where you are in Alabama. You are familiar with St. Charles Avenue?"

"In New Orleans?" said Stella.

"Yes," he said. "New Orleans, Louisiana. I have ... uh, members of my family there. The house is in a very desirable part of the city known as the Garden District. You know of it?"

"Yes, of course." But Stella had never known the man to have any affiliation—business or personal—in New Orleans. The uneasy feeling that accompanied de Campos like a shadow began its familiar dance up Stella's spine.

Does the man get a kick out of sounding sinister? Could it be a cultural thing? If so, I should find out exactly where in South America he's from—so I will never go there!

Though Stella couldn't say exactly why, despite Andrew's endorsement, de Campos still gave her the willies. However, the fact that the project was a two-hour drive from Bayview made it very appealing. Also, de Campos informed her that "important business and long travels" would keep him from any personal involvement in the project. She was the only person he could trust with the fate of the grand house.

Stella informed him that before she could even consider the proposition, the señor must agree to a more established method of payment than suitcases of cash. De Campos laughed good-naturedly and agreed.

Due to Andrew's claim that the South American was a legitimate—if unorthodox—businessman; the man's promised absence during the project; his assurance of conventional payment methods and the fact that the architect for the project was one Stella had dreamed of working with, curiosity won out. She agreed to take a look at the property and the proposal. De Campos was headed to Mexico City for a week or two, he said, but would call her upon his return.

Next she emailed Andrew.

This is all so crazy. And sad. I don't know how I feel about any of it. Please don't contact me. I will call you soon.

As she pressed the send tab, she realized that in spite of referring to her as "his dearest," Andrew had not mentioned love—let alone marriage—in the email.

And who attempts to repair a monumental breakup with an email?

Well, I wasn't exactly receptive to his last call. But he also seems more interested in my relationship with Señor de Campos than in my relationship with him.

Weary of arguing with herself, she shrugged. Then sighed.

Because that's how she and Andrew had always been—the elegant, collected couple others saw and wanted to be. Avoiding crass emotional displays and petty squabbles, Andrew and Stella nurtured shared tastes in art and music and food, until their relationship became a sophisticated waltz of mutual interests and admiration.

It was Andrew's cool sophistication, his appreciation of her work and his apparent delight in her southern ways that intrigued her in the beginning. She'd never met anyone like him. They enjoyed the same vacation destinations and restaurants and music if not always the same people. They laughed together, as if on cue, though never with the innocent joy of simply being together in the moment as she and Sam had.

The changes had been subtle. When had Andrew begun to encourage her to "lose the accent," reprimand her for "chatting up the staff" and frown until she'd replaced her easy laugh with a cool smile? The partnership (because really, that's what it was) was so satisfying, that incredibly, she'd barely noticed.

Until Anika, the high-flying paramour, there was rarely any friction. Or spark, if she were to tell the naked truth. Not that sparks are essential to a relationship, she reminded herself.

The no-sparks aspect actually fit nicely into Stella's blueprint for the kind of serene, adult environment she'd been dreaming about since junior high. Gris had supplied the few essential splashes of color and caprice to her domain. But without her devil-may-care mentor, everything else in that D. C. world faded into a lackluster palette.

Was this a blinding flash of the obvious? Or simply grief casting its shadows? She had to find out. It was part of the reason she'd returned to Bayview and part of the reason she'd agreed to go into business with Marilee. Stella desperately needed the color.

25.

Scary Stuff

Stella picked up the phone several times to call Buck. But she couldn't decide whether to mention Kitty's alleged presence in the Biloxi Fashion Emporium. Though the woman had lied (or was at the least, extremely evasive) about having been in New Orleans and, according to proprietress, Edna Oster, had most certainly been in the Fashion Emporium with Carmen (the prime suspect in the possible murder of Floyd Finger), Stella just couldn't believe Kitty was involved in these nefarious doings. Elliot's safety was of primary concern, of course, but it was obvious that Kitty, prevaricating, voodoo-practicing sidekick to a murderess or not, was devoted to the child.

With all these disparate thoughts playing tag in her brain, Stella decided she had to make at least one proactive move—even if it was a compromise of sorts. She found Buck Early's card, put her thumb over the creepy eye and dialed the number listed below.

"Who? Oh, Stella Gray! Stella … sure. I was just going to call you, believe it or not." (She didn't.) "We got ourselves… well, kind of an unpleasant development. I was told some information. It was in confidence, you understand. So this is between us, okay?"

"Sure."

"Seems some remains have been found floating in the Mississippi Sound. Looks like it could be your buddy, Finger."

"My what? Oh! Oh, no! Why do you think it might be Floyd?"

"Well, the remains seem to have been burned. However, there was a fire at the shipyard about the same time that the RV exploded. They thought everyone was accounted for at the shipyard but who knows? Stranger things …"

"When will they know who the remains belong to?"

"Well, not to get too graphic but the remains are kind of minimal if you know what I mean. I'll let you know, but I'm betting somebody who wasn't s'posed to be at the shipyard was at the wrong place at the wrong time. Think about it. If Floyd did meet his maker in that RV, how'd he get in the sound?"

Stella pictured a fiery Floyd skyrocketing through the roof of the RV and landing with a splash in the Mississippi Sound.

She immediately put the grisly picture out of her mind and said, "I have no idea."

She told Buck about her meeting with Detective Luckett at the Biloxi police department, and her visit to the Fashion Emporium. She relayed the plus-sized proprietor's description of Carmen, but could not bring herself to mention Kitty.

Buck was quiet for a few seconds. Then he said, "You know, one of the main benefits of hiring a private investigator is that you don't have to do the investigating yourself. Sticking an inexperienced nose into things, well, you might just get it cut off. Do I make myself clear?"

Stella assured him that he'd made himself abundantly clear. She gave a little shiver as she put the phone on the counter. It rang immediately, causing her to jump. She took a deep breath and answered it.

"Hey, this is Sam. Remember the duplex I asked you about?"

"The one that's just plain ugly?"

"That's the one. I thought maybe you'd take a look at it. Just to see if you might be interested. This offer includes dinner at the restaurant of your choice."

It had been days since she'd talked to Sam. She relaxed against the kitchen counter and smiled. His voice is like sunshine, she thought.

"An offer I can't refuse," said Stella. "When do you want to go?"

"Anytime. You name it."

"Tomorrow afternoon?"

"Pick you up at two."

The following morning, Stella met Helen for their appointed hour-long walk. She noticed that in the short time they'd been exercising regularly, Helen had picked up her pace. Stella also shared a recipe for a lo-cal salad dressing, and instead of wrinkling her nose, her buddy had not only prepared and eaten it, but described it as not horrible.

"And these pants?" said Helen. "They're new. And they're a size fourteen, which, believe it or not, is an improvement."

Stella hurried home to shower because she had an appointment with Vickie at Hair Now. She was contemplating a bold move. Vickie agreed with the idea, and after a bit of discussion, Stella's shoulder-length waves began drifting onto Hair Now's floor. By the time Vickie had holstered her blow dryer, Stella had a bouncy, wavy, shining chin-length bob. As her hairdresser looked on proudly, Stella examined her new do from every angle, finally declaring that she'd never felt so stylish.

When she opened the door for Sam, he grinned his approval and said, "Whoa, look at you!" He made her turn all the way around, then said, "I like it. I really like it."

As encounters go, Stella would have described her conversation with Buck as pretty scary. But that was before she saw the duplex on Park Boulevard. It was a little patch of sixties blight festering in the middle of a delightful, circa 1930's block. Renewed interest in wide streets, towering shade trees, charming curb appeal and good deals had this area, which was also close to town and the bay, on its way back. One by one, the neighboring houses had been reclaimed, which only accentuated the ugliness of Sam's potential purchase.

The restored treasures sported the crisp exterior and trim colors sanctioned by Bayview's historical board. Swings and overflowing planters once again graced the ample porches. Yards were neatly mowed, clipped and edged, as was the expansive green median cleaving the boulevard.

The duplex, on the other hand, was an indeterminate, nausea-inducing color—probably the result of mixing leftover cans of pink, tan and yellow paint. The trim was chocolate brown. Cheap siding and aluminum windows enclosed its porches. The roots of a gnarly magnolia took over one side of the front yard, while weeds claimed the other.

As unappealing as it all was, Stella knew there had to be even more negatives lurking behind the house's unsightly face. It didn't take much vision to know that there were darn good reasons the last, inexpensive fixer-upper on this charming street hadn't been snapped up.

When they entered the front door, Stella's fears were confirmed. The place was worse than just plain ugly. It was complicated ugly. Originally one two-story house, it had been butchered in an attempt to transform it into a rental cash cow when the once-fashionable area surrendered to suburb mania back in the day.

Inside, flimsy walls sectioned off the stairway leading to the second floor residence. Every room, it seemed, had been altered from its original purpose—closets built into the corners of parlors and hallways, a kitchen rigged into an upstairs bedroom. The upstairs balconies had even been closed in for use as makeshift closets. A rusted water heater lived on the back porch. But the house was starting to speak to her.

"Some renovation, huh?" said Sam.

"More like vandalism," said Stella.

Cockroaches the size of mice (only a slight exaggeration) scrabbled toward the shadows as Stella and Sam entered the bizarre rooms.

"Aaag!" yelled Sam and Stella as one scampered over his shoe. "God, I hate those things," said Sam. "The first night I came in here they were flying all over the place."

"Oh, my God! Flyers? They're the worst!"

"Yeah, and there were dozens of them. We're talking nightmare stuff." Sam shook his head at the memory and actually looked a bit pale.

"They really bother you, don't they?" said Stella. "I mean like a real phobia."

"I never liked them. Then when I was about six or seven, Buck locked me in a shed. It was full of them." He shuddered. "I was in there for hours with those things."

"Buck, as in your cousin, P.I. Buck Early?"

"One and the same. But he didn't realize. Anyway, I hate roaches." He smiled at Stella. "I get the feeling you're not crazy about them, either."

"Our house on Pine Street where I grew up sits beneath an enormous live oak. I love the tree, but in spite of regular visits by the bug man roaches were everywhere. Mom said they were a nuisance we had to learn to live with."

"But you never did."

"Right. My mother and sisters can swat a roach and step on it without a second thought, but I swear I can't look at one without getting all creeped out. I tell myself it's ridiculous, that they can't hurt me, but still.

After their confession of a mutual phobic loathing for cockroaches, Sam said, "Okay, change of subject. What do you think of the place?"

"You say the house is structurally sound?"

"Believe it or not, it is."

"If you'll consider turning it back into a single-family house, and hiring a draftsman—and an exterminator—I'll be happy to help you. We can do a lot of what we did on Whimsy Court to modernize it. Then it's just a matter of what Gris used to call paint and powder."

"So you'll work up a price?"

"Yes, and I'll draw up some preliminary plans. We can go over them, compare them to your ideas, make changes and then send them to the draftsman. I'd like to use Katie Myerson. She's young, but very good ... thinks outside the box."

"I like outside the box," said Sam.

"Good." Stella smiled. "And don't worry. You can afford me."

Sam put out his hand and Stella shook it. He smiled like a kid on his birthday, again reminding her of Elliot. The faces of a contrite Andrew and an eager de Campos popped into Stella's consciousness. Knowing she should sort out her relationships with those two (not to mention the ones between Sam and Danielle, the sexy Biloxi belle, and Sam and hyena woman and Sam and Lord only knew who else) before getting involved any further with her adorable neighbor, she shook the whole pile of unpleasant images out of her head and said, "I think you've got a deal."

She didn't want to let go of his hand. And she didn't want to keep secrets from him any longer. Stella's conversation with Marilee in the Crab Shack's parking lot played in her head. She'd taken her friend's well-intentioned advice concerning Andrew and de Campos and Buck (well, for the most part, anyway). In addition to coming clean with Marilee, she'd fessed up to Detective Luckett. And with each encounter she'd felt freer of worry and more in control of her life. It was a good feeling.

On the way home from Park Boulevard, the conversation turned to Elliot, and Stella decided to tell Sam what she knew about Kitty. Which meant she had to tell him the whole sordid story of Floyd Finger.

When she finished her tale she had included every weird detail and the corroborating pictures Marilee had snapped of voodoo Kitty at the Lafayette Cemetery.

Sam sat in stunned silence for a full minute then asked why she didn't tell him about her involvement with Floyd that first night they'd discussed it. If you remember, it was the night she'd nearly fainted in his kitchen. Stella took a deep breath and let it out slowly.

"Sam, I saw you hurrying away from the scene—with a date, I guess. It looked like you were running away. Surely it was another coincidence. But I didn't know what to think, and remember I didn't know you at all then. It seemed better not to say anything."

"Wow," he said. "Looks like it's my turn. That was Danielle—the girl I was with in Biloxi. We just happened to be walking the strip when the RV exploded. It upset Danielle … she was already on edge because Buck was staying at her place while working a case. It makes her nervous when he's on a job, so we grabbed the first cab back to her condo."

"Wait a minute. Buck was staying at your date's place?"

"Danielle is Buck's little sister."

"So she's your?"

"Cousin." He smiled at Stella. "First cousin. Not my date. Anyway, like I said, Danielle has a condo in Biloxi, and since

Buck was over for a few days, she invited me to join them. When Buck got in that night, he told us everything he'd heard from the Biloxi police. And told us not to say anything.

"I should explain that this is classic Buck. He's good at what he does, but he doesn't get that many real cases, so having the inside story on things … well, it builds up his ego. He'll give you a little confidential info supposedly from his buddies on the force, then swear you to secrecy."

"So we both had good reasons for keeping secrets," said Stella. "I didn't want to implicate Kitty, possibly get her fired, when she was in all likelihood innocent. Besides, she seems devoted to Elliot. I can't believe she's guilty of anything."

Sam sat mulling things over for a while. Finally, he said, "You know your association with this Finger guy could've gotten you and Marilee killed. I don't understand why you felt the need to find out what happened to him. He is … or was … a cheap crook who tried to swindle you and Marilee."

Stella shook her head. "It's hard to explain. Partly it's because I know Floyd was in that RV. He couldn't have gotten out. And no one believes us. Worse than that, no one seems to care one way or the other if he's dead or alive… or murdered, even. Also, in spite of it all, Floyd, the womanizing, alcoholic con man is a likable guy."

"You're kidding," said Sam.

"No, I'm not. From what Buck tells me, Floyd's not all bad. And I believe that." At this point she shared the story of Floyd's tenderness toward the little cat family in New Orleans. "He had a rough childhood," Stella continued, "And has made bad choices.

"Then there are so many other odd things going on like seeing Kitty in New Orleans and her all but denying it. And then finding out she—or someone of her exact description— was in Biloxi with Carmen, Floyd's scary girlfriend. There's the note in Spanish … probably from Carmen. But if not, then from whom? Tell me truthfully, Sam. Could you have just let all of that go?"

Sam smiled at her, shook his head and said, "Probably not. But I'm a guy … a big guy who's been in a fight or two and knows one end of a gun from the other. And yet I would hesitate to get mixed up in this. Besides, you've got cousin Buck looking into things. He's a character, but he knows what he's doing. Take his advice and Detective Luckett's advice. And my advice, for what it's worth. Let this go, Stella."

"Okay," she said, but as the word left her lips she knew the only way to stop thinking of Floyd Finger going up in smoke was to get to the bottom of what really happened to him.

"Now that that's settled, when and where would you like to collect on that dinner?" he asked.

Stella thought about Lena and the other women orbiting number four like love-starved moons.

"Sam, are you sure you want to do this? Like you said, if things don't work out, it could get very uncomfortable with us being neighbors."

"Believe me, I've weighed my options. A lot."

"And?"

He smiled at her. "I've decided it's worth the risk."

"What about the other women in your life? I'm sorry, but I just can't see myself as one of your ... regulars."

"To tell you the truth, I'm getting a bit weary of the regulars. So what do you say?"

Stella realized that she had no choice. She was in too deep already. If she didn't take a chance on Sam Poole, she would always regret it.

And so she smiled up into his lovely hazel eyes and said, "Okay. How about Friday? At Bay Bistro."

"Excellent choice. I'll reserve a table outside. And they're having the monthly art walk near the restaurant—something right up your alley, I believe."

"Definitely up my alley," said Stella. "Any good art?"

"I wouldn't know. I've never been." He smiled at Stella. "You're my first artsy date."

Stella pictured Jennifer, the brainy beauty queen, Lena, the vacuous blonde with the unfortunate cackle and finally, Danielle, the hot, not-date from Biloxi and was not at all surprised.

26.

The Dinner Date

Stella turned this way and that in front of the mirrored closet door in her bathroom, pulled a just-purchased crimson sweater over her head and added it to the pile on her dressing table chair. "Too hot," she muttered. Next came a sleeveless cobalt blue blouse. Remembering that "arms were the new legs," she held her arms out to the sides like a ballerina. She swung them back and forth. "Ugh!" Sleeveless cobalt blue joined the reject pile.

Finally, she wiggled into a long-sleeved, creamy silk top that graced the hips of her new black skinny pants. It was perfect with the new haircut. Black suede wedge heels, comfy for walking, came next. She vetoed the black pearl choker given to her by Andrew and added the long chain and locket bequeathed to her by Gris. It had belonged to his mother.

Why was she making such a fuss anyway?

She told herself it was because of Bayview's fickle weather. She didn't want to be too cold or hot while dining alfresco, wandering Bayview streets and ducking in and out of frosty galleries. And it was her first dinner date with anyone other than Andrew in almost ten years. She smiled at herself again, hearing Gris say, "You look like two million and counting, kiddo."

Because she did look good. The shorter haircut made her appear and feel younger. She'd ramped up the exercise and healthy eating right along with Helen, and though the shadowy scars remained on her cheeks, the sadness plaguing her countenance for months had all but vanished. Noting these pleasant developments gave her confidence a very nice boost. She decided to stop analyzing and worrying for this one evening at least. And just give in to the moment.

"Who are you kidding, girl?" she teased her reflection. "You have a date with the cutest, hottest guy this side of the Mason-Dixon Line. You better look good!"

She gave herself a mental thumbs-up and spritzed on her old stand-by, Chanel No. 5 just as her neighbor rang the doorbell. Stella grabbed a short jacket of silvery suede and hurried down the stairs.

It appeared that Sam also considered their date worth "getting got up for," as her daddy might say. His tan slacks and pale blue shirt were pressed, his loafers polished and the cashmere sport coat he wore looked brand new. He smelled faintly of pine soap.

"Wow," they both said at once. They laughed, then said simultaneously, "You look very nice/great."

In Stella's experience, October weather was variations of pleasant everywhere in the world, and Bayview was no exception. The evening air was salty-soft and cool on the wide deck of Bay Bistro where creamy lights reflected on the bay below. Candlelight danced across white tablecloths set for gloriously long meals. Waves lapped at pilings, and sailboats' lines pinged gently against masts in the marina nearby. A young woman played classical guitar from a shadowy corner by the bar.

They decided on a wine and perused their menus.

"I feel guilty just reading about all of this," said Stella.

She told Sam about Helen, swearing him to secrecy when she came to the part about the Jehovah's Witnesses. He couldn't help but laugh though he sympathized with the door-to-door evangelists.

"When I was in high school, I had a summer job selling magazine subscriptions ..." and soon Stella was laughing at his tales of slammed doors, amorous housewives and lost paperwork as a teenaged entrepreneur.

"I like the sound of your laugh," he said as the server poured their wine.

"Really? I don't think anyone has ever told me that before," she said, remembering Jennifer, Sam's mirthless ex and Lena, his cackling admirer. It was no wonder he appreciated a normal chuckle. "I'm glad you approve," she said.

His expression softened and said, "Really. Your laugh is … musical. I never get tired of hearing it." As if embarrassed by this declaration of affection for Stella's laugh, he picked up his menu and said, "I hear the crawfish beignets are really good."

The dinner progressed nicely from there. The taste of perfectly prepared crispy red snapper, celery root puree and fennel salad finished off with key lime soufflé was enhanced by her and Helen's recent meals, most of which were compilations of Tutta's lo-cal recipes. But truly, if the food had been fat free cottage cheese and water Stella wouldn't have cared as she basked in the afterglow of setting sun, romantic ambience and Sam's good company. She just had to keep reminding herself not to get carried away by his approval of her laugh.

Maybe that's what happened to Lena!

The area where Palmetto Bay carved a crescent into Bayview's sandy shores had, like so many wonderful, discarded things, been rediscovered. Now everyone was asking themselves how malls fronted by acres of asphalt had ever been preferred to store fronts open to catch breezes and passers-by. What mind-altering substance had the citizens been smoking back in the day that caused them to tire of leafy parks and sidewalks and bike paths?

But the folks had come to their collective senses, slapped their foreheads in successive aha moments and headed down to the neglected bay front. Galleries, eateries and boutiques began springing up like mushrooms after one of Bayview's tropical downpours. It was here that Stella Gray and Sam Poole wandered after dinner, happily discussing mostly mediocre art, the weather and anything else that popped into their heads.

They lingered in one small, dingy space that nevertheless had a certain appeal with its wind chimes and lights strung across the opening and funky art on the sidewalk. They accepted a glass of wine from the proprietor and had a look inside. Sam bought a book on seashells for Elliot and crystal wind chimes for Stella, saying, "That's what your laugh sounds like to me."

Well, the gift and the sentiment were the most romantic things anyone had ever given to Stella. In fact it was just about the most romantic thing she'd ever heard of.

"What a nice thing to say. And do. I can't wait to hang them," she said.

It was all she could manage because tears were pricking at the backs of her eyes. That's how romantic she thought it was.

27.

Romantus Interruptus

By the time Sam pulled up in front of number two Whimsy, Stella was feeling all floaty and about as happy as an oyster at high tide. It wasn't surprising, considering the romantic attentions of sweet, funny, handsome Sam Poole stoked by several glasses of chardonnay and the uber-romantic wind chime gift. So of course, when he walked her to the door, took her in his arms and kissed her like she'd never been kissed before, Stella wanted nothing more than to take him by the hand, lead him up to her bedroom and dive between the sheets with this wonderful man. Instead, she simply invited him in.

The spell of new romance, soft night air and hoped-for, soon-to-be-requited love had the duo so bedazzled with one another that neither of them noticed a figure scowling at them from the shadows of the oak tree in Stella's side yard. Nor did they pay any attention to beams of a car's headlights winking through the Whimsy oaks. All Sam and Stella could do was grin at one another as they slipped into the house and shut the door behind them. The mystery car slowed to a stop in front of number four and doused its lights.

The time enjoying each other's' company, of sharing thoughts and stories culminating in such magnetic mutual admiration was quite naturally manifested in sexual attraction. Sexual attraction simmering like Mount Vesuvius. And it erupted that evening right there in Stella's lovely living room because Stella and Sam couldn't wait long enough to climb the stairs to her bed.

Luckily, Stella had followed Gris's steadfast sofa rule: The perfect sofa is forty inches deep, sixty inches long and thirty-six inches high with arms big enough for a guest to perch upon. So love on the couch—though a bit cramped—would be every bit as sublime as they'd both envisioned. After which they would fall asleep in each other's arms wearing the serene, besotted smiles of requited lovers. Such were Stella Gray's thoughts as Sam Poole kissed her mouth, gently at first.

Sam and Stella were well into the thrilling throes of one another's charms when the scowling prowler slipped quietly from the shadows to peek through the mullioned window where moonlight illuminated the lovers. After several minutes the enraged interloper ran to the front porch and burst through the door, yelling at Sam and calling him the worst names you ever heard.

Sam leapt to his feet. Stella tumbled to the floor over-turning her ultra-chic acrylic and metal coffee table. Books, a large Chinese bowl and a vase of white hydrangeas crashed down after her. When Sam looked to see if Stella was okay (which she wasn't), the intruder took his chance and punched Sam in the face.

•

The driver of the car parked in front of number four was getting sleepy and running out of patience. She got out and was heading to the door when she noticed Sam's truck in the driveway of number two. Thanks to Elliot, she was well aware of Stella Gray. She was trying to decide on a course of action when she saw a man slip from the bushes and let himself into the house.

"What the …?" she was asking herself as cursing and crashing sounded from inside the house. She darted back to her car, retrieved a hand gun and charged number two Whimsy like it was the Alamo.

As she entered, she could just make out what looked to be a naked woman with a very cute haircut rising from the floor. The woman was staring at the male intruder in horror.

"Andrew?" was all she said. Again and again.

"This is Andrew?" yelled Sam. "The guy who cheated on you with the flight attendant? Buddy, you've got some nerve."

That's when the gun-toting woman noticed that Sam, also naked, but holding a silk throw pillow in front of himself with his left hand was cradling his bloody nose with the right.

Groping for the light switch, she pointed the gun at Andrew and demanded, "Just what is going on here?"

"Don't shoot," yelled Andrew and Sam simultaneously.

•

"You can shoot me," groaned Stella, because this night had brought personal mortification to a whole new level for poor Stella. "Just please don't turn on the light." She grabbed a saffron-colored cashmere throw from a chair and wrapping it tightly around her like a sarong, she said tearfully, "What are you people doing in my house?"

Sam looked at the woman expertly holding a gun in her French-manicured fingers and said, "That is a very good question. What the hell are you doing here, Jennifer?"

"I thought you were being killed," she said matter-of-factly.

"But what are you doing … here?" Sam asked, waving his bloody arm in a gesture meant to include his home, his neighborhood, his love life.

"I needed to talk. George called our engagement off. I don't know what I'm doing wrong. I just needed to talk," she said again. With no emotion. Like a recording or a bad actor trying to get through her lines.

Stella and Andrew could only stare.

But Sam? Stella noticed that he was actually looking sympathetic!

"How did you get in here, Andrew?" asked Stella.

"The fake rock? I mean, come on." He turned to Jennifer. "And lady, please put that gun away."

"Sorry about that," said Jennifer, flashing her dimples at Andrew. She was still in desperate need of someone to talk to and figured her ex-husband was not a good candidate on this particular night. "Do you need a ride?" she asked Andrew.

"Uh, yeah. Actually, that would be good," said Andrew, suddenly wanting to be anywhere but number two Whimsy Court and wanting it so badly that he was willing to take a chance on the gun-toting ice queen who was somehow connected to the man who'd almost just defiled the woman meant to be his.

He looked at Stella, who he noticed was downright alluring wrapped in her saffron sarong/throw with her new, short hair all tousled and highlighted by a shaft of moonlight, and he tried his darnedest to come up with words that would somehow put things right between them.

But in the end, the best he could come up with was, "Do you want me to put the key back in the rock?"

"Just leave it on my broken coffee table," Stella said.

28.

Lunch Therapy

Stella took a long sip of her frozen blackberry mojito and shook her head, remembering. "She looked like one of Charlie's Angels—all statuesque and confident, shaking her beauty queen hair out of her eyes and holding that gun on us," she said.

"Did she hold the gun with two hands?" asked Marilee.

"What?"

"You know, like they do on TV. I'm trying to picture the scene."

"Yes, as a matter of fact, she did," said Stella. "I'm telling you, it was impressive."

"So, did you even get to …?" Marilee made a little hopeful face.

"No, I did not," said Stella. She didn't even attempt to hide her irritation.

"And Andrew actually caught a ride with Jennifer? That's the part I can't get over," said Helen, who figured it was high time to change the subject of non-consummation to something slightly less personal. "Have you heard from him?"

"Andrew? Yes. He's staying at the Bay House Hotel, waiting for me to call him. But I'm not."

"Here we go again," said Marilee.

"You have to call him," said Helen. "Put an end to all of this. You do want to put an end to it, don't you?"

"Going back to my old uncomplicated life with no ex-wives, no kids with problems, no wacky relatives … it has its appeal.

Especially after that horror show the other night." Stella sighed and dropped her face into her hands.

Marilee rolled her eyes and blew out a slow breath. As far as she was concerned Andrew was one big Windsor knot. But she bit her tongue. Because there was always the chance that Stella might actually resume that ice box of a relationship she had with Andrew.

Following a desperate call from Stella, Helen and Marilee had picked up their friend and taken her to lunch at Marilee's club. The previous night's embarrassment factor alone called for lunch and drinks. The fact that it had happened to Stella who shunned complication like a plaid recliner, was downright mind-boggling.

"The real problem is Sam," said Stella. "Do I want a relationship with a man whose ex still calls him with her problems? I mean she wouldn't be calling him if he weren't sympathetic. Which he is. I saw the way he looked at her. The expression on his face was—not exactly pity but … sympathy, at the very least."

Helen and Marilee looked at each other.

"Sympathy is good," said Marilee. "So many men are totally unsympathetic when it comes to women's problems. And face it, she is the mother of his child. And according to Georgiana … You know, the one who works with Jennifer, he is the one who ended the marriage. All in all, the sympathy is a good sign. In my opinion."

"I agree," said Helen. "By the way, have you heard from Sam?"

"I haven't returned his calls either."

They sat in silence for a minute or two.

Finally Marilee said, "Would you really choose a man who, after a ten-year relationship and after cheating on you, still hasn't proposed marriage? A man who hasn't used the word love one time in all his calls and emails?"

"He did fly all the way down here," said Stella. "He's not comfortable with emotions."

"How many times has he bought you a wind chime because it reminds him of your laugh?" asked Marilee

"I'm betting precisely never," muttered Helen.

"Or sung to you?" continued Marilee. She gave an ecstatic little shiver. "I love that. Helen told me all about it."

"He was singing to everyone," Stella reminded her.

"It sure didn't look like that to me," said Helen. "As a matter of fact, I think he forgot the rest of us were even there. The bigger question, however, is how important are wind chimes and guitars under the stars to you?"

Stella sighed again. Very dramatically. "The biggest question is do wind chimes and guitars under the stars last?" she said.

"I believe it's possible," said Marilee. Her words floated out on a sigh. Bringing herself back to earth, she added, "Okay, you have to decide. The security of the known—secure if Andrew doesn't stray again, that is, versus taking a chance on something wonderful—possibly forever wonderful. But unknown. With a few complications." She held up her left hand. "Safe." She held up her right hand. "Exciting. And wonderful. Possibly forever. But somewhat complicated. Only you can decide."

Stella felt certain that Andrew would not be unfaithful again. It was an aberration. He'd ventured off into the exciting, wonderful unknown with Anika. And it was a terrible mistake. Yes, she was sure Andrew had learned his lesson. She was also sure that there would never be guitars and wind chimes with Andrew. He was a known. A plus in the Andrew column. She sighed. And also a minus.

Were guitars under the stars an aberration with Sam who had women clinging to him like pilot fish? Was he simply her version of Anika? A day trip into the titillating unknown? The allure of excitement and head-over-heels romance had her commiserating with Odysseus and his futile resistance to the Sirens' song.

Somebody tie me to the mast, already!

"Now, I hate to change the subject," Marilee was saying, "But are you ready for Birmingham?"

"Birmingham?" Stella was genuinely confused.

"Omigod! You are not ready? You really are not ready. We are leaving for Birmingham to participate in the Jubilee Mistletoe Marketplace on Main in a matter of days, missy."

Helen snorted. "Missy? Calm down, Marilee. In the time it

takes you to pick out your underwear, we can be ready."

"We? You're going, too?"

"I promised Tutta."

"Mama asked you to go? I don't believe it."

"I hate to break it to you, but the events of last night, well …
they're pretty much common knowledge by now."

Stella shouldn't have been surprised. She'd heard from both
her sisters that morning. Alice thought the whole thing was a
hoot, and was not one bit surprised that men were fighting
over her smart, beautiful sister. Ann Olive, on the other hand,
was all about damage control, but at least she blamed the
entire "debacle" on Andrew and would make "damned sure"
everyone knew it.

But Stella groaned, envisioning the town gossips sacrificing
their last free cell phone minutes and multiplying her
humiliation at lightning speed.

"It just keeps getting worse, doesn't it?" she said.

"Tutta didn't exactly say she'd heard anything," said Helen.
"She just suggested it might do you good to get out of town
with friends. And you two have been so helpful with my
weight loss regimen. I've lost four more pounds, by the way,
and I can actually do downward dog without cramping up. I
mean it's the least I can do!" she said. "Besides, I'll get a little
Christmas shopping out of the way."

Marilee gave her cousin a look that said you are lying
through your teeth, but of course, she said nothing. Dealing
with the fickle, lovesick Stella while trying to manage a booth
in the biggest Christmas show in the southeast was beyond her
abilities, and she knew it.

Actually, Tutta was aware of the previous night's events
minus a few of the more prurient details, thank goodness.
In the ensuing texting frenzy, the version passed to Stella's
mom fell somewhere between OMG and TMI. I would like to
report that this was out of kindness or respect, but the truth is
that even the wickedest gossips weren't dumb enough to risk
banishment from Tutta's gastronomic largesse. So there was no
mention of firearms or nudity in the tale Tutta was told.

However, fearing that another mishap while in Birmingham
with Marilee would "do Stella in," Tutta had enlisted Helen

as a chaperone. Helen, who would rather eat rice cakes for a month than attend the Jubilee Mistletoe Marketplace on Main, agreed that her friend's mental state was too delicate to be left in the hands of her disaster-prone cousin.

So, braced by her plan to secrete a box of family-sized Hershey bars in her make-up case, Helen put a smile on her face and promised to go along.

29.

Lessons from SpongeBob SquarePants

Stella allowed herself a few more hours of steeping, saturating, all-consuming self-pity before calling Sam.

"You've reached Sam Poole. Leave a message."

The sound of his voice had her wanting to track him down, throw her arms around him and plight her trough with his forever. Or at least for the afternoon. Simultaneously, she was light-headed with relief that she would be able to put off the inevitable conversation that was certain to involve ultimatums of some kind.

"Beep."

"Hi, Sam. It's me. It's Stella. Sorry I missed you. I know we need to talk. But I'm headed out of town. With Marilee and Helen. To the Mistletoe market in Birmingham. I'll call you when I get back. And Sam, I'm so sorry about the other night. It was wonderful until well, until … it wasn't. I hope your nose is better. Okay. Bye."

She put her face in her hands and shook her head. "That was so inept," she said aloud. Her voice echoed in the emptiness of her kitchen. She wasn't just alone, which she enjoyed for the most part. For the first time in her adult life, she felt desperately lonely.

And not alone, after all. A small, strange figure was walking through her backyard. He wore pint-sized jeans, a Roll Tide sweatshirt and yellow swim goggles that had pushed his red hair straight up in the back. He was bare-footed and carried a brown paper bag.

Stella went to the back door and opened it.

"Elliot?" she called.

"Yeth, ma'am?"

"Whatcha doin'?"

He was at the fountain now, emptying the contents of the bag into the water.

Stella walked over to him and knelt down in the grass. Now they were almost the same height.

"Good grief," she said, pointing to a tiny figure spiraling toward the bottom of the fountain's trough. "That looks just like SpongeBob SquarePants."

"It ith. Patrick and him had a fight."

"Oh, gosh. I'm sorry about that. But I bet they will make up. Friends almost always do."

He bobbed his head in the affirmative. The goggles were fogging up. "They like it in the water," he said. "They thould all play in the water together."

"Ellll-i-ot?" It was Kitty, coming down the drive.

"We're back here," called Stella.

Kitty walked over to Elliot, gently removed the foggy goggles, took his glasses out of her pocket and hooked them on his ears. She rubbed his back as she quietly reprimanded him for going off without telling anyone.

Stella figured that Kitty knew what was going on—at least in Elliot's life. The gentle tone she used with him told her that. Did she also know about the farce that had played out in Stella's living room just two nights ago?

And was it possible that she also knew what had happened to Floyd Finger and his girlfriend, Carmen, the Cuban firecracker? Stella wondered if Sam had asked Kitty about being in New Orleans with the voodoo crowd or in the Biloxi Fashion Emporium with Carmen.

Before Stella could say anything, Kitty took Elliot's hand. "Elliot, thank Ms. Stella. Boy, we got to get you back in time for your mama. Get your toys out of Stella's fountain and let's go."

But Elliot, obviously stuck on the horns of a child-sized dilemma, didn't move.

"Elliot, would you like SpongeBob and his friends to stay and play in the fountain for a while?" asked Stella.

"Yeth, ma'am. I would," he said, and allowed Kitty to lead him quickly across the yard and out of sight.

If and when Sam quizzed Kitty, had he mentioned Stella? He'd promised not to. Judging from Kitty's frosty attitude, it was a definite possibility. Of course, it was also possible that she had guessed. Stella remembered her clumsy interrogation of Kitty concerning New Orleans. Buck Early was right. Stella was no detective.

She had hung the wind chimes from a low branch near the fountain. A new breeze set the crystals tinkling softly. Their music soothed her overloaded psyche as she turned the recent humiliation over in her mind and weighed various theories concerning Floyd Finger. She finally decided the most likely scenario was that Kitty knew something of the crazy ménage in Stella's living room. Was Kitty afraid of jeopardizing her job by letting her boss (Jennifer) find Kitty and Elliot in Stella's back yard?

Stella looked at the cartoon figures at the bottom of the trough and thought about Elliot. She rolled up her sleeves, reached in and picked up SpongeBob and Patrick.

Such a peculiar duo.

She put the quarrelsome buddies back in the water, arranging them so that they faced each other. Yep, they were talking things out, clearing the waters, so to speak. She hoped Elliot would find the weird, little friends like that—and imagine them all made up—when he returned to get them.

The thought made her smile, and she realized it was the first time she'd relaxed since Andrew burst in on the most romantic night of her life. The calmness felt good. And the self-pity party was growing tiresome. She could just hear her daddy saying, "It's time to shake it off, Stella."

Besides, if a five-year-old can try to fix his world armed with only a sweet soul and his SpongeBob figures, then I—a forty-six-year-old woman of the world—can act like a big girl and sort out my life.

And so Stella began to feel like she might actually have the energy to box up stacks of Two-A-Tee dresses, pack the car, make the drive to Birmingham, decorate a double-wide booth with bolts of netting and ribbons, check into the Vulcan Suites and man the Two-A-Tee booth for three straight days while subsisting on junk food and prepackaged samples sold at the gourmet stalls.

Yet as she headed back inside to pack her clothes for the trip, she had no idea what lay ahead — in Birmingham, in her personal life, in her career. It was all as big a mystery as the spectacular demise of Floyd Finger.

Some of it was out of her control, but not all. And as sure as Patrick and SpongeBob would make up their differences, she wasn't going to leave anything to chance. So once she'd packed her suitcase and tended to a few necessary household chores, she called Sam again. This time, he answered.

"Hi, Stella," said Sam. "I was just listening to your message. I couldn't be sorrier about what happened."

"I know. Me, too. It was insane."

"Yeah. Completely insane."

"And so … embarrassing."

"I know," he said. "I hate it for you … for us. But I promise you that as far as my end of things goes, it will never happen again."

"Lord, I hope not," said Stella. "And I can promise you Andrew will never … either. How's the nose?"

"Not broken, but still a little swollen. It'll be fine. Look, I've got to take Elliot to his mom. Kitty's not here … it's kind of a long story. Could I come over after I drop him off?"

"I'm on my way out of town. To the market in Birmingham. And I promised to help Marilee. We have a stack of dresses to finish. There's just no time."

"I need to see you, Stella, even if it's just for a few minutes. Can I stop by in an hour? I won't stay long."

An hour later, Stella and Sam stood in her kitchen, neither of them speaking. (They were both avoiding her living room where the broken coffee table sat as a reminder of the crime of almost passion.) But after the commotion of their previous meeting, this was an easy, welcomed silence. It allowed them to simply be together alone.

Finally, Sam leaned over and gently kissed her cheek. Of course, the next thing Stella knew, she was wrapped in his arms, and the urgency of the upcoming market was dissolving into thin air. All she could think about was Sam's mouth on hers, his breath in her hair.

Thanks to Marilee, she was jolted back to reality before the point of no return. Because just as her responsibilities to her friend disappeared from her lust-filled brain, the phone on the counter began to chime.

"Omigosh! Sam, I'm sorry, but ..."

'It's my fault. I promised to stay only a few minutes." He smiled and added, "Guess I got carried away."

Stella smiled at him. "Yeah. Me, too." She looked at the phone. "It's Marilee. I'll have to call her back. But what were you going to tell me? Something about Kitty?"

"That was one thing. I asked her about Floyd Finger and his girlfriend. She denied knowing them, but she was evasive when I asked her about being in New Orleans and Biloxi." He shook his head. "I hate to say it, but I got the feeling that she's hiding something. On the other hand, I took your advice and went to her church a few times. Everyone there loves her and looks up to her. They're nice people. I don't think they would hang out with Kitty if she were—I don't know—anything other than what she claims to be. But then as soon as we finished talking, she asked if she could have some time off. She'd already cleared it with Jennifer who's lined up some replacement sitters. I said it was fine. She didn't offer an explanation, and I didn't ask."

Could she have a split personality? wondered Stella. *There's church-going nanny and there's voodoo nanny.*

But the idea was too silly to mention to Sam. He might think she was making fun of a serious situation. Besides, her brain was brimming over with "to do's" for the market. Figuring out the Kitty conundrum would have to wait.

"Maybe it will sort itself out while I'm in Birmingham," she said. "I hope so because I like Kitty, and she's good with Elliot. But what else did you need to discuss?"

"Well, the most important thing ..." He smiled at Stella, and as usual, melted her heart a little. "... is us. But it will have to wait. It's not a discussion I intend to rush through. I just needed to see you and make sure you were okay, that we were okay."

Stella returned his smile. "We are," she said. She looked at her watch. "I hate it, but I've got a lot to do if I'm going to be ready for the market."

"There's one other thing," he said. "Be careful."

"I will."

"I'm serious, Stella. Promise me you won't start playing detective when you get to that market. Don't go asking questions about any of it. Especially about Floyd Finger. And don't mention Biloxi to anyone, okay?"

"I promise to be careful." She smiled reassuringly. "Besides, I doubt there'll be anyone in Birmingham that has the slightest connection to Floyd Finger." She made a little face to show just how silly the notion was. "It's not that kind of market."

30.

Two-A-Tee Goes to Birmingham

The following morning, which was the day before B day (Birmingham day), Shirley Esposito showed up with a half-dozen coral-colored dresses fresh off her smoking sewing machine. Since these coral creations were their best-sellers, Stella, Marilee and Stella's sister, Alice met in Marilee's playroom to decorate them.

They chose the crab and starfish designs, which were the simplest and also the most popular. Alice ironed on the fabric designs while Marilee and Stella finished the edges with silver and gold acrylic paint. When the paint was dry enough, they all frantically but carefully sewed sequins and beads into the designs.

Well after a late supper, Marilee's enormous, bottle green SUV was packed with luggage, collapsible racks, hangers, booth decorations, Two-A-Tee signs, business cards and of course, the "must-have" dresses. Marilee draped the recently-painted creations on top of everything else and said a prayer that they would dry completely by departure time.

Fake palm trees wrapped in clear plastic were strapped to the roof. This gave the car a jungle camouflage appearance. Helen was (rightly) worried that this would distract the other drivers flying up I65 and cause wrecks. Marilee pretended not to hear her.

At six AM, Marilee stopped in front of number two Whimsy. Helen was in the front seat. Stella, balancing a mug of coffee and a piece of toast, crammed her overnight bag into the rear compartment. She then squeezed herself into the backseat alongside boxes of dresses and wedged her purse between her feet.

As they pulled away from the curb, Helen said, "I wonder who's visiting Sam Poole at this hour?"

Sure enough, a black Mercedes was parked squarely in front of Sam's house.

"It's Lena's car," said Stella dejectedly.

"The laugher?" asked Marilee.

"Yep. Either she's a very early riser or she spent the night over there," said Stella. Her voice caught as she uttered the second, more logical explanation.

"Didn't you say that Sam was just at your house promising no more embarrassing situations?" said Marilee.

"Yes. And warning me not to ask any more questions about Floyd. Or to mention Biloxi to anyone. Which was out of concern for my safety, of course." Stella's last statement was swimming in sarcasm.

"Well, I forbid you to jump to conclusions," said Marilee.

"I agree," said Helen. "The man can't help it if he attracts more women than a shoe sale at Nordstrom's. Honey, if he's the one, you're going to have to learn to trust him. Even though it's hard after the way Andrew behaved."

Stella let out a large sigh. "Okay. I choose to believe there's a logical reason for Lena's car to be parked at Sam's house at six o'clock in the morning. And that the only reason he's warning me off the Floyd Finger case is because he cares."

But the little voice of reason in Stella's head was saying something else entirely.

Mid-morning found them stepping over boxes and crates and dollies of merchandise until they found booths One F & One G, recently vacated by Tiny Tots Angel Wing Hair Products.

Tiny Tots must have been with the show since its inception because the booths were front and center—directly across from the show's main entrance. At seven o'clock that evening, the doors to the main entrance would be thrown open to admit a select five hundred, formally-attired shoppers. Their staggeringly expensive but tax-deductible tickets guaranteed them first crack at the latest, greatest gift items and their fill of libations and gourmet nibbles.

The booths on either side of Two-A-Tee's prime spot had their curtains drawn and tied. Marilee had learned that one was occupied by the jeweler, Paula Grant, whose designs could be found in high-end boutiques all up and down the East Coast.

Remember the emerald and diamond starfish pin that ended up in Floyd Finger's doomed RV? It was a Paula G original. There would be no diamonds at the Jubilee Mistletoe Marketplace on Main, Stella was certain, but the more mainstream Paula G baubles surely would be.

When Helen asked why someone of Paula Grant's stature would allow her jewelry in such a plebeian setting, Marilee explained: Proceeds from the market went to the children's hospital. Paula Grant was on the hospital's board. Having a Paula G booth would draw a crowd.

"I wouldn't be surprised if Paula Grant, herself doesn't attend the preview party!" added Marilee.

The neatly-tied curtains on either side of them suggested that the organized proprietors of One E and One H had already set up. Stella pictured them soaking in bubble baths somewhere while she, Marilee and Helen (who kept complaining of hunger pangs) worked like bees on speed to get their Christmas Beach Boutique in shipshape. Marilee looked at her watch.

"How will we ever be done in time?" she muttered.

The good news was that this time there was an actual booth with actual tables and chairs. There were technicians to help with lighting and volunteers bringing coffee and doughnuts! And change!

Since they'd inherited a double-booth (at double the price), there was plenty of room for racks of dresses and the cutest cardboard Two-A-Tee attired mannequin you ever saw. The sea colors and metallics Marilee had chosen for decorations were gorgeous—as well as a nice diversion from the redundant red and green motifs going up in the other booths.

Marilee had silvery ornaments and sandy, silvery bows for the palm trees, which stood like the sentinels of a summer Christmas on either side of the booth opening. She rolled dresses and tied them with silver and blue and green, and placed them in clear beach bags with sandals and sunglasses and good beach reads. Dresses were hung neatly on racks, and boxes of extras hidden beneath tables draped in sand-colored burlap.

They had just enough time to get across the street to the Vulcan Suites, shower, slip into their most flattering Two-A-Tee dresses and get back to the trade center before the preview party. When they entered the cavernous building, they simply could not believe the transformation.

Though a few vendors were still stashing boxes out of sight and tweaking shelves, the place was a fairyland. Caterers had set up here and there in the wide aisles. Ice sculptures and sparkling wine glasses shone beneath faux candle light. A string quartet was tuning up next to the Barnes & Noble Bookstore booth where best-selling authors were readying their pens to autograph books.

A pretty African-American woman with short, curly hair was parting the drapes on booth One H. Two young women were assisting her. Stella and Marilee were happy to see that the Paula G booth was also done in silver and pastel tones. The booths shimmered together seamlessly.

The woman wore a strapless pink cocktail dress accessorized by a bracelet and necklace of seed pearls. Almost-matching drop earrings studded with tiny amethysts hung from her ears.

When she caught Stella's eye, she smiled and said, "Hi, I'm Paula." She nodded to the young women and added, "These are my assistants, Becka and Janie. "And girl, we love your dresses," she said.

When Paula Grant smiled she went from pretty to dazzling. She was funny and energetic with a sparkle in her eyes. So of course, the Bayview girls, as Paula referred to them and the bauble peddler from Atlanta, as she referred to herself, became friends right away. When Marilee admired a pearl and shell necklace, Paula insisted she wear it. It was perfect with her lavender dress—the one with the watery mermaids on it.

"You'll be good advertisement for me," said Paula. "Helen and Stella, please select something, if you like."

With guidance from Janie and Becka, Stella chose a necklace. Just as the string quartet started up and the champagne began to flow, Helen decided on a pair of turquoise and silver stick earrings. Minutes later, the doors were thrown wide and a happy, tony crowd of men and women poured in.

Being next door to the Paula G booth was a Godsend. While shoppers waited to peruse the jewelry, they inspected the dresses. There were a few negative remarks about beach dresses being sold at a Christmas market, but it wasn't long before the savvier shoppers began snapping them up.

"We'll be in the keys this Christmas. These will be perfect!" said one designer-attired woman.

Her dowdier companions looked at one another and decided that they needed Two-A-Tees for their traveling daughters and nieces. As the wine flowed, the grip on credit cards loosened and more clear, Two-A-Tee bags circulated through the place advertising the dresses.

Whenever there was a lull in the action at her booth, Paula G would say something like, "Girl, have you seen those cute Two-A-Tee dresses next door? But don't touch that pink octopus. That one's mine!"

The "Bayview girls" took turns mingling with the crowd, checking out the other booths and getting some nourishment. Helen, whose stomach would not stop growling, went first. She returned sated, but with a plate of lobster kabobs—for later. Then it was Stella's turn.

She had just polished off two beef tenderloin biscuits and three tiny trout tacos when she noticed some familiar-looking pottery. Sure enough, it was Babs, the potter from the shrimp festival who had told her about Floyd and his Cuban girlfriend, Carmen. Babs had her gray braid twisted up into an approximation of a chignon and wore a gold lame shift with her Birkenstocks. She was working alone and selling turkey platters like hot cakes. When the crowd thinned a bit, Stella fixed another plate of appetizers and took it over to her.

"Bless your heart! I'm starvin' and can't leave the booth. My old man … you remember Freddie. He can't stand these bashes."

"Really?" said Stella who was not the least bit surprised.

"Yeah, he hates the skimpy food, hates the fruity wine, hates the snooty folks and won't put on a tie for nothin'. I told him he's the snooty one." She rolled her eyes and let her mouth hang open in feigned exhaustion for a few moments before adding, "But who wants to listen to him complain? I'd rather do it all by myself." When she'd finished the last asparagus spear, she said, "Weren't you the one askin' about that no 'count Floyd and Carmen Miranda?"

"Yes, I was. Floyd stole our dresses, remember?"

"Right. It's comin' back to me now. I believe I suggested you stay clear of the both of 'em, but in case you're the type who don't take good advice—and I believe you are that type— you might be interested to know that Carmen is in town."

"You're kidding!"

"I don't kid about the likes of Carmen Miranda. 'Cause that woman is crazy as a sprayed roach. Anyway, she has wormed her way into Rygood Barber's booth—it's called Hearth Matters. Carmen talked him into giving her a piece of it when he came down with appendicitis last week. Back row next to the bathrooms. Not a bad location, believe it or not."

"Thanks, Babs." The women exchanged cell numbers. Babs promised to text Stella with any interesting developments concerning Carmen. "Now I've got to relieve Marilee. See you later."

Stella returned to the Two-A-Tee booth via the back row. She needed to avail herself of the convenience anyway. When she arrived, the line to the bathroom stretched all the way to the Hearth Matters booth, so she was able to observe Carmen at her leisure. She was careful to do this in the most surreptitious manner, however. Getting on Carmen's bad side (did the woman have a good side?) was to be avoided at all costs.

Babs was right. It was not a bad spot. There's always a line at the ladies' and one of the few things that can take a girl's mind off her bladder is a good deal on a one-of-a-kind fireplace screen or a graceful pair of andirons. Or in Carmen's case, not-bad-art made from a fifty-gallon oil drum.

I would love to report that Carmen was a mousy, anorexic brownette, but in fact she was the stereotypical, seen-better-days-but-still-got-it Latin dream girl; in-your-face, dark, flashy, buxom, lots of black hair, tight dress, yada, yada, yada. The woman was as formidable as her sculptures were scary.

But Stella had to admit it. The twisted things possessed a certain surrealistic beauty. Kind of like the artist, herself. Stella could just see Carmen in a tight jumpsuit—it would have a plunging neckline, of course—the sheen of her perspiration reflecting the fire from her welding torch.

Not surprisingly, a group of waspish, tuxedoed men were discussing the merits of Carmen's creations with the artist. A man who identified himself as a children's dentist chose two of the intimidating masterpieces—for his clinic waiting room, no less! As Stella looked on, the overzealous admirer of Carmen's—uhh, *art*, wrote a check and folded it sensually into Carmen's hand.

Stella pictured Elliot quivering in front of the monstrous sculpture as he waited to have his baby molars inspected. The very idea infuriated her. As if going to the dentist isn't scary enough for the kiddies, this man intended to hang a huge, black flower with a dagger in it on his waiting room wall!

Finally, it was Stella's turn at the loo. She was in and out in two minutes flat and raced back to the Two-A-Tee booth. She told Helen and Marilee about Carmen. Between selling, wrapping and accepting payment for dresses, they discussed the situation. A decision was made to further discuss it after the show and revisit the Hearth Matters booth the next morning.

31.

Look Who's Here!

When the preview party finally came to a close, the vendors tidied up, gathered their earnings and closed the curtains on a very lucrative night. The Two-A-Tee threesome was headed to the door when they remembered that they still wore Paula G's jewelry. Retracing their steps, they met Paula on her way out.

"Keep them till the show's over. Or if you like, we'll work a trade. I wasn't kidding about that octopus dress."

Marilee laughed. "I put the last one up for you just in case."

"I'll let Becka and Janie choose one, too. They deserve a bonus." She grinned and rolled her eyes. "I worked 'em pretty hard tonight."

Like the Two-A-Tee girls and most of the other vendors, Paula was staying at the hotel across the street. It had a cozy bar with comfy chairs and tables. The women were so keyed up from working the show, unwinding over a light libation seemed just the thing. They sank into swiveling club chairs arranged around a coffee table and ordered four glasses of white wine.

Paula possessed a wealth of merchandising info which she graciously shared. Her stories of things she "learned the hard way" interspersed with tales of Marilee's misadventures had the women laughing so hard they could barely drink their wine.

They were deciding whether to indulge in a second drink when Stella, who was facing the bar entrance, noticed a familiar figure enter the hotel's lobby. The figure belonged to who else but Carmen Miranda! The woman glanced this way and that, her piles of black hair flying behind her like something alive. When she spied the four women, she narrowed her eyes, threw her impressive shoulders back and headed straight for their table.

"Holy Moly," said Helen. "That wouldn't be Carmen Miranda, would it?"

"Ohhh, yeah," said Stella.

"Oh, my God," squeaked Marilee.

Paula's eyes shot from one woman to the other, but she wisely said nothing.

Carmen was at the table in a flash. Her hands—actually her fists—were on hips even more impressive than her shoulders. A vein pulsed in her neck. She was breathing hard.

Talk about your anger management issues!

"Okay, wheech one of you haf been asking questions about Carmen and Floyd Feenger?"

Believe it or not, it was Marilee who spoke first.

"Now listen here Ms. Miranda …"

"Whaa?"

"Her name's not really Miranda," muttered Stella like an inept, panicked ventriloquist.

Marilee began again. "Now listen here, Carmen. We are the ones whose dresses were stolen by Mr. Finger. And we were the ones who almost got blown—"

"That's right," interrupted Stella. "We have every right to try and find out what happened to our merchandise."

That's when Carmen leaned down, placed her hands on the arms of Stella's chair and inches from Stella's face, hissed, "I see you watching my booth tonight like a hawk. I geeve you a piece of advice." Her breath smelled like spearmint gum and rum. "You forget your leetle dresses." She poked a very long, very red fingernail at Stella's chest. "And you forget Floyd Feenger. You got it?"

In the deep curve between Carmen's breasts and hips Stella could see Paula. The woman was on her cell phone!

How can she be texting when Carmen Miranda is about to kill me?

Paula put her phone down as a bouncer-looking dude

with an earphone in his ear approached the table. "What's the problem here?" he said in a flat, scary tone. Stella noticed he wore a pin on his lapel identifying him as hotel security.

Carmen straightened up, smiled at the guy and said, "There eez no problem. For now." After glaring at each of the women in turn, she pivoted on her five-inch heel and went to the bar where she sat on a stool, crossed her curvy legs and ordered a rum and coke.

Paula turned to the security guy and said, "Thanks for coming so fast."

"Any time, ladies," he said and tapped his earphone. "I'm here all night."

The women picked up their drinks and moved to the far corner of the bar—as far away from Carmen as they could get.

"Okay," said Paula. "How did three nice Bayview ladies get on the wrong side of that woman? And do I need to triple-lock my door tonight? Because from the look she gave me, I think I'm on her enemies' list right along with y'all."

The Bayview girls looked at one another.

"She's right," said Helen. "We owe her an explanation. Besides, it was her quick thinking that kept Carmen from doing bodily harm to Stella with those nails of hers."

"It's a long story. Sure you want to hear it?" said Stella.

"Are you kidding?" said Paula. She motioned to the server and asked for another round of drinks. "These are on me," she told him.

Stella felt only slightly guilty about breaking her vow of silence to Sam. I mean, he had some serious explaining to do concerning the jovial Lena. So she and Marilee, with a little help from Helen here and there, just went ahead and blurted out the whole, sad convoluted saga of Floyd Finger.

"I know he was in that RV when it exploded," said Stella. "And I don't think it was an accident."

Paula shook her head. "And to think it all started with my starfish pin. I figured there had to be more to your involvement with the likes of Carmen than some missing dresses," she said. "But this ... this is some story." She was quiet for a few seconds, thinking. Then she said, "But tell me, why do you want justice for a guy who ripped you off and almost got you killed right along with him?"

"I can't get the picture of that RV exploding out of my mind," said Stella. "I've just got to find out what happened."

"And from the looks of Floyd's trailer, somebody was after something," said Marilee. "They might have seen us that night and be biding their time …" She gave a little shiver.

"A wise man once advised me never to give unsolicited advice," said Paula, "but I'm doing it anyway. It sounds to me like y'all are in waaaaay over your heads. I think you should leave the investigating to your detective friend, Buck, and the cops."

She smiled at Stella. "And no offense, but it sounds like your surveillance techniques could use a little work. I'm just sayin'."

Marilee sighed. "It's true, Stell. Everybody says so."

Helen, whose surveillance techniques were far superior to her friends' had purposely seated herself in a chair where she could keep an eye on Carmen. Due to the lounge's poor lighting and a strategically placed Ficus plant, Carmen was unaware of Helen's watchful gaze.

The woman was making phone calls every few minutes. It was obvious she was getting no response because after every call she would leave a short message and slam her cell on the bar. In between the calls, she kept turning toward the women in the corner. It was as if she was checking to see if they were still there.

Was she calling for evil backup?

Finally, her phone began to play salsa-sounding music. She snatched it up and engaged in what appeared to be an actual normal, non-confrontational conversation. She then slid off the barstool and walked toward the lounge's wide entrance, not even glancing toward the women in the corner. Helen watched as she motioned to someone coming her way.

"Ladies," said Helen, "You are not going to believe who's here now."

32.

Surveillance Snafus

But by the time the others turned to look, the doorway was empty.

"Who was it?" said Marilee.

"I swear it was Kitty," said Helen. "I only saw her for a second, but it had to be her. I think she and Carmen just left the hotel."

"Kitty, the voodoo nanny?" asked Paula, who was having some difficulty keeping the details of the Finger caper straight.

"One and the same," said Helen.

"Well, what are y'all waitin' for?" said Paula. "My car's parked out front."

Wasn't this the woman who'd just given them the unsolicited advice to leave it to the professionals?

But Paula was heading toward the hotel entrance where a silver Acura was illegally parked. They all followed.

"We could really use a designated driver," muttered Helen as she slid into the back seat with Marilee.

Paula gestured toward a white SUV heading away from the hotel. "Is that them?" she asked.

"I think so," said Stella. "But I'm not certain."

"It's worth a shot," said Paula, and she pulled away from the curb.

It was near midnight, so traffic was light, but their quarry zipped and leapt around the city's hills like a NASCAR contender. Paula stayed a good distance behind the alleged Carmen and Kitty, hoping her silver Acura wouldn't be noticed. They wound through a neighborhood of lovely, old homes nestled atop sloping gardens, then exited onto a main thoroughfare which curved into a village of shops, restaurants and bars. Good food smells and music floated out into the night air that had grown crisp and chilly.

The white SUV took a left onto a side street and slipped into a parking space beside the Miami Bar and Grill. A neon sign advertising the Cuban Sensation Sandwich glowed in the window.

Paula took the next left and continued around the block, slowing until she could see Carmen's and Kitty's vehicle. She found an empty space in the shadow of a big cedar tree and stopped. The white SUV was empty, its occupants undoubtedly inside the Miami Bar and Grill. Paula switched off the ignition and turned to the others.

"Okay, ladies. What now?"

They all looked at one another. They had no idea.

Finally, Marilee said, "Oh, I know. We'll have a stake out."

Helen groaned. "I'm too tired to stake out anything. And remember, we've got to be back at the market at eight in the morning. Maybe we should just go in there and … and order a Cuban."

"We're supposed to be clandestine," said Marilee. "Let's give it a half-hour, then if nothing happens we'll go back to the hotel and go night-night."

Paula wondered if the phrase night-night had ever been used on a stake out, but said nothing and like the others, agreed to give it another half hour. Ten minutes into said stake out, however, they began feeling the effects of the drinks they'd had earlier. Stella was the first to voice her discomfort.

"I hate to tell y'all this, but I've got to find a ladies' room."

"Me, too," said Helen, who had popped a diuretic an hour before.

It was decided that they would take turns visiting the Village Pub, which was on the main road. The plan was to circle the long way around the block to avoid running into Kitty and/or Carmen exiting the Miami Bar and Grill. Stella promised to be quick and slipped out of the car before Helen could beat her to it.

The Village Pub was obviously the place to be for the newly legal on Thursday nights because Stella could hardly make her way through the throng of young bods to ask directions to the loo. Finally making herself heard over the music, she followed the bartender's directions to the rear of the establishment where the line was predictably long.

She'd left her phone in the car, but wouldn't have been able to hear it anyway, so she filed in behind the giggling queue and waited her turn. There were more than a few annoying stares from the gaggle of co-eds waiting ahead of her. If they didn't smile at her with pity, they were glaring at her. Stella figured they thought she was a desperate cougar after their boyfriends, a curfew-Nazi mother or possibly an undercover cop preying on the under aged, so she smiled back at them and tried not to think about her bladder. By the time she made her way back out to the street, she'd used up most of the allotted stake out time.

Helen's gonna kill me, she thought. *Because it's gonna take us the rest of the night just to go to the bathroom!*

She tried to remember one female TV detective who had had this problem while on a stake out. She ran through the list from Angie Dickinson to Angie Harmon and couldn't come up with one. It seemed that besides nerves (and buns) of steel, bladders of steel were an important prerequisite for the job.

Stella shook off thoughts of gorgeous gumshoes and decided to take a chance on running into the surveillees. Attempting to look as inconspicuous as possible, she started down the side street which was the shortest route back to Paula's car. She'd just headed down the street's far side when she noticed a dark green truck tucked hood-first into an alley across from Carmen's SUV. Though most of it was camouflaged by shadow and not visible from Paula's car, it occurred to Stella that the truck's rear view and side mirrors would afford any occupants a nice eyeful of the white SUV parked across the street.

Stella walked quickly back toward the main street, crossed the side street and, keeping to the shadows she inched along toward the Miami Bar and Grill. If Carmen and Kitty exited the restaurant, there was no way she could avoid them. The thought of Carmen's hot temper, cold threats and killer nails ran a small shudder up her spine. But she was determined to find out if the truck hiding in the alley was the same one that called number four Whimsy home.

She crept along the sidewalk until she could just make out the Wildlife Federation tag on its bumper. A tall, broad-shouldered man was sitting in the front seat. He was staring into his side view mirror at the Miami Bar and Grill. It was as if … well, as if he was on a stake out.

"I don't believe it!" she muttered and started toward the truck.

But common sense got the best of her. At which point she flattened herself against a stucco wall, took a deep breath and surveyed her options like an Alcatraz escapee. That's when she spied Paula heading for the Village Pub. Hoping that Sam wouldn't see her, she darted across the village's main street and intercepted Paula just as she was entering the pub.

"Where in the heck have you been?" yelled Paula over the music.

Stella explained, directed Paula to the ladies' and took Paula G's phone outside to call Helen and Marilee.

It was one AM by the time they'd all relieved themselves and reconvened in Paula's Acura. Stella told them about spotting Sam hiding like a snake in the alley.

"How could I have been so stupid!" whispered Stella dramatically. "To think I came this close …" She held her thumb and forefinger an inch apart, then narrowed the gap by half. "… this close to—" She couldn't bring herself to finish.

Paula frowned. "Whoa, girl, you don't mean?"

"Yep," said Marilee.

"He makes Andrew look like a choir boy," said Stella.

"Okay, Andrew is the one from D.C. who took off with the flight attendant?" asked Paula.

"Right," said Marilee.

"Uuh, uhh," said Paula.

"But if Sam is in cahoots with Kitty and Carmen, then why isn't he in there with them? Chowing down on a Cuban Sensation? With fries and homemade slaw?" said Helen.

"There's no honor among thieves, Helen," said Marilee sagely. "They probably had a falling out. And sweetie, you've got to get your mind off food. We have to come up with a plan."

It was at that moment that Carmen and Kitty emerged from the Miami Bar and Grill. Carmen unlocked the doors with an audible click, but she didn't get in. Instead, she swiveled her head with that wild mane of hair flying and looked all around. It was as if she could smell their presence. And as if on cue, each of the four women slumped down in her seat, their eyes just visible at the open windows.

But Carmen was looking the other way! She was looking in the direction of Sam's truck. While Kitty wisely held her ground, Carmen Miranda staggered angrily out of view. The Bayview girls and Paula let out a collective sigh of relief.

Almost at once they heard a barrage of Spanish.

Stella then heard Sam's voice yell, "Hey, slow down. No comprende!"

"What should we do?" whispered Marilee. She's gonna kill Sam!"

"Not soon enough," said Stella.

Helen reached over the seat and patted Stella's shoulder.

Paula was rummaging in her purse. She produced her phone and began punching in a number.

"Who are you calling?" whispered Helen.

"I think it's time to bring in the ambassadors," she said.

33.

The Ambassadors

Okay, how much do we really know about Paula Grant? Just because she's a big-time jewelry designer (and seems nice enough), that doesn't mean she's not nuts. I mean who has ambassadors'—plural!—numbers in her phone?

Such were the thoughts of Paula Grant's new friends as she calmly waited for an ambassador to answer her call at one-thirty in the morning. Finally, one of them did. Really.

"Hey. Yeah, it's Paula. Sorry. I thought you might be on duty. Darn. Oh, you are? Two blocks? Be right there."

Paula turned to the others. "Okay, my cousin, Ambassador Jenkins is off duty, but she's working her night job not two blocks from here. She's going to try and get in touch with Ambassador Fifty-nine. I told her I'd be right over."

Marilee, Stella and Helen looked at one another in total incomprehension.

Finally Helen said, "Oh, the ambassadors! Of course!" She turned to Stella and Marilee. "The Ambassador Force is a hospitality and public safety group that assists visitors to the city."

"Right," said Paula. "They work with the police. They wear uniforms and ride those Segway things."

"Marilee, why don't you go with Paula," said Helen. "Stella and I will keep watch."

Feeling relieved that her cousin had gotten her mind off food and was back in command mode Marilee was prepared to follow orders without question. Before she could open the door, however, Carmen was back in their field of vision. She stood next to her own vehicle for a brief period, still yelling a combination of English and Spanish curses at Sam. Or Kitty. Or the city of Birmingham in general. Who knew?

Anyway, she flung herself back into the car and slammed the door, catching a quarter of her wild tresses in the door. Too mad or inebriated to care, she and Kitty disappeared into the now-frosty night, Carmen's raven curls flapping in the wind.

"That woman is something else," said Marilee in a voice tinged with fear and a smidge of admiration.

A frantic, whispered conversation ensued. Should they follow Kitty, follow Sam or wait for Paula and Marilee to visit the ambassador. Indecision narrowed their choices to the latter two because by this time Kitty and Carmen were who knew where.

"So why isn't Sam following them?" said Stella.

"Maybe it wasn't them he was following," said Helen.

"But who?" asked Marilee. "You mean—"

"Right," said Helen. She looked at Stella. "He must be following us. Well, actually… you."

"Now, wait a minute," whispered Paula. "You mean the guy Stella came this close …" She held up a thumb and forefinger a half-inch apart. "… to doin' it with is a stalker?"

Stella looked as if she might cry.

"I don't believe it," said Marilee. "Helen, what do you think?"

"I don't believe it either. But we can't discount it. There's too much we don't know about all of this."

They fell silent, each lost in her own wine-muddled, sleep-deprived thoughts.

Finally, Paula said, "Okay, Marilee, let's go."

They were just about to hop out into the night when a soft whir floated their way on a chilly breeze.

"What in the world?" said Stella, squinting into the darkness.

She assumed the day's physical and emotional exertion had finally taken its toll on her sanity because a disembodied pith helmet appeared to be floating through the shadows toward them. As it neared the car, they could see that it was a large, extremely dark-complexioned woman in uniform. The uniform included the pith helmet. The woman was riding a Segway.

"It's Fifty-nine," said Paula. "Ambassador Jenkins must have called her."

As Fifty-nine breezed by their car they all began waving and hissing, "Ambassador Fifty-nine! Stop! It's us!"

Paula flashed her headlights for a split-second, and Fifty-nine expertly and calmly executed a turn and headed back in their direction. She pulled up next to the car and stopped.

"Is one of you Paula G?" she asked, poking her head in the front, passenger-side window.

Paula raised her hand. Fifty-nine held up a thick wrist. A silver bracelet studded with clusters of seed pearls encircled it.

"Oh, it's one of mine!" said Paula. She forgot to whisper, and they all shushed her.

"Jenkins gave it to me for my last birthday," said Fifty-nine. Now what's the trouble?"

By the time Ambassador Fifty-nine had it sorted out she determined that the guy in the truck around the corner—one Sam Poole from Bayview, Alabama—was possibly a dangerous stalker and definitely a suspicious character. As the eyes and ears of the police force, she was duty-bound to call the cops.

Seconds later two policemen, Ambassador Fifty-nine, Paula G and the Bayview girls were assembled on the now-deserted village street staring at a snoozing, snoring Sam Poole. One of the officers, whose name was Jeremy indicated that the women should move out of harm's way. When they had complied, Jeremy tapped on Sam's window, rousing him from deep slumber.

He seemed not to know where he was, and Stella could imagine him wondering if he'd been dreaming, if he was still dreaming. Sympathy for her almost-lover filled her soft heart and overflowed so that it was all she could do not to jump in the cab of his truck, throw her arms around him, kiss his sleepy, bewildered face and take him back to her bed at the Vulcan Suites.

A rumpled, unshaven Sam finally exited the truck. An embarrassing pat-down and search of Sam's truck followed.

When Jeremy asked if and whom he was stalking, Sam threw a weary look at Stella and explained that yes, he had followed her to Birmingham. But it was because he was worried for her safety.

"Um, hmm," said Fifty-nine, rolling her large dark eyes.

Stella figured she'd heard that before.

Sam and Stella then gave an abbreviated version of the explosion in Biloxi. Stella explained that Carmen might have been involved in the explosion that had possibly killed Floyd Finger. When Jeremy learned that an actual body had not been found in Biloxi, he warned them all to leave police work to the police, thanked Fifty-nine for her professional handling of the matter and, shaking his head, joined his partner in the squad car. The women walked down the street a little ways leaving Stella alone with Sam. Fifty-nine cruised off into the darkness.

"For God's sake, Stella, you thought I was a stalker?"

"No. I really didn't. It just got all blown out of proportion. But you know what? I do have another problem."

"You saw Lena's car in front of my house this morning, didn't you?"

She had forgotten about that!

"Now that you mention it, I did!"

"Believe it or not, she showed up at my door late last night. She'd had a few drinks so I called a cab to take her home. She left her car at my place. While we waited for the cab on the front porch, I explained to her that I was seeing someone. Exclusively. I dropped her keys off at her office on the way here."

"Really?"

"Really. So what was your other problem?"

Relief at his plausible explanation for the presence of Lena's car in front of number four at dawn chased most of the indignation from her.

Finally she summoned up enough righteous anger to say, "Do you really think I need a keeper?"

"No. No, of course I don't think you need a keeper. I've got some timber business up here that I've been putting off. I thought I'd tend to that and at the same time be available in case … in case you and Marilee got into trouble."

"Marilee and I don't always …"

She stopped when she saw the look on his face that said, *Seriously? You're going to deny it?* And well, she couldn't deny it.

"When I saw who I thought was Kitty leaving the hotel, I was going to speak to her," said Sam. "Before I could, she got into a car and took off with that crazy Spanish woman. Then I saw y'all take off after them." He shrugged. "I wasn't about to let you go off in the middle of the night in a strange city… obviously in hot pursuit." He shook his head and ran a hand through his hair. "Good grief, Stella. You have got to let this Floyd Finger business go. It's getting obsessive. And dangerous."

Stella was exhausted, embarrassed, frustrated and overwhelmed with emotion for Sam Poole. And so she began to cry. Like the female swoon, womanly tears bring out the manly, protective instincts inherent in the DNA of all southern gentlemen. And Sam Poole is nothing if not a southern gentleman.

He wrapped his arms around Stella and kissed the top of her head. He took the tail of his shirt and dabbed at the tears on her cheeks, trying not to further smudge her mascara. He kissed the corner of her mouth and massaged her tired back with his hands. There was an audible sigh from Helen, Marilee and Paula whose belief in men and romance for the over-forty female was momentarily restored. Having gotten their romantic fix, they headed back to the car. Stella relaxed against Sam and let her mind rest. But only for a minute.

Then she pulled away. "Sam, what did you mean who you *thought* was Kitty?"

"What?"

"You said, 'When I saw who I thought was Kitty leaving the hotel.'"

"Yeah, that's the odd thing. That wasn't Kitty. She looks enough like her to be her twin, but …"

They stared at one another.

"Twins!?" they both said at once.

"That would explain a lot," said Stella. "Could Kitty have a twin sister?"

"She's never mentioned one. But then, she keeps a lot to

herself." He sighed. "It's pretty far-fetched."

Headlights flashed on the trees at the end of the street.

"I think you're out past your curfew," said Sam. "And I'm too tired to think straight. Talk to you tomorrow?"

"Sure."

Sam kissed her cheek and got into his truck. As Stella walked away he said, "Hey, Stella. Double-lock your door, okay?"

34.

The Partnership

Stella offered to open the booth alone the next morning and explain to Paula's young assistants, Becka and Janie that their boss would be a couple of hours late so that her friends/accomplices could sleep in. It was the least she could do after keeping the women out chasing Carmen Miranda half the night. They all protested, saying it was the most excitement they'd had in years, but gave in quickly and fell into their beds. Stella was up by eight. She showered, dressed and was manning the Two-A-Tee booth by eight-thirty, in time for the early wave of shoppers. To stay awake, she loaded up on the cinnamon rolls and coffee being passed around by the market volunteers.

Mid-morning there was a text from Babs, the potter.

The Hearth Matters booth hasn't opened. No sign of CM, it said.

Where in the world is Carmen Miranda? thought Stella.

It could have been the caffeine or the sugar or the once-and-for-all vindication of Sam Poole, but Stella got a second wind, put a smile on her pretty face and sold the heck out of fancy T-shirt dresses that morning. Eleven o'clock—the appointed time for the second shift—got there before she knew it. A grateful, well-rested Marilee and Helen took over. Paula picked up her pink octopus dress and joined Janie and Becka in the Paula G booth.

Stella took one cautious peek at the Hearth Matters booth. Still no sign of Carmen Miranda. She then made straight for her bed at the Vulcan Suites. She kicked off her shoes, slipped beneath the covers and was asleep before her body hit the sheets. Three hours later the phone woke her from a dream in which she was eating a Cuban Sensation with Kitty. It was Sam. Like her, he'd slept through lunch and was starving.

They met at a deli down the street from the Vulcan Suites. When they'd finished hamburgers, fries and iced tea, they split a piece of apple pie.

"I think I feel human again," said Sam.

"I'm not quite there yet, but close," said Stella.

"Do you feel up to filling me in on the case of the missing Finger?"

"I'm glad to see you've recovered you sense of humor ... such as it is," laughed Stella.

"Me, too. It was pretty much in the dumper last night. Okay, I have a proposition to offer you."

"Another proposition?"

"Right. Since we'll be working on the Park Boulevard property together, and it's obvious that you aren't going to let this thing with Floyd Finger go, why don't we join forces in finding out what happened to the guy?"

"You want to play detective with me."

Sam's face grew serious. "Not play, Stella. This isn't a game."

"I know," said Stella. "But you don't have to worry." She told him about Carmen not showing up at the market. "I think our prime suspect has skipped town, so there'll be nothing for me to do but sell dresses." She sighed. "Frankly, I could use the help. Detecting, that is. Thanks."

"Don't thank me. I want to know what's going on with Kitty. I have to for Elliot's sake."

"You haven't heard from her?"

"Not a word. It's made me realize how much we all depend on her." He was quiet for a few seconds before adding, "And I worry about you chasing around after these ... these characters." He reached across the table and took her hand. "Stella, if anything happened to you, whether you like it or not, I'd feel responsible."

"Oh. I appreciate your concern. But I was hoping for something a little more romantic than responsibility."

"Work with me here, Stella. I'm trying to keep the various compartments of our relationship compartmentalized. We're neighbors, business partners, possible partners in crime-solving, if you agree to it ..." His face softened. His eyes twinkled. Stella loved that. "And I'm hoping sooner than later ..."

"What?" asked Stella with a flirty grin.

"When we get back to Bayview ..." Sam started to smile.

"Yes?"

"I'm going to bolt all the doors ..." Bigger smile.

"Really? And then what?"

"And then ..." Really big smile. "I'm gonna let you have your way with me."

By now they were grinning at each other like a couple of college kids on spring break.

"Mr. Poole, you've got a deal."

"So no detective work without me?"

Stella held up her right hand. "I promise," she said.

Sam checked the time on his phone. "Sorry, but I've got to see a man about some trees. I really do have business up here." He motioned to their server for the check. "Then I've got to get back to Bayview and meet with the draftsman one more time. I want to start the initial demolition on that duplex next week."

Sam dropped Stella off in front of the crowded entrance to the trade center with a quick kiss and a promise to make good on a redo of their ruined romantic evening.

The shoppers were mostly women, of course, and they were either lining up to buy tickets or bustling out loaded with packages. Stella noticed several juggled Two-A-Tee bags among their holiday purchases. She showed her vendor pass to the ticket taker, took a deep breath and entered the fray.

According to Paula, this group of afternoon shoppers was made up primarily of the carpool crowd. They'd picked up the kiddies at three and brought them along. Accordingly, the sno-cone, popcorn and frozen yogurt booths were selling goodies as fast as they could make them. The other vendors had subtly moved their wares away from sticky hands as best they could. Stella made a final reconnaissance to the Hearth Matters booth. Still no Carmen. Next she stopped by Babs, the potter's booth.

"No, I ain't seen hide nor hair of her. I check every time I hit the ladies', too. I just wonder who's gonna take the booth down come Sunday mornin'. 'Cause you get a heck of a fine if you're not cleared out of here by six PM sharp."

Stella finally got to the Two-A-Tee booth. A very large woman was holding a size medium dress in front of her. Stella could see Marilee struggling to explain to the woman that they did not have anything that would remotely fit her.

As Stella slipped into the booth, Helen stepped up to the plus-sized shopper and said, "I'm sorry, but I think it's obvious we don't have anything in your size."

The woman threw the dress onto the table and waddled off.

Marilee gave her cousin a look that said, "Really, Helen?"

"She's in denial about her weight," sniffed Helen. "You can't enable these people."

"Good grief, Helen. I really don't think it's our job to point that out to random consumers … especially ones who are nice enough to take an interest in our dresses," said Marilee, who was turning pink with indignation. "But when I get into the therapy business I'll be sure to let you know."

She caught Stella's eye and motioned to the trash can with a nod of her head. The receptacle was full of Popcorn, yogurt and even corn dog wrappers. Helen had obviously taken a colossal tumble off the wagon and was now likely suffering roaring cases of remorse and indigestion.

Poor Helen! This place is to the weight-watcher as an open bar is to an alcoholic, thought Stella.

What she said was, "Okay, which one of you wants to get out of here and get a little fresh air?" meaning, *Okay, Helen, go walk off the junk food and the attitude, and stop taking it out on our customers!*

Helen evidently got the message because she said, "If you don't mind, Marilee, I could use some fresh air. I'd like to take a walk."

The storm in Marilee had quickly blown itself out, as usual. She sighed, smiled at her cousin and said, "Sure. Take your time. The crowd's starting to thin out a bit anyway."

The action did indeed thin out between the carpool crowd and the after-work crowd so Marilee and Stella decided to take turns shopping. Stella's first stop was Paula's booth where she was able to simultaneously fill Paula and Marilee in on her lunch agreement with Sam. After Marilee wandered off, she also found things for all the adult females on her list, including Marilee and Helen. She branched out from there, finding something for each of her nieces and nephews and everyone on Tutta's list. Though her mother had lowered herself to giving cash to her family, she still bought Christmas mementoes for members of her various bridge, tennis and lunch groups.

Stella sauntered up and down the aisles, perusing merchandise at almost every booth. She bought a blueberry gelato cone. She chatted with the author of *Creek County, Alabama — Bound for Home* at the Barnes & Noble book corner. Since Scratch Ankle was mentioned on the flyleaf, she had the author sign it to Sam and Elliot. She then headed back toward the Two-A-Tee booth.

For the first time since the beginning of the preview party she listened to the cacophony of happy female voices, breathed in the smells of new merchandise, food and Christmas-scented candles and really saw the decorations and signs and merchandise hanging from every available surface.

She then thought of her small, quiet office next to Gris's in Washington, of her Bayview patio with the wall fountain that she and Tutta had found at Bingham's Statuary. She remembered the night at Sitaspel when she and Sam had listened to a breeze ruffling the pines and stood still as statues to watch deer in the moonlight.

Stella knew then and there that she would not be present for the Atlanta Annual Spring Festival or Springfest in Emerald Shores or for a return performance at the Shrimp Festival the following fall. It was time for Stella Gray to get back to what she loved. And what she did best.

Which was creating spaces of comfort, beauty and serenity that reflected the tastes and lives of her clients—spaces that beckoned after a day in a place like this cave of a trade center with its sensory overload. The truth was that Stella missed delighting people with what they didn't realize they wanted.

But how in the world would she tell Marilee that the Jubilee Mistletoe Marketplace on Main would be her swan song?

35.

Quittini Time

Believe it or not, she didn't have to worry. And really, she should have known. Because as we all know by now, no amount of success holds Marilee's interest for long. While Stella's mind had been on Sam Poole, Andrew, Señor de Campos, Floyd Finger and Carmen Miranda, Marilee's eyes had been wandering next door—to Paula G and her fabulous jewelry.

And while Stella was at the Vulcan Suites, sleeping off an exhausting night of detection followed by an early morning at the market, Marilee and Paula had got to talkin'. Paula thought a boutique featuring her jewelry would do well in Bayview. She just needed someone who knew the clientele; someone with a flair for accessorizing; someone who could decorate a boutique so that no one could pass it by without dropping in; someone who could sell dope to the Pope; someone like—Marilee!

"Oh, it's been ages since I've had a shop," Marilee had told Paula, clapping her hands. "Running a boutique has always been my first love!"

However, Marilee was well aware that running a boutique and selling someone else's creations would not suit her business partner.

How will I ever tell Stella?

And so it was with a mixture of pride, shame and trepidation (emotions, which always accompanied Marilee's, um, transitions) that she decided to leave Two-A-Tee, LLC and throw in with Paula G.

Close of market occurred at five PM Sunday. Before it opened at eleven AM that morning, Marilee had struck a deal with Babs the potter. Babs could have all of their beachy Christmas decorations—including the faux palm trees—in return for dismantling the Two-A-Tee booth. Babs, who was a bit of a hoarder and had a thing for palms, jumped at the deal.

By five-thirty PM on Sunday, Helen (who hadn't been this miserable since the last time she'd gone swimsuit shopping) had checked them out of the Vulcan Suites and personally lugged the money bag, clothes racks, plastic containers and four remaining dresses to the car where she had their luggage waiting.

Marilee and Stella had each confided to Helen their desire to abandon the Two-A-Tee venture. Helen advised each of her buddies not to worry. They would discuss it on the ride home she'd said, and added that she had a feeling everything would work out fine.

She was right, of course. Relief washed over the two old friends when after talking around the problem for a half-hour or so, they realized that they both felt it was time (business-wise, anyway) for each to move on. By the time they made their first pit stop an hour out of Birmingham they were laughing about it all, and Marilee was promising them a family discount on Paula G originals.

They agreed to blame the dissolution of Two-A-Tee Casuals on one another. Though he was bound to be used to it by now, Marilee always dreaded telling her husband about her career changes. It made her feel better if she had a somewhat legitimate reason. In this instance, she would simply explain that without Stella, her heart was no longer in it. She intended to wait a while before bringing up the Paula G enterprise.

In Stella's case, it was her sister, Ann Olive who was most likely to criticize. She'd probably see it as one more impulsive and faulty decision on Stella's part. Ann Olive, who practically wallowed in the reflected glamour of her highly successful sister, was still getting nauseous every time she thought about Stella's abandonment of the fulfilling, lucrative (not to mention, celebrated) interior design career in Washington, D.C. to move home and start painting T-shirt dresses. When you think about it, she had a point.

Once the inevitable reprimands began, Stella planned to roll her eyes and remind Ann Olive that it wasn't Stella's fault. As usual, Marilee was on to a new project—one Stella knew nothing about. Since Ann Olive admired (and demanded) loyalty in others, Stella would add that she'd decided to be a good sport about it all and not stand in her friend's way.

Mama Tutta and Stella's other sister, Alice would get the truth and a good laugh. Besides, they would all be so relieved that Stella had decided to make a clean break with Andrew, her short-lived stint in the T-shirt business would hardly register on their radars.

"But what about Shirley Esposito?" said Marilee, suddenly remembering their faithful employee. "She won't have a job!"

Helen smiled at her cousin as if she were a dim-witted child, and said, "Not to worry. Just before we left, I had a call from Shirley. My Spanish isn't that great, but it didn't take me long to figure out that between dickeys and last-minute orders, y'all are driving the woman crazy. She wants to quit, but is worried about letting you down. I suggest you give her a nice bonus and one of those leftover dresses and call it a draw," said Helen.

Stella told them Sam's explanation concerning Lena's car at his house in the still-wee hours. Helen and Marilee both decided it was not only plausible, but commendable and a testament to his character that he'd called the woman a cab.

"A lot of men would have taken advantage of that situation," said Marilee, and her eyes got all slanty just thinking about it.

Stella next relayed Sam's conviction that the woman with Carmen at the Vulcan Suites was not Kitty. On this particular point, her friends were skeptical. Stella was hesitant to voice the idea that it was Kitty's evil twin, but finally asked their opinion of the notion.

Helen snorted. "If they are identical, how would he tell it wasn't her?"

"I think he's just not used to seeing his child's nanny in different surroundings," said Marilee.

"Or wearing voodoo clothes," said Helen.

"He seemed so sure," said Stella. "Maybe they're almost-identical twins," said Stella.

"It's just too far-fetched," said Helen.

"Sorry, Stell, I agree with Helen.

In spite of Helen and Marilee shooting down her and Sam's twin theory, the dissolution of Two-A-Tee Casuals had Stella feeling a weight she hadn't known was there lift from her shoulders. Her list of worries was shrinking!

Of course there was still Andrew to deal with. She'd decided it was totally, absolutely over for good. But Andrew's emails, texts and calls had become increasingly persistent, and when Andrew got persistent, he usually got his way. Stella figured that nothing short of an exorcism would convince her ex that his chapter in her life was as over as the lava lamp.

Then there was Gilberto de Campos. She had to make a decision about his enticing offer. Could she pursue a dream job in New Orleans with the phenomenally talented architect, Edgar Beche while helping Sam with the dilapidated duplex in Bayview? More important, what would happen to their budding relationship in her absence? Would it die on the vine? She remembered Lena's car parked in front of number four Whimsy and frowned. There would always be some woman willing to keep company with Sam Poole.

And then there was Floyd. Stella had to find out what in the heck happened to Floyd Finger.

36.

Return to Whimsy

The morning after Stella's adventure in the Magic City (a.k.a. Birmingham), her phone rang. As she had hoped, it was Sam.

"I'm looking for a pretty interior designer who does a little detective work on the side. You wouldn't know anyone like that, would you?" teased Sam.

Stella laughed. "I do, but she's kinda busy right now … helping her cute neighbor with his duplex."

"Cute neighbor, huh?"

"Yes. Extremely cute."

"How does the pretty detective feel about bribes?"

"She loves them. What exactly did you have in mind?"

"I was thinking of a romantic dinner for two at number four Whimsy Court. Tomorrow night. The chef does a pretty good filet. Do you think she'd be interested?"

"Oh, I'm pretty sure she would," said Stella.

"Great. And Stella?"

"Yes?"

"I have very good locks on my doors so there will be no uninvited guests."

Stella giggled. "Now that is very good news."

"And if you don't mind a little business, I'll show you the preliminary plans for Park Boulevard."

"I can't wait to see them," said Stella.

And she meant it. Now that she'd decided to get back in the 'ol saddle, she couldn't wait to get going. That meant starting out with a clean slate. So after saying goodbye to Sam she turned her attention to the first item on that slate. Andrew.

Stella retreated to the serenity of her bedroom to tackle the chore. She sat at the mahogany escritoire bequeathed to her by Gris. The little desk was situated a sideways glance away from French doors, a tiny balcony and the graceful limbs of the oak in Stella's side yard. A breeze was stirring things, including the tree's swags of Spanish moss. Between the sounds of cars traveling down LeMoyne Avenue, she thought she heard the tinkle of wind chimes. The view was so captivating that it was difficult to concentrate on one's correspondence.

But Stella forced herself to focus on the job at hand. She pulled a box of her best stationery from the drawer and copied the final draft of the goodbye-forever letter to Andrew. She licked the envelope, placed a stamp on its ecru face and slumped back into another of Gris's bequests, a Louis the Fifteenth fruitwood and cane side chair.

She looked out at the oak and the lacy shadows the breeze painted on the wall beyond and gave herself a mental pat on the back. The note was concise, polite and clear-cut with no room for misunderstandings. She'd chosen a hand-written note because the occasion certainly called for it. But in addition, whenever she'd had trouble getting her point across to a client it was Andrew's repeated admonition—his mantra, almost—to Stella to "put it in writing. That way they'll know you mean business."

Having written Andrew off, so to speak, Stella felt downright empowered and decided to tackle another prickly item on her to-do list. Buck Early.

Buck, it seemed, was working in direct proportion to what she was paying him. Which was nothing. She dreaded calling him because her adherence to his insistence that she stay out of the mysterious case of Floyd Finger's disappearance was in direct proportion to Buck's apparent interest in the case. Again, this amounted to none at all. Besides, as we all know, Stella would go around the block to avoid confrontation of any sort.

"Buck Early here."

"Hi, Buck. It's Stella Gray."

"Stella Gray! Just getting ready to call you."

"Really."

"Yep. Had an interesting development. That body I told you about … the one they found floating in the sound?"

"The … the burned one?" Stella shivered at the thought.

"Right. Turned out the deceased was a disgruntled shipyard worker who most likely started the fire that killed him. It was definitely not Mr. Finger who I would guess is living it up in Mexico or the Bahamas as we speak."

"So there's been no word on Floyd at all? I just can't believe no one cares where he is."

"Look, Stella, it's not like your missing person is some nine to five family man who kissed his wife goodbye, dropped the kiddies off at school and never made it to the office. Finger's a drifter and a con man. Even if he'd died in that explosion, there's no reason to think many folks would be crying over it. Or that it was anything but accidental."

Stella took a deep breath and told Buck about her run-in with that hot-headed Cuban, Carmen. Though he'd promised not to discuss the case with his cousin, Stella figured it would be a miracle if the subject of the midnight misadventure in Birmingham didn't come up the next time he and Sam talked. Besides, she hadn't kept her promise to Buck to let the professionals handle things. And she knew Sam was in no way involved with the explosion in Biloxi. So she might as well tell all to Buck.

When she'd finished, Buck said, "Look, Stella. Carmen is the female version of the bar room brawler. Violence and confrontation get her garters going, if you get my meaning. The woman's a psycho. She got into it with you because you were handy. Lord, Stella, didn't your mama ever tell you to stay clear of people like that?"

Stella sighed. Buck's words made perfect sense. But she'd seen Floyd in that RV! She'd seen the threatening note! And if Babs, the potter, was to be believed, Carmen had already tried to kill Floyd once with a piece of her metal artwork. There was no reason to think that during one of her anger management lapses, she hadn't tried it again. And there was more to Carmen's determination to stop Stella from finding out what happened to Floyd. The woman was hiding something. Stella was sure of it.

"Stella? You there?"

"Yes. Just thinking. I guess this means you're off the case."

"Stella. There. Is. No. Case. Let it go, okay? Look, if you promise to drop this … this obsession with Finger, I'll keep looking into it."

"Really?"

"That cousin of mine would never forgive me if I let anything happen to you. Now have we got a deal?"

"Yes. And thanks, Buck."

She put the phone down and uncrossed her fingers.

Stella mentally crossed Buck off her list and picked up the letter addressed to Andrew. She skipped down the stairs to the front door and wedged the missive into the mail slot. Minutes later, the doorbell rang. She opened the door to find Elliot standing on her front porch. He grinned at her and held her letter to Andrew up proudly.

"Hi, Mith Thella. You got a letter."

Good grief! All I need is Elliot making off with this letter.

"Thank you, Elliot, but I was mailing that," she said a bit more sternly than she'd intended.

His face fell as she took it from him and returned it to the slot. So she smiled at him, and once she was assured that he'd gotten permission to be there, she said, "Would you like to come in? I have some of Tutta's chocolate chip cookies in the kitchen."

He bobbed his head, pushed his glasses back up onto the bridge of his little nose and followed her into the kitchen where he took two cookies from the proffered jar.

"Thank you. I came to check on Thponge Bob and Patrick," he said.

Stella had completely forgotten about the little figures in the trough of her fountain.

"Oh, I hope they've made up by now," she said. "Let's go see."

They walked through the garden. When they got to the fountain, Stella and Elliot peered into the trough. By some miracle, the two tiny figures were standing where she'd placed them before leaving for Birmingham.

"What do you think?" asked Stella, sitting next to the

trough.

Elliot smiled at her. "Yep. They made up."

She held his remaining cookie while he reached in for the figures.

He knocked them together in some approximation of a male show of affection and said, "Yea! You guyth are friendth again!"

He handed the little rubber buddies to Stella, dried his hands on his jeans, took back his cookie and sat very close to her. It had grown chilly, and she supposed he was cold so she put an arm around him. His warm kiddie body felt good to her, and it was all she could do not to snuggle him into her lap.

Instead, she listened as he told her the latest problems facing SpongeBob and his underwater world. She asked him questions about the characters and their interactions. He was surprisingly adept at discerning underlying themes and relating them to his own earthly domain. Elliot was one intelligent preschooler.

When they stood up she noticed that the child's face was flushed, and his pale eyes looked weak behind the glasses.

"Elliot, do you feel okay?"

"I thort of don't," he said. "Inthide my neck hurth."

"Do you mean your throat?"

He nodded, patted his chest and added, "And my cheth. I think I need my mommy," he said.

For some reason, the words surprised Stella. She was horrified to realize that the words hurt a little, too.

Of course he wants his mother! She chided herself. *That's just as it should be!*

But Elliot's comment was another reminder that a relationship with him—and his father—would be an emotionally tricky one. She looked at Sam's wind chimes, waiting for their song to offer encouragement, but they hung mutely from their branch.

Stella walked Elliot to the door of number four and informed Sam that the little guy wasn't feeling well. It wasn't until she was back at her own front door that Stella realized Elliot hadn't used a single "preacherism" since he'd been there.

Like Sam, Stella had nothing against preachers. She was

a friend and great admirer of the minister at her Episcopal church in Washington. But let's face it, Elliot's evangelical phrases were odd in a child his age and (combined with a lisp) would certainly alienate him from his peers.

This fact of the nature of kindergartners is not fair, of course, but as Tutta often remarks, it is what it is. So as far as Stella was concerned, Elliot dropping the preacher-speak was a positive step on the road to becoming a well-adjusted kid.

Was this development a result of Kitty's absence?

The question led her once again to the mysterious nanny. Was she a bad influence or good? A wild voodoo practitioner and best bud of possible murderess, Carmen Miranda or a mild-mannered, faithful disciple of Big Welcome Baptist Church? Or, as all the facts indicated, some freaky combination of the two?

37.

Down for the Count

The next item on Stella's checklist took care of itself. Gilberto de Campos called to ask if Stella would be available to survey his newly purchased property in New Orleans.

"It is a fine house," he said. "A great house with much history. Casa Chartier it is called."

He told Stella that he'd lined up a meeting with Edgar Beche at the house on Prytania Street in two weeks' time.

At the drop of the architect's name, a thrill of anticipation filled Stella. Trying not to sound like a star-struck amateur, she agreed to meet the two men at the house on the New Orleans Garden District's Prytania Street.

On impulse she added, "I am currently working with someone on a project here in Bayview. Would you or Mr. Beche mind if he joined us?"

This was somewhat unorthodox, but having been on the receiving end of a boatload de Campos' unorthodox behavior, Stella decided the South American owed it to her. If Sam Poole continued to invest in properties like the duplex on Park Boulevard, and if he and Stella continued to work together, observing someone like Edgar Beche would be invaluable.

De Campos assured Stella that any associate of hers would be welcome. Before ending the conversation, he added, "Mr. Beche is looking forward with great pleasure to meeting you."

"Really?" said Stella.

She couldn't help it. Though this was typical of de Campos' over-the-top flattery and likely an out-and-out lie, she wanted to hear more.

"Oh, yes," he said. "Working with you was a stipulation for him working with me. So you see we have the mutual admiration, yes?"

"Uh, yes. Thank you Mr. de Campos."

Could this be true? Edgar C. Beche wanted to work with her as much—or almost as much—as she wanted to work with him?

Stella couldn't wait to tell Sam the good news. As soon as de Campos wrapped up his typically elaborate and lengthy goodbye, she dialed Sam's number.

After asking about Elliot and hearing Sam's assessment that "he's definitely coming down with something", Stella relayed her plan for them to meet Edgar Beche in New Orleans.

"I can't thank you enough," Sam said. "Wow, Edgar Beche."

"I know," said Stella. "I've always wanted to work with him."

Sam's voice grew serious. "I'm proud of you, Stella."

"I'm proud of me, too," she giggled.

"You should be," he said, laughing. Then he added, "You know, nobody should visit New Orleans without having at least one good meal. What do you say to dinner after our meeting? We can head back the next morning."

"The next morning?"

"Yeah. If that's okay."

"It's perfect with me," she said. "But I hope you're still feeding me tomorrow night."

"Absolutely. There's a filet with your name on it in the fridge." Stella heard Sam's doorbell chime in the distance. "Sorry," he said, "But I've got to go. Jennifer's here to pick up the patient. See you tomorrow."

The next morning Stella woke with visions of that evening's romantic dinner dancing in her head. But as the day progressed she began to feel tired. By lunchtime, her head pounded and her nose began to run. She drooped like a wet sock. By mid-afternoon, her throat felt as if a green pinecone—and you know how prickly they are—was lodged in it.

She called Sam.

"Hi," she croaked. "I'm afraid I've come down with

something."

"Oh, no," he groaned. "You caught Elliot's cold."

"I guess. But I could've picked it up anywhere."

"What can I do? Oh, I know. Chicken soup. I'm bringing chicken soup."

All Stella wanted was to get into bed, but Sam insisted. It was the least he could do, he said, since she'd been infected by Poole germs.

Stella picked up what seemed like a thousand damp, crumpled tissues she'd left around the house, threw open some windows and sprayed her new Lavender Linen air freshener around. She forced herself into a very hot shower and had just donned her least ratty but still comfy yoga duds when Prince Charming showed up with soup and every conceivable cold remedy one could purchase over the drugstore counter. But the best medicine was the look of genuine dismay on his handsome face when Stella opened the door.

"You really feel bad, don't you?" he said.

Stella answered with a sneeze that she caught in the hem of her yoga shirt. She realized that it was the first time Sam had seen her without her make up. As if her red nose and weak eyes weren't enough, the fierce acne scars would be staring him in the face. If he was surprised at Stella's naked face, he didn't show it, so Stella shook off the old feelings and said, "How's Elliot?" Because she hated to think of the sweet, little guy feeling half as bad as she did.

"Jennifer took him to the pediatrician. He got some medicine and is in bed sound asleep. Which is where you should be." He felt her head and ordered her to her room. He warmed the soup which he served to her on a tray. Then, mercifully, he left her to sleep off her miseries.

Elliot was back at school in three days, but it was a week before Stella returned to the land of the living. In the meantime, Sam caught the bug, and Stella wondered if the gods were conspiring to keep them apart. Shrugging off the self-pity, she returned the favor of the chicken soup and meds delivery to Sam and even cleaned his kitchen and did two loads of clothes. She then tended to her own neglected house-cleaning, bill-paying and social duties. She also paid a visit to Park Boulevard.

Happily, the substandard materials enclosing the porches were gone. It was as if the place had been freed from a prison of junky siding and cheap aluminum windows marring its pretty façade. The notion was silly, but Stella thought the place looked happy—as if it was aware that it was getting ready for a new lease on life. It was a feeling she could identify with, and she was smiling as she entered the front door.

A faint chemical smell and a few monster roach corpses told her that the exterminator had been there. One extra-large critter, its hairy legs still twitching in the air reminded Stella of Babs-the-potter's description of Carmen. *The woman's crazy as a sprayed roach.* A vision of the Cuban firecracker raging around Birmingham filled her head, and she had to agree with Babs' assessment. Though the Park Boulevard roaches had crawled—or God forbid, flown—their last, Stella shivered at the sight of them. Because creepy Carmen Miranda was still out there waiting to fly out of the shadows when you least expected it.

As Sam had promised, the interior had been gutted. Stella now had her blank canvas. Best of all, the house was no longer a duplex! The roomy foyer was now a showcase for the stairway with its charming landing. Sunlight streamed through the formerly walled-off rooms, and Stella began to envision paint colors, window treatments and furniture.

She went upstairs where more disfiguring alterations had been excised. A few faded scars were the only reminders of the remodeling nightmare that had been visited on the house's lovely second floor. Trees and sunlight were visible through French doors now that the balconies had been opened up. The place could breathe again!

Satisfied that things were progressing smoothly on Park Boulevard, Stella returned home and turned her attention to the other project on her drawing board—the house in New Orleans. First, she familiarized herself with any and every thing Edgar C. Beche had been up to in the last year.

Next she located both dated and recent pictures of de Campos' Louisiana purchase as well as a lengthy history of the house. In its long life nestled among the mansions of Prytania Street, the place had been home to many of New Orleans' famous and infamous.

The first and most notorious was Bernard Louis Chartier, a gambling, womanizing cotton merchant who was murdered with excruciating precision by his long-suffering wife, Elnora. Legend has it that Bernard, along with his other nefarious traits, was renowned for his stubbornness. He wasn't going to let a petite detail like death deprive him of his grand domicile and/or retribution for his unpleasant demise. Once his ghostly presence had driven the widow Elnora mad, she'd thrown herself, appropriately enough, off the house's widow's walk. Folks figured scores had been settled once and for all, and they'd seen the end of the spooky doings in Chartier House.

But Bernard, irascible to the end and beyond—and now joined by the ghost of his psychotic wife—was determined to haunt the halls into eternity if need be, fighting with the deranged spirit of Elnora and seeking vengeance on any subsequent mortals foolish enough to inhabit his home.

More than one report blamed the black-hearted poltergeists for the house's reappearance on the market every year or so. But the nail in the coffin of its marketability was hammered home with the inclusion of Chartier House in the *Top Ten Garden District Haunted Houses Bicycle Tour.*

Because there were actual reports of ghostly activities from several of the cycling tourists, the *Garden District Haunted Houses Bicycle Tour*, in turn, became one of the city's top (alternative) tourist attractions, beginning as it did at dusk with cocktails at Saints Bar on St. Charles Avenue and ending whenever with complimentary cocktails at a hole in the wall called Sixth Street Tavern.

While seated in the tavern's attractively shabby courtyard, patrons have a view through the stately iron gates of Lafayette Cemetery Number One. On moonlit nights, moss-draped oaks bathe the ancient mausoleums and markers in ghostly ambience. For those who shell out fifty-five bucks apiece to set their spines a-tingling, the Sixth Street Tavern finale is the ultimate howl.

Convincing tales of hauntings and apparitions at Chartier House and the popularity of the haunted bike tour along with a tanking real estate market resulted in the haunted money pit's repossession by the bank. It was put on the auction block where it was snapped up by a somewhat sinister South American who paid for it with cash.

Stella guessed that the dwelling's sketchy history only increased its appeal for Gilberto. In a skirmish between de Campos and an evil spirit or two, Stella's money was on de Campos. Not that she believed in ghosts. She absolutely, unequivocally did not. Still, feelings of dread overcame her. Something was going on over there—something very real and probably very expensive.

This is why I didn't want to get involved with de Campos!

It seemed that clouds lurked behind every one of Gilberto's silvery promises, and they usually manifested themselves in shadowy dealings that weren't apparent until some gullible person had committed to one of his propositions. Well, she hadn't signed a contract yet. And Edgar Beche or no Edgar Beche, if there was anything to the "paranormal" occurrences at Chartier House she would have no part of it.

38.

Major Revelations

Stella waited until Sam was on the mend before sharing her findings about Chartier house. She figured he was apt to take the news better without a fever. To her surprise, he laughed the whole thing off.

"Husband and wife ghosts still going at it after death? Doesn't get much scarier than that."

"True," Stella agreed. "Kind of sounds like one of Dante's circles of hell."

"If it's not, it should be," he said. "But seriously, have you ever wondered why only old places are haunted?"

"Not really."

"Well, when was the last time you heard about a haunted condo, for instance?"

"Hmm ... never? And I guess that's because most ghosts turn out to be loose wiring, bad pipes or bats in the attic. Which happen predominately in old places."

"Exactly."

"Look, Sam, I don't believe in ghosts any more than you do. But that kind of thing can upset subs, undermine work and run up costs," said Stella. "Every time the costs go up, clients start making changes on my end. It can be a real nightmare. That's what worries me when I hear about unexplained bumps in the night."

"I understand. And I agree. But remember, Edgar Beche has signed on to the project. I'm sure he knows everything about the place, and it hasn't scared him off."

"Good point. But there's one other interesting thing about this. I did a little research on Edgar Beche. His middle name is Chartier."

"No kidding?"

"No kidding. That's got to figure into his decision to work with the likes of de Campos. And to ignore the ghost stories. And there might be more to the frequent resale of Chartier House than bats in the attic and overactive imaginations."

Stella sighed. "I'm very leery of getting involved with de Campos. Things get complicated with him. This ghost story is one big, ol' red flag."

"It's only a preliminary consultation, Stell. At the least we'll meet the great Edgar C. Beche and see an interesting, old house."

Another very good point, she thought.

"Okay," she said, shaking off the negative vibes. "You're absolutely right."

"And don't forget." She could hear the grin in his voice. "I have an outstanding evening planned for us. Dinner at Galatoire's and a room at a new boutique hotel a friend of mine told me about. It's a beautiful place not far from Prytania Street."

"And you're sure you feel well enough to go?"

"Yes. By tomorrow I'll be fine. Stop worrying. It'll be great!"

"It sounds wonderful. Really. I guess I'm just afraid to get my hopes up. The fates are against us," she added in a spooky voice."

Sam laughed. "I know it seems that way. But keep the faith. No matter what happens in that meeting, we're going to have a great time. I promise."

His enthusiasm was contagious. In a matter of seconds Stella's outlook progressed from hopeful to downright positive, not only about her romantic evening with Sam but about the de Campos project as well.

"I can't wait," she said.

"So I'll pick you up at seven in the morning?"

"I'll be ready."

But at seven that evening just when she had narrowed her New Orleans wardrobe down to eight possible outfits, her phone rang. It was Sam.

"Hi, Stella. It's me. There's someone here I think you might want to talk to."

Minutes later Sam, Stella and Kitty Petite were seated around Sam's patio table. Subtle outdoor lighting and a flickering candle in the table's center glinted off the mysterious nanny's gold-framed front tooth. The séance ambience had Stella half expecting voodoo Kitty to whip out a Ouija board or at the very least a deck of Tarot cards.

Kitty's attire pretty much dispelled the eerie vibes, however. Instead of sporting her voodoo garb, Kitty was in jeans and a long-sleeved T-shirt—much like she'd been whenever Stella had seen her in the neighborhood. Voodoo Kitty was nowhere in sight.

"Kitty asked me to call you," said Sam.

"I owes everybody explanations," said Kitty, shaking her head. "I knows how much y'all loves Elliot, and I hates it that I worried ebbody. Specially you, Sam. You been fair and square with me. I knowed when Sam asked 'bout me bein' in N'awlins with them voodoo folks what was goin' on. First off, that wasn't me. It was my sister, Pup."

"Oh, my gosh!" said Stella. "You really do have an identical twin!"

"Pup ain't my twin. But she might as well be. Guess I ought to start at the beginnin.'"

Kitty and her sister were the fourteenth and fifteenth children born to her parents. The first thirteen were boys. Kitty's daddy doted on the girls so much that the boys accused them of being their daddy's pets. They gave them the nicknames Kitty and Pup. Throughout their lives the sisters were so alike in looks that they were mistaken for twins.

But there all similarity ended. Though the sisters were devoted to one another, the elder Kitty was as introverted as Pup was outgoing. Soon Kitty was known as the good sister, Pup the mischief-maker. This turned out to be one of those self-fulfilling prophesies.

As they grew into their assigned roles, a kind of competition evolved and escalated. Kitty became more involved with her church, so Pup dabbled in the occult. This had Kitty, who was raised Catholic and presently affiliated with Big Welcome Baptist, speaking in tongues, saying novenas and dousing Pup with holy water. Because as far as Kitty was concerned, Pup was throwing in with the devil, himself. She feared for her sister's very soul.

"I had to go see about her," Kitty said.

"Why didn't you just tell Sam?" asked Stella.

Kitty shook her head. "I was scared of gettin' fired. I know folks who lost good jobs for less than havin' a crazy, voodoo sistah."

Sam assured Kitty that he didn't know enough about voodoo, hoodoo or any that stuff to have an opinion one way or the other, and that she certainly wouldn't lose her job because of the actions of her sister.

"So did you find her?" asked Sam.

"I did. Took me awhile, but I did. She was in N'awlins, all right. It was Pup who Stella saw at the Marie LeVeau convention." She shook her head. "Nothin' but black magic and temptin' the devil."

"I'm sorry, Kitty," said Stella. "I know how you feel about voodoo."

"Thank you, Stella. I'm happy to say the good Lord has answered my prayers. Pup has quit her walk on the dark side." Kitty chuckled. "After one of them night meetin's in the cemetery, Pup said she had enough. Said them folks was startin' to spook her. She's still dressing in scarves and necklaces and such, though. Says the look suits her." She smiled. "And it do. It suits her. Anyway, she's waitin' tables at the African American Museum restaurant, and got her a little place over there. I think she goin' be fine."

Hearing such good news quashed any qualms Stella had about asking the question that had been on the tip of her tongue since she'd walked into Sam's backyard and seen Kitty sitting at the table.

"Kitty," asked Stella, "Do you know a Cuban woman by the name of Carmen?"

"Yes, I do, and I owe a lot to that woman."

"Really? How on earth …"

Kitty laughed. "I'll tell you. Carmen and Pup got to be

friends sometime last year. It worried me to death because that woman ain't nothin' but bad. She just about got Pup into some heavy stuff. Big trouble. As usual, Pup slipped out just in time. But she told me it taught her somethin'.' 'I need new friends and a real job,' she said. 'It's time for me to grow up.' And it look to me like that what she done.

"But she say something else, too. She told me it's time I come down off my high horse. 'Spouting religion and thinkin' everybody else is sinners ain't God's way,' she said. And I knows she right. So I'm thinkin', if Pup can change her ways, then I guess I can, too. I tell you the Lord's ways is mysterious, girl."

"Wow, they sure are," said Stella. "I'm glad things worked out for you and Pup. Does this mean you're back on the job with Elliot?"

"That's just what it mean. I been missin' that boy." She smiled at Sam. "I been missin' all y'all."

An hour later Stella was back on the horns of her wardrobe dilemma. First she decided on black ankle boots, jeans and a striped silk tee with a short leather jacket. This would do for the ride over, lunch at Clancy's and the all-important meeting with Edgar Beche. Sensible-yet-chic attire was de rigueur for meeting highfalutin clients in low places such as Edgar Beche in Gilberto de Campos' crumbling, supposedly-haunted, two-hundred year old mansion.

Next she chose brown slacks, an avocado sweater and a mink-trimmed cashmere shawl for dinner at Galatoire's. She smiled as she pictured Sam and her among the convivial diners reflected in the restaurant's mirrored walls. She closed her eyes, savoring the vision and breathed deeply and ecstatically. A dreamy sigh escaped her as she folded a creamy silk nightgown and new, lacy undies into her suitcase.

What can I say? The woman was smitten! Not to mention she was going to have actual sex with the dreamy object of her affection.

A busy day, the meeting with Kitty and packing her suitcase for a second try at the most romantic night of her life was pretty exhausting, so after treating her hair with exotic oils and exfoliating her entire body, Stella Gray said a quick, hopeful prayer and fell into bed.

39.

News from Buck

At a quarter past seven the next morning, Sam—obviously a morning person—hummed as he stowed Stella's overnight bag and computer case in the back seat of his truck. He wore jeans, a yellow buttoned-down shirt and a sports coat. A tan baseball cap covered his dark hair. All signs of the past week's illness were gone. As a matter of fact, he looked better than ever. And when he smiled at her like she was the best thing he'd ever seen, it all but took her breath away.

"Man, what a beautiful day!" he said.

Stella, smitten though she was, was not a morning person. Still a bit groggy from getting up at six, she responded with a sleepy smile. She climbed into the truck with two oversized mugs of steaming coffee and handed one to Sam, which he thanked her for with a kiss.

They had just turned onto I10 when Sam got a call from none other than his investigator cousin, Buck Early.

"Hi, Buck. Yeah, Stella and I are on our way there right now."

Sam outlined their plans for the next twenty-four hours, giving Buck the addresses of Chartier House and the Hotel Delphine where he and Stella would be staying.

He ended with, "Okay, I'm putting you on speaker."

"Morning, Stella," Buck drawled. "Buck Early here."

"Good morning, Buck," she said pleasantly, but she was dying to know what he was calling about.

"I've got some news concerning your buddy, Finger."

The hair on the back of Stella's neck began to twitch.

"What is it?"

"There's been a sighting in New Orleans."

"A Floyd sighting? Someone has seen Floyd?"

"That's right. A living, breathing Floyd Finger."

Stella thought about this for a few seconds. Then, influenced by the developments in the Kitty/Pup mix-up, she added, "Not just someone who fits his description?"

"Nope. It's the real deal. But I figured you'd be skeptical, so I've come up with a plan to put this thing to bed before you get your pretty self in some real trouble."

"Let's hear it," said Sam. It appeared he was as anxious as Buck to keep Stella out of harm's way.

"Okay. Seems that Finger has been back in his home town of New Orleans for a month or so. Got himself a job as a streetcar conductor."

"Floyd Finger is a streetcar conductor," said Stella, repeating Buck's words for authenticity.

"Actually, Floyd Finger alias Fouche was conducting a streetcar … a streetcar by the name of Desire, believe it or not. I just rode it all the way down St. Charles Avenue and made the acquaintance of his replacement, Mr. Marcus Brown. Mr. Brown had a lot to say about Floyd Fouche. It seems that ol' Floyd got fired just a few days ago. An altercation with a female passenger. No surprise there."

"How does that conductor … uh, Mr. Brown, know all this?" asked Stella.

"Streetcar scuttlebutt best I can figure. Like me, Mr. Brown isn't in the habit of revealing his sources."

Stella looked at Sam and rolled her eyes. Sam shook his head. But he was smiling. His cousin was obviously enjoying the "Finger caper." It made Stella wonder just how many real cases Buck investigated.

"However, I am on my way to meet an acquaintance of Mr. Brown's who just may be able to lead me to the extremely undead Floyd Finger," Buck continued.

"I can't believe Floyd's alive," said Stella. "I saw…"

"I know. I know," said Buck as soothingly as if he were talking to Elliot. "But if it was Finger you saw in that RV, he got out before it blew."

"He's a women's clothing rep, Buck—not Jason Bourne!" said Stella.

"Listen, Stella, my daddy always told me, 'Don't believe anything you hear and only half of what you see.' It's real good advice." Buck paused to let his daddy's counsel sink in, then said, "Okay. I got to run. On my way to grab some breakfast at the Camellia Grill. It only holds about twenty customers, you know, and there's always a line."

"So, Buck, are you going to tell us your plan or not?" said Sam.

"Oh, right. The plan. I got to thinking. What is it that Floyd cannot resist?"

"Hmmm. Easy money," said Stella.

"And difficult women?" offered Sam, remembering the volatile Carmen.

"Right on both counts. I know Stella isn't going to let this go until she sees Floyd and finds out what happened in that trailer. To tell the truth, I'd like to know myself. So I'm gonna set up a little sting. But first I have to find Floyd and dangle the bait. I'll give you a holler when I know something."

And he was gone.

Stella was frowning and shaking her head.

"What? asked Sam. "I thought you'd be glad to know Finger's alive."

"Oh, I would be. If it were true. I just don't believe it. How many times do I have to say it? He could not have gotten out of that RV."

"If he was actually in it," Sam said gently. "Like Buck said, you can't believe everything you see."

Stella began rummaging in her purse—the one with all the great compartments that she'd bought from poor, heartbroken Edna Oster at the Biloxi Fashion Emporium.

"What are you looking for?" asked Sam.

"My phone. It's got to be in one of these pockets. I'm sure I didn't leave it at home."

"Should we go back?"

"No, I'll just use yours if I have to." She sighed. "I must be getting old," she said. "I never forget my phone."

Sam grinned at her. "Well, you're the best-looking old lady I've ever seen."

Stella smiled back at him.

Who wants to be interrupted when she's out with the likes of Sam Poole, anyway?

40.

Meanwhile Back at the Boutique

About the time the New Orleans skyline came into Stella's and Sam's view, Marilee and her new business partner, Paula Grant (aka Paula G) were scoping out a tiny but well-positioned retail space in Oak Corners, Bayview's hottest, newest, trendiest shopping district. Though small, the space would easily accommodate a variety of Paula G baubles, Two-A-Tee dresses (Marilee had decided to continue producing the dresses on her own—for a while, anyway) and other accessories. Another plus was that it was wedged between a wine bar and an upscale women's shoe shop.

The space had recently been vacated by Oh, Baby!, an outrageously expensive infant and toddler boutique carrying such horrors as tiny fascinators and pint-sized mink jackets for infant girls and tuxedo onesies for males (size zero to three months, no less). Since Bayview mothers tend toward day gowns and smocked dresses for their offspring, and the weather rarely dips below freezing, Oh, Baby! had progressed little further than a twinkle in its owner's eye.

The two women were discussing the merits of steaming versus painting over the silvered pink and blue zebra print wallpaper when there came a frantic knocking at the door.

"Probably someone needing a kiddie cocktail dress," muttered Paula.

But it was Helen.

"Sorry to barge in," said Helen, "But y'all have got to see this."

Helen flashed her phone in front of Marilee and Paula.

"Look at this picture," she said.

It was a photo of a crowd in what looked like an opulent hotel lobby. A smiling woman waving a fistful of cash stood grinning at the camera.

"Is that your sister-in-law?" asked Marilee.

"Sure is. She won three hundred bucks on a dollar slot machine. But look at the couple behind her," Helen instructed them.

Marilee studied it for a moment. "Oh, my gosh!" she said. "Is that who I think it is?"

"Who?' said Paula.

She snatched a pair of tortoise-shell cheaters out of her hair, slipped them on her nose and squinted at the phone. She zeroed in on a couple in the background. They were involved in conversation and either unaware or unconcerned that they were being photographed.

"Well if it isn't Carmen Miranda, the you-know-what from you-know-where!" said Paula. "Who's the tall dude she's with?"

"That," said Helen, "Is none other than Buck Early, Stella's private investigator. The one who to my knowledge has never told Stella that he has ever made the acquaintance of Carmen."

"Uh oh," said Paula. "And he's the one who's also Sam Poole's cousin?

"Yep."

"And Sam Poole is the hottie we met on the midnight stake out in Birmingham? The one who Stella has gone to New Orleans with?"

"One and the same," said Helen.

"How did you get this picture?" asked Marilee

"It's a random photo from Marty's Facebook page. She had it taken in front of the Beau Rivage in Biloxi.

"I'm getting a real bad feeling," said Marilee. "If Buck is keeping stuff from Stella, Sam probably is, too. And to think we encouraged her to believe Sam! Helen, you call her right now."

"I've tried. It goes to voicemail. I messaged the picture to her. I just hope she looks at her phone before anything bad happens."

"Or anything good," said Marilee. "Bless her heart. She's all excited about her romantic evening with Sam. Oooh, I just hate this."

"Could there be another explanation?" asked Paula.

Helen and Marilee looked at one another each hoping the other would come up with something positive in this latest love snafu of Stella's.

Finally Helen said, "Umm. Maybe. But I sure can't come up with one. You, Marilee?"

Marilee shook her head. "And she's with Sam right now."

Helen checked the time on her phone.

"They have that meeting in a few hours," she said. "I know the address." She threw a sheepish look at Marilee.

"Oh, Lord," said Paula. "I'm smellin' a road trip."

"Do you mind, Paula?" asked Marilee. "We can finish our meeting later."

Paula thought back to the bumbling stake-out in Birmingham. She couldn't let her new friends take on a crooked P.I. alone. Besides, she hadn't had that much excitement since Oprah bought a Paula G toe ring.

"Mind if I tag along?"

Helen was also remembering their escapade in Birmingham. Paula had coolly summoned hotel security when Carmen Miranda threatened them. She had tailed the speeding Carmen around an unfamiliar city in the dark after two glasses of wine.

She had cousins who were … ambassadors! Helen looked at Marilee, her sole partner-in-crime-prevention—Marilee, who was on the verge of her umpteenth career. In a former store for infant fashionistas.

"Paula, pack an overnight bag and meet me at Marilee's in half an hour," she said.

41.

Imagine the Possibilities

Clancy's is a true neighborhood cafe in uptown New Orleans. The atmosphere is laid back and convivial, the service excellent and the food is … well, you've just got to try it.

After waiting a mere twenty minutes, Stella and Sam found themselves at a table on the first floor not far from the bar. It was obvious that most of the patrons were locals. They table-hopped and chatted with fellow diners and/or neighbors. Some even shared their meals, passing butter plates with samples between tables.

"I want everything on the menu," said Sam.

"Me, too," Stella laughed. "All I've had is coffee. Just remember, we'll be eating at Galatoire's in six hours."

"True." He grinned at Stella and patted his exceptionally trim middle. "But I'm up for the challenge."

And so he ordered like it was his last meal—a large green salad, plenty of French bread, smoked soft-shell crabs and risotto with lobster and mushrooms. And on top of this obscene quantity of food, crème caramel for dessert. This was all washed down with iced tea.

"I hear they have a great wine list, but I guess we should keep a clear head for our meeting," he said.

Stella took her own advice as well as Sam's and ordered a crabmeat salad and tea. Besides, alcohol was superfluous. Sam Poole and Stella Gray were pretty much inebriated with one another. As they laughed and talked and shared bites of Clancy's tantalizing delicacies, their intoxication grew. By the time Sam tipped a spoonful of crème caramel between Stella's lips, the temperature at the table for two near the bar had risen significantly.

After lunch they located the Hotel Delphine, which was as charming as promised. A converted mansion, the Delphine is nestled in tropical grounds complete with private balconies overlooking lush courtyards. The room Sam requested wasn't quite ready, however, so they left their bags at the front desk.

"Probably just as well," grinned Sam. "If we got into that room, we might forget the meeting altogether."

Stella, blushing becomingly, agreed.

Although she couldn't wait to be alone with Sam—she'd had a taste of him that disastrous night in her living room, remember—she didn't want to rush their time to finally be together. Besides, there is a lot to be said for delayed gratification.

People who jump in the nearest sack at the drop of an attractive pheromone miss out on all the delicious expectation of, for lack of a less archaic term, courtship. Words to live by, compliments of Tutta Gray.

"I hate to admit it," Sam was saying, "But you were right."

"I'm sure that's true," teased Stella. "But about what exactly?"

"Lunch. I ate too much. I need to walk it off. What do you say we head over to Chartier House? It's only eight blocks, and we can check it out before the meeting."

"Good idea. This warm sun has me feeling sleepy."

They set off over cracked, roller coaster sidewalks in the direction of Chartier House. Sam took her hand, and they walked companionably, admiring a balustrade here, a towering banana tree there. But after weeks and weeks of sexual tension, the nearness of him, the sensation of her hand in his had her feeling positively giddy. When he looked at her and smiled, she knew he was feeling the same.

For heaven's sake! I've got to get my mind on something else or I'm gonna drag him into that clump of jasmine and …

Presently visions of dreamy sex on a bed of jasmine vines floated into her psyche.

Think about the scenery. That should clear your head.

As Sam had gorged himself at lunch Stella now binged on her surroundings. Over the decades, architecture, landscape and color had softened and spread, merging into a world of perfect imperfection not unlike impressionistic renderings of the original scenes.

"It's so beautiful here," she said.

"It is," Sam agreed. "But can you imagine trying to maintain some of these places? It could become your life's work."

In spite of introducing practicality into Stella's reverie, the sound of his voice had her back in the jasmine. She forced herself to pay attention to the subject at hand.

"It's like the people around here know just where to draw the line between charming ambience and depressing decay," she said.

"They seem to really revel in their surroundings. Good taste grows like moss around here."

"Very well put," said Stella.

"Well, thanks. I kinda liked it myself."

"Seriously …" She smiled up at him. "You're right. I'm overthinking it. It's simply a matter of that all-important intangible known as taste."

Sam stopped and took both Stella's hands in his. He looked into her eyes then kissed her gently on the cheek.

"Keep overthinking. I love that about you." He kissed her mouth softly and smiled. "Tonight," he said.

She grinned at him. "I can't wait," she said.

Minutes later they were standing on an especially lovely block of Prytania Street staring at Chartier House.

"Wow," said Sam. The house was a double-galleried, slate-roofed pile of crumbling grandeur. "This makes the Park Boulevard duplex look like a cakewalk."

"It's a challenge, all right," said Stella. But if de Campos is willing to throw enough money at it … and keep his ideas to himself … and if Beche agrees to take it on, this can be one impressive house again."

"You're not even put off by it, are you?" said Sam. "Doesn't it seem overwhelming?"

Stella laughed. "Yes. It does. But if I get involved with it, I'll do what I always do. This may sound silly, but I listen to what the house tells me."

"So you've worked on other haunted houses?"

"No. No haunted houses. We don't believe in them, remember? It's just that after I spend a little time with a place, a style and palette evolve. Then, well ... I just take it room by room."

"And the individual rooms? Do they speak to you, too?"

Stella looked to see if he was teasing, but his face showed only polite curiosity, so she continued.

"Yes. Some more than others, of course. But when I really connect with a space and its owner, that's when my job gets to be fun. A lot of designers feel that their work should be a reflection of them ... sort of like a writer's voice, I guess. but Gris thought the work should reflect the client's personality— with flare. And I agree. Seeing it turn out like I envisioned and the look of gratitude on a client's face ... well, it's priceless."

"Very well put," said a male voice heavy with Cajun.

They turned to find none other than the famous architect, Edgar C. Beche standing behind them. He held a hand out to Stella.

"Ms. Gray, right? Ed Beche. Welcome to N'awlins." He gestured to the house. "And to Chartier House."

"Thank you. It's a pleasure to meet you. This is my associate, Sam Poole."

"Glad you could join us, Sam," he said, smiling up at Sam and shaking his hand. "I apologize for eaves-dropping, but I wasn't sure it was y'all. Until I heard Stella talking, that is. I was a great admirer of Brian Grissom. Such a talented, entertaining man. I know you miss him, Stella." He turned to Sam. "So you're in the renovation business, too."

"The timber business, actually. I've only recently gotten into restoring old places in Bayview." He nodded toward Chartier House. "Nothing as half as grand as this, though."

"With Stella helping you, you can't go wrong. She's a very talented lady."

Sam smiled at Stella. "Yes, she is," he said.

Edgar Beche was a charming, down-to-earth, sixty-ish year old Louisiana Cajun. His full head of hair and impressive mustache were thick silver. He stood about five and a half feet tall and by the look of him, was no stranger to his city's gastronomic abundance.

After a few minutes of chit chat, "Ed" checked his watch and said, "de Campos must've gotten held up. I have a key. What do you say we have a look?" And he started up the front steps.

As Beche fiddled with the lock, Stella took in the house's small front garden. It was a jumble of abandoned azalea, palm and magnolia corralled by rusting wrought-iron. The houses on either side sported freshly painted clapboard, manicured lawns and signs of family life—a tricycle on a walkway here, a teenager texting from a porch swing there.

The disarray of Chartier House, not to mention the Haunted Bicycle Tour, must drive the neighbors crazy, thought Stella.

They'd gotten no farther than the entrance hall when a door slammed somewhere above them and reverberated off the marble floor. They all jumped and turned to peer into the gloom at the top of the curved staircase.

"The infamous spirits, no doubt," said Beche. But he was smiling. "I assume you've heard the tales."

"Oh, yes," said Stella.

She and Sam smiled, too, just to show what they thought of infamous spirits.

Due to a soaring ceiling and the imposing stairway the hall was impressive in spite of its small dimensions. Enormous double pocket doors led to the usual twin parlors with floor-to-ceiling windows and marble mantle pieces. It was a wedding cake of a house from the scrumptious heart pine floors to the ormolu-accented moldings to the solid brass chandeliers suspended from frothy plaster ceiling medallions.

Stella looked around her and sighed. As impressive as it all was, the unhappiness of Bernard and Elnora Chartier lurked in the dusty, dusky nooks of the place. Stella felt as if she'd stepped into another time—another realm, really. She looked at Sam and Ed and could tell they felt it, too.

It was surprising that in the parade of owners of the house, not one had gotten rid of the throwbacks to the 1800s. Maybe they were preparing to, and the "spirits" would have none of it, resorting to paranormal mischief in order to keep their beloved haunt intact.

Not that I believe in "hants," Stella reminded herself.

But whatever the reason, she was glad to see these vestiges of New Orleans' golden age, the days after the Louisiana Purchase when nouveau-riche cotton brokers began building their mansions, were still intact. The challenge would be in retaining these architectural details and the historical integrity of the place—maintaining its unique personality—while freeing it from the shroud of heaviness peculiar to homes of this era. Chartier House's added legacy of marital mayhem, compliments of Bernard and his homicidal bride, only added to its shadowy ambience.

It is the nature of old houses that they settle and creak, but Stella now heard a faint crackling noise. Sam glanced her way, and a smile of forced nonchalance flittered across his face. But he seemed poised for an imminent attack from out of the gloom. Ed looked from Sam to Stella, then cocked his head, as if listening for (or to?) something other worldly. He turned abruptly and started down the hall.

"Where are you going?" asked Stella.

"Pantry," he said, continuing toward the rear of the house.

All traces of affable Ed seemed to have vanished.

Sam and Stella followed Ed beneath the curve of the staircase to see what was up with the pantry. Ed went directly to a barely visible door in the paneled wall and opened it. Sure enough, it was a pantry. Tiny shadows disappeared across curling shelf paper into the shoe molding.

Ed smiled, his affability restored. "Mice," he said.

"And I thought I had done my homework," said Stella. "Ed, do you know where every cupboard and drawer in this house is?"

"Pretty much," he admitted.

"I hope you don't mind me asking," said Stella though she knew the answer very well, "But what is your middle name? What does the C stand for?"

He turned to Sam. "Your associate is very perceptive, Sam. And has obviously done her homework. My middle name is Chartier, of course. Bernard and Elnora Chartier are my ancestors."

"So that's it," Stella said softly.

Sam moved closer to her, started to put an arm around her then changed his mind. After all, Stella had introduced him to Ed as her business associate.

Beche's admission confirmed Stella's suspicions.

So that's why the great Edgar C. Beche wants in on this. It probably has nothing to do with working with me … like that con man, de Campos said. And it isn't that he's not worried about the "ghosts" of his ancestors. He knows as well as I that the haunting will materialize as some unfathomable structural problem. As for working with de Campos? He's considering the job in spite of Gilberto's reputation. He either can't afford to sink his own money into the place or simply doesn't want to.

Beche looked at his watch again. "I can't imagine what's keeping de Campos," he said. "As excited as he was about this project, you'd think he could be on time. In the meantime, let's finish our tour."

"Good idea," said Sam. He smiled encouragingly at Stella. "After you."

And so the threesome trouped up and down staircases and in and out of rooms while Stella took notes and pictures. Some work had been started by previous owners, and thankfully, most of it was sensibly done. If there was one thing Stella hated, it was tearing out the new and the bad. Such a waste of time, effort and money!

When they had thoroughly inspected everything except the attic, they ventured onto the back porch and stood looking out to the garden. It was surrounded by a high brick wall inset with the most beautiful wrought-iron panels. One of these insets was a cleverly concealed gate, apparent only because it was ajar.

The space was predictably overgrown. But like the cloistered garden of a monastery, the secluded serenity was palpable. The space was hidden from neighbors and strolling tourists by a row of Crepe Myrtles, clumps of banana and several palms, now backlit by the late afternoon sun. Like the wonderfully time-worn wall, a small swimming pool and its brick surround were covered in algae and moss. The patio was barely visible beneath leaves and limbs and broken pots. Standing there amid the chaos and serenity, Stella was seduced.

She mentally swept away leaves and plant debris, filled the pool with sparkling water and removed most—but not all—of the moss growing on the bricks. She imagined pots of color in puddles of sunlight, pictured a boy Elliot's age and his parents dining at a table near the pool. Like the house, the garden was starting to tell her things. She smiled and almost imperceptibly nodded her head. The men watched as Stella imagined the possibilities, and they smiled, too.

42.

Uninvited Guests

"So what do you think?" asked Sam.

"I admit I'm intrigued." said Stella. "It's a wonderful house. There are some serious negatives, though."

Beche chuckled. "Like rumors of ghosts, a dubious financier and an architect who's emotionally involved with the project?"

"Honestly, yes. And I hope you don't mind me asking, but speaking of de Campos, why didn't you buy the house yourself when the bank auctioned it?"

"I'm getting too old to keep up a place this big. I don't want to live in it, and I don't want to sink my money into it if I can help it. I only want to restore it. And get to the bottom of the ghost stories. How would you like it if your ancestors were known as slave-traders, philanderers and murderers? The ridiculous haunted bike tour has turned me into a freaky celebrity. They've even started riding by my house on St. Charles! I'm just tired of it."

"Good Lord," said Stella. "I had no idea. Ed, you know I would love to work with you. Gris would love the idea. He and I both admired your work. And I would like to help you get to the bottom of your ghost story. But I'll have to think about it. How about I get in touch with you in a few days? Who knows, we may even hear from de Campos by then."

"Oh, I plan on speaking to the señor, I assure you. But if you can give me a few more minutes, there's one space we haven't seen. I want to check out the attic." He looked across the garden to the setting sun. "I think we have time before it gets too dark."

The threesome headed back through the house. The interior rooms had grown damp and cold and heavy with shadows masquerading as ghostly sensations. Stella began to wonder if Beche was interested in the attic for professional reasons or for signs of his ancestors.

They followed him up stairs and finally through a back hallway that ended in a narrow door leading to the attic. They started up, single file, Ed Beche leading the way. Something flew from one wall of the enclosed stairs to the other.

"Just a roach," said Ed.

He swatted the thing down to the floor and stepped on it with a sickening crunch.

Stella shivered. Sam took his baseball cap from his coat pocket and put it on. "Man, I hate those things," he said.

"Comes with the territory," said Ed.

The attic was floored. Exposed beams, wiring and ductwork were everywhere. Several dormer windows admitted enough daylight to see. Stella looked for mementos left behind by previous occupants, but surprisingly, there were none.

Ed and Sam examined the beams and exposed studs, making predictable comments like, "Look at that joist. They don't build them like this anymore." Ed explained the architectural significance of Chartier House, with its mixture of Greek Revival and Italianate details.

A door slammed somewhere below them. Sam and Stella, who were already spooked by the killer cockroach on the stairs, jumped. Stella let out a tiny scream.

Ed simply smiled and said, "Probably de Campos. I'll be right back. Check out the view from that front window while I find him."

And so they did. The district, located on a former sugar cane plantation, was laid out in a grid of squares heavy with arching oak and delicate crepe myrtle. In each square a Greek Revival, Queen Anne or Italianate Victorian mansion erupted from profusions of foliage. Many had outbuildings of one type or another—former servants' quarters or stable here, a garage or pool house there. Glimpses of double porches and balconies, the railings throwing filigreed shadows on patios and fountains and pools, were visible through the jumble of green.

Many of the residents had attempted to keep the bounty of vegetation in check with neat lawns and hedges and more manageable shrubbery choices. Others, content with runaway jasmine and wisteria, towering banana and copious fern opted out of the battle with Mother Nature, fixed themselves a drink and watched things grow. To Stella, all of it was so gorgeous that it just about took her breath away.

But the sun was turning things rosy and Sam was checking his watch, so Stella pulled herself away from the window.

"I wonder what's keeping—"

She was interrupted by a loud crash, the slamming of a door and what sounded like curses delivered in a mixture of English and Spanish. It was the unmistakable voice of—you guessed it—Carmen Miranda. And it was coming from the hallway below.

Stella and Sam ran to the head of the stairway. Which was now as dark as pitch.

Sam unnecessarily put a finger to his lips—no one could have heard anything over the scuffling and cussing outside—and started down the steps. That's when they heard the shots. Three of them. They seemed to be coming from right outside the attic door. They were followed by male and female screams and some serious expletives.

Stella darted into a corner of the attic. Sam crossed the attic's expanse in a flash and crouched behind the furnace.

Carmen was screaming, "Are you crazy?"

Another voice, vaguely familiar, said, "Now baby, put that gun away."

And there was crying. Strangely enough, the sobs were also familiar. It was at this moment that Stella felt a slight vibration. It was coming from her purse which she was clutching to her chest. Her phone! She dug through the maze of pockets and compartments cursing its confounding orderliness. She finally found the phone, its ringer turned off, wedged between the pages of a Magazine Street shopping brochure. Her hands were shaking as she attempted to dial 911 and instead zeroed in on the umpteen messages from Helen and a picture of some people in a hotel lobby. The Beau Rivage Hotel lobby.

Is that Helen's sister-in-law? She looked more closely. *And Buck? And Carmen? Together?*

Stella forgot about 911. She looked across the attic where Sam was huddled in the near darkness, his handsome face illuminated by his phone.

Buck, Carmen, Buck, Sam. If Buck is mixed up with Carmen, then Sam must be, too!

So who was he texting? Or calling? The police? Or cousin Buck, whose motives had also become very questionable?

The piles of discounted evidence against Sam Poole flashed before her eyes. She looked over at him again, heard another sob and realized it came from her. Sam heard it, too. He listened for a second then dashed across the attic to where Stella was hiding.

Sam crouched down beside Stella and wiped a tear from her cheek with his thumb. She was too numb with fear and disappointment to object. By now the room was nothing but shadow upon shadow and her eyes blurred with tears. She couldn't see Sam's face, couldn't read his expression or see if truth or deceit filled those beautiful hazel eyes.

Something small fluttered above them and landed on a wall with a soft click. Then several small shadows began flying above their heads. She cringed and felt Sam flinch. His breathing quickened. Were they having simultaneous panic attacks? Stella put her hands on her head and tried not to imagine roaches flying into her hair, their prickly legs getting stuck, her trying to pull them out.

She remembered Tutta's advice the time her mother found Stella crying under her covers, held hostage by two of the flying monsters in her bedroom.

"Pretend they're something pretty," she'd advised while dispatching the critters with her bedroom slipper. "They're a fact of life where we live so play like they're lightening bugs or dragonflies. A bug is a bug, honey."

Sam gently pried Stella's hands from her head, took off his hat and placed it on her. He removed his jacket and placed it around her shoulders leaving himself vulnerable to a massive cockroach attack. And Stella knew. Sam Poole would slay dragons (or in his case, flying roaches) for her. If that wasn't true love, Stella didn't know what was.

Could it be that Sam and I owe the final validation of our love to the lowly cockroach?

Stella made a mental note to discuss this theory with Sam. If they lived long enough.

The crying had started up again outside the door. Stella looked down at the purse in her lap, and it came to her. The sobs belonged to Edna Oster, proprietor of the Biloxi Fashion Emporium!

What is she doing here? And where is Edgar Beche? Lying dead with three bullets in him? And who else is out there?

As if reading Stella's mind, Edna blew her nose and said, "I thought I killed you, Floyd."

Floyd Finger? He really is alive! And present in the hallway!

Stella's surprise morphed into relief as she heard Edgar Beche say, "Who are you people?"

Before anyone could answer, a South American voice demanded, "What is the meaning of so many people in my house?"

It seemed that Gilberto de Campos had finally arrived.

They all ignored him.

"But why? Why'd you do it, baby?" said Floyd, who sounded even more bewildered than Ed and Gilberto.

Has the man never heard of hell's fury and scorned women? wondered Stella.

"You broke my damn heart," sobbed Edna. "And don't call me baby, you …"

Carmen, who was no fool and knew to side with the person holding the gun, interrupted with, "The man eez a dog! A lying, dirty dog!"

"Hey, tone it down, sister," said Floyd.

"You are a dog and you know it is truth," said Carmen. "Tell them, Buck."

Buck is out there, too?

"Well, now …," Buck drawled, but he, too was interrupted.

By the sound of sirens. Blue lights began to bounce off the beams of the attic.

"Did you call the police?" Stella whispered from beneath Sam's jacket.

Sam swatted at a roach and croaked, "Yeah. I sent a text. If they don't get up here, I'm taking my chances with the gun. These roaches are everywhere!"

"I know. One just ran over my foot! If one gets up my pants leg, I'll have a stroke."

"Oh, God," moaned Sam. "I hadn't thought of that." He quickly stuffed his pants legs into his socks.

"Just remember, Sam. Roaches can't hurt you. Think of them as … as dragonflies."

Silence.

"What?" said Stella.

"I hate those, too."

Stella started to laugh.

Okay, now I'm officially hysterical.

"How do you feel about butterflies?" she asked him.

Stella's hysteria was evidently contagious because she heard Sam's chuckle in the darkness.

"They're all right," he said.

"Then try butterflies. That's what I'm doing."

Stella's visions of monarchs fluttering above her head were interrupted by hurried footsteps and yet another voice. Believe it or not, it was Marilee's.

"Edna, is that a gun?"

"Yeah," Edna sobbed. "I'm getting ready to kill Floyd."

"Well, I wouldn't blame you one bit if you shot him. Floyd, you know you deserve it. But honey, do you really want to spend the rest of your days in an orange jumpsuit?"

Edna sniffed in the ensuing silence as she thought this over.

Next, they heard Buck say, "You made the right decision, Edna. I'll take the gun."

"Let's get out of here," said Sam, helping Stella to her feet.

They hurried down the dark stairway to the door. Sam pushed it open.

"Oh, my God, I forgot about Stella and Sam," said Ed Beche.

The door swung open and there stood Ed and de Campos and Edna and Carmen and Buck and Marilee and Helen and Paula G. And Floyd Finger—as alive as the day he was born. Stella noticed that they were all dusted with varying amounts of plaster. She looked to the ceiling and sure enough, there were three holes where Edna had fired her warning shots.

But right now it was all Stella could do not to snatch Floyd the faux rep by his black shirt and shake him. Before she could put the big questions to Floyd, however, the group was joined by two of the Crescent City's finest. They had their service revolvers drawn and their serious cop faces on.

Per their instructions, Buck very carefully laid Edna's gun on the floor and stepped away from it. Which wasn't easy, it being so crowded in Chartier House's back hallway. When the officers asked for an explanation, they all looked at one another. No one knew where to begin. Floyd Finger, himself finally spoke up.

"It was all just a misunderstanding, sir. That lovely lady there with the cerulean eyes mistook me for a burglar instead of the man who's in love with her."

"Oh, Floyd," wailed Edna, who had to be getting dehydrated from her record sob-a-thon.

Carmen glared at Floyd.

"Why, you son of a—"

Surprisingly, it was Gilberto de Campos who calmed her down by saying something in Spanish that Stella could only guess at. He said it with a sly smile in a throaty voice. Carmen's eyebrows lifted pleasantly. She actually smiled at the South American and seemed to calm down.

Everyone else simply nodded in grateful, dumb agreement.

The cops verified that the legal owner of the property was indeed Gilberto de Campos, who wasn't pressing charges against anyone for anything. I mean does a dirty pot call a kettle black? When they learned the identity of Edgar C. Beche, one of the city's most prominent citizens, they talked football (the Saints) for a few minutes before bidding everyone good-evening and taking their leave.

43.

Apps at Edis

They all began talking at once, of course. Edgar Beche silenced them with a raised hand.

"All in good time," he said, taking his phone from a pocket. He made a series of quick calls. Then armed with the flashlight app on his phone, carefully led the gang through the dark house. As they filed out onto the front porch and finished making introductions, a van pulled up.

"Good evening, Mr. Beche," said the driver. "Where to?"

"My house, please."

Twenty minutes later, they were seated in the scrumptious paneled den of Edgar C. Beche holding drinks and New Orleans take-out, which consisted of shrimp and grits, fried oysters, asparagus with curry sauce and tiny, blue cheese biscuits. Ed insisted that no one speak of "tonight's strange events" until after they'd eaten.

When everyone had cleaned their hors d'oeuvre plates and used Ed's fabulous powder room with its lacquered walls, marble basin, aged brass wall spigots and Louis XV mirror, Ed freshened glasses and took his place as group moderator. He first addressed the gun-toting Edna who had stopped crying long enough to inhale a mountain of appetizers. She and Floyd now shared a leather loveseat while she sipped vodka and cranberry juice, and Floyd enjoyed a Budweiser.

"Ms. Oster, would you like to start?"

"Well, Mr. Beche," she said, dabbing at her mouth with an icy green linen cocktail napkin, "To begin with, I am a somewhat emotional person."

Somehow Ed kept a straight face.

"The night of the explosion, I went to the RV to have it out with Floyd. I heard him and that …" She looked at Carmen with hatred festering in those amazing eyes of hers. Ed, fearing a cat fight, raised a warning eyebrow and Edna rephrased. "I heard Floyd and Carmen going at it. Carmen said Floyd owed her money and had been unfaithful. She was taking the place apart. She shoved Floyd, and he went down like a sack of bricks."

Carmen proudly nodded in agreement. Floyd looked at the toes of his boots and shook his head at the memory.

"I was standing out in back of the RV. The wall is rusted clear through, and I could see the water heater. The gas was on and the pilot light had went out. I started smelling gas, but I was so heart broke I took off, left Floyd and Carmen to their fate."

"So it was you I heard you running around like a snake in the grass!" said Carmen. "That's why I left you, Floyd. I was afraid! I never smell the gas. I was on the other side of the parking lot when your leetle camper blew up. But I saw those nosy women in there." She turned to Stella. "You! Poking yourself into others' business!" The vein in Carmen's neck was starting its ominous pulsing. Her eyes bulged furiously.

Paula reached into her pocket, plucked out her phone and said, "Carmen, I'm calling 911."

Carmen scowled at Paula, but regained her composure and slumped petulantly in her chair. Paula slipped the phone back into her pocket.

Stella couldn't take it anymore. She stood up, threw her arms wide and said, "How did you get out of that RV, Floyd?"

"Well, when Carmen here shoved me, I took a lick on the back of my head. When I came to my senses, I smelled gas, but I figured Carmen might be waiting for me outside the door so I used my escape hatch."

Carmen started to object, but quieted when Floyd said, "Woman, you been writing me threatening letters, beating me up, what do you expect?"

So it was Carmen who'd written the note on the betting sheet, thought Stella.

"You have an escape hatch in your RV?" asked Buck.

"Right. Years ago I had a misunderstanding with some boys over in Bay St. Louis ... you know how it is. So I had a trap door installed in the floor of my RV. Just in case.

"When I came to that evening and smelled gas, I was laying right next to my escape hatch. I knew that thing would come in handy one day." He smiled and shook his head at the improbability of such good fortune. "Anyway, I just lifted it and rolled out. When I hit the night air, I got my strength back and took off toward the beach. I wasn't halfway there when the thing blew up. What with folks trying to kill me, it seemed in my best interest to let myself stay good and dead."

"Good grief," said Sam. "A trap door. It never occurred to any of us."

"Man, oh, man," said Buck.

Stella rummaged in her bag and found her phone. She showed Buck the picture of him and Carmen at the Beau Rivage.

"Why didn't you tell me you knew Carmen?"

"Because I didn't ... at least not until you asked me to take your case. He looked at the picture fondly. A smile played at the corners of his mouth. "When this was taken, I was performing a little undercover work."

Still wearing the smile, he winked at Carmen. Carmen shrugged and began inspecting her fingernails.

"What I'd like to know," said Sam, "is how you all ended up in the upstairs hall of Chartier House."

"Yes," said de Campos. "How does this happen?"

Silence fell over the group who were all looking at one another for answers.

"I think I know part of it," said Buck. "Carmen, you heard rumors that Floyd was in New Orleans and talked to Mr. Brown, the street car conductor, didn't you? He told you where he'd sent me. And you followed the trail. All the way to Chartier House."

She didn't answer, and they all took that for a yes.

"When Floyd and I got inside," said Buck, "we heard voices upstairs and found Mr. Beche in the hall. Carmen followed us."

He turned to Edna. "And you followed Carmen, right?"

Edna shot the snake eye at Carmen. "Yes, I followed that—"

But Ed Beche cleared his throat authoritatively, and Edna straightened up.

Sam turned to Helen. "What about you three? How did you end up here?"

"When we saw that picture of Buck and Carmen and couldn't get in touch with Stella, we hopped in the car and came directly here. Sorry, Sam, but it looked to us like you and Buck were hiding something. We took a chance that y'all were still at Chartier House."

Buck clasped his hands together. "I guess that's a wrap," he said. "Mr. Beche, thank you for your hospitality."

Stella got the impression that Buck preferred to keep any further details of his part in this little drama to himself. She didn't press him, but sooner rather than later she was going to get every last detail out of him.

"Not so fast," said Marilee. She hopped to her feet and walked over to Floyd where she stood with her hands on her hips. She leaned in close to his face.

"Floyd, do you know the trouble you have caused? My friend, here …" She motioned to Stella. "… was so worried about you being murdered and it going unsolved that she has employed a private detective and put her own safety, not to mention her love life, in peril to find justice for you. And this is after you stole from us!"

Floyd looked back at his boots and shook his head sadly. "I have much to atone for. All you ladies have suffered mightily because of me. But I swear I am a changed man." He raised his right hand and looked up into Marilee's eyes with intense sincerity. "And I don't mind telling you almost getting blown to smithereens was one heck of a eye-opener. Floyd Fouche… uh, Finger is a changed man." He nodded for emphasis. "I'm going straight. And if she'll have me, I'm doing it with the lovely Miss Edna Oster."

This, of course, started Edna sniffling again.

"I hope you're telling the truth, Floyd," said Marilee, "Because if I hear of you stepping one toe out of line, I will personally see that you get what you deserve."

They all knew she wasn't kidding.

"One more thing," said Stella. "What happened to the cats?"

"Cats?" the group murmured.

"Oh! The mama kitty and her kittens," said Floyd. "As far as I know they're chasing mice at Peggy's Hair Affair in Mobile. I found 'em a good home before the RV—" He looked at Edna and left the thought unfinished.

Ed called cabs for everyone. Helen, Marilee and Paula decided they deserved a luxurious night at the Windsor Court Hotel in the French Quarter. Floyd, Edna and Buck made a beeline to Bourbon Street. de Campos and Carmen shared a cab, but their destination remains unknown.

Stella and Sam went directly to the Hotel Delphine where a bottle of Veuve Clicquot awaited them in their suite. A card on the tray read, *Thank you for the most interesting evening I've had in years!* It was signed, *Ed*.

I'd like to tell you Sam and Stella enjoyed the champagne, but the truth is when dawn streamed in through the French doors of their bedroom the next morning, the champagne floated unopened in its bucket.

When Stella opened her eyes, she wondered where she was, why she felt warmer and more satisfied than she could ever remember. Then Sam pulled her to him and nuzzled her neck and kissed her hair.

"Did I mention that I'm in love with you?" he said.

"Yes, you did. Several times." Stella snuggled into him and well, you know the rest.

44.

Clarification over Coffee

When the couple emerged from their suite, they wore the unmistakable look of new lovers. An adoring twinkle filled Sam's eyes whenever he looked at Stella, amazed that this enchanting woman had given herself to him. And with such enthusiasm! Vignettes from their previous night kept popping into his brain, and he would realize he was grinning like an idiot. But when he looked at Stella to see if she had noticed, she was smiling, too.

The aura of just-requited love was one the staff at the tres romantique Hotel Delphine knew well, of course. But when a lovely, mature couple like Sam Poole and Stella Gray recaptured the glow of first love, even the veteran concierge who'd been at his desk since midnight had to smile, his appreciation of the power of love and the marvel of romance reinvigorated.

When Sam and Stella emerged, the air itself—a gentle sixty-two degrees—seemed to confirm their good fortune. The sun was warm and the sky blue. There was even a hint of fall color in the crepe myrtles and popcorn trees. It was the kind of November morning that almost makes up for the city's sauna-like days of August.

"Another beautiful day!" said Sam. "You up for beignets and coffee?"

"Always," said Stella.

"I still owe you a meal at Galatoire's," said Sam.

"How about we split an order of beignets and have a late lunch at Galatoire's?" suggested Stella. "Do we have time before you have to be back?"

"Absolutely." He grinned at Stella. "Get in the truck, woman. I'm starving."

Café Du Monde was a mélange of tourists, locals, bustling waiters and the irresistible smell of coffee and fried pastries. They grabbed a table near the sidewalk and minutes later were sipping café au lait and biting into the French Market's famous sugar-dusted beignets.

As Stella scanned the crowd, a man at a nearby table lowered his newspaper.

"Look, Sam. It's Buck. I know we agreed not to talk about Floyd until after breakfast," she said, "But I think we should ask Buck to join us. I'm dying to know... well, everything."

Sam caught his cousin's eye and motioned him over.

Buck dropped his paper on the table, picked up his coffee and chair and sauntered over to Sam and Stella.

"Morning," he said.

"Morning," said Stella. "Have a beignet?"

"Had my fill, thanks."

"So, Buck," said Sam. "Why don't I order some more coffee, and you can tell us how in the heck you got Floyd Finger to Prytania Street yesterday."

Sam signaled to their server, and Buck began.

"You remember the last time we spoke I was on my way to meet an acquaintance of Mr. Brown, the streetcar conductor, in the hope he'd lead me to Finger."

Sam and Stella nodded.

"This guy did indeed point me to the elusive Mr. Finger. The short version is once I'd verified his whereabouts I befriended a pretty redhead named Amber who happens to be employed by the Garden District Haunted Bicycle Tour, LLC. I did her a quick favor ... got a picture of her boyfriend and well, that's another story for another day. Anyway, two hours later Amber, per my instructions, accidentally on purpose bumps into Finger and chats him up. She turns the conversation to employment, and Floyd admits he's out of work. She tells him there might be an opening as a tour guide, exaggerates the pay and offers to personally show him a bit of the bicycle tour route. Also as instructed by me, she takes him immediately to

Chartier House."

Buck stopped long enough to empty two packets of sugar into his coffee and chicory. He took a sip, reconsidered Stella's offer of a beignet, and took a bite out of the pastry. Powdered sugar showered his shirt and pants, but he didn't seem to notice and finally, continued his tale.

"I tried to time the thing so that it would take place while y'all were at Chartier House. I wanted Stella to see Floyd in the flesh, you know. So to pick up the story, yours truly happens by, Amber takes off, and I impress upon Mr. Finger the futility of him attempting to remain deceased. After applying a small amount of pressure, Floyd agrees to accompany me inside. That's where we met Mr. Beche. I didn't offer these details last night because I promised the lovely Amber I would keep her name and that of the haunted bike tour out of it. And Buck Early keeps his promises. Right, Sam?"

Sam nodded.

"Little did I know but Miss Edna Oster has come to the realization that Floyd is still among the living. Then I get a call from one of my associates in Biloxi … she's been keeping an eye on the Fashion Emporium for me. It turns out that Carmen paid a recent visit to the Emporium, insulted Edna, told her she was meeting Floyd in New Orleans, even told her all kinds of bull about how Floyd made fun of Edna. I knew enough about Finger to know that wasn't true. I mean the guy has his standards. They're pretty low, but still …

"So insecure Edna, she believes the lies, gets emotional … no surprise there … closes up the store, packs her gun in her purse and follows Carmen to New Orleans intent on killing Floyd. And Carmen, too, for all I know. They both end up at Chartier House. And then that de Campos guy shows up." He shook his head and pressed his thin lips together. "Don't know how I missed those two women tailing me. Just goes to show…"

He didn't finish the thought, and Sam and Stella didn't ask. Buck resumed his story.

"Okay, so we all follow one another upstairs. About this time Edna whips a gun out of her purse. Carmen pushes Edna into the door and starts screaming … mostly in Spanish. God only knows what she's saying, but it ain't, 'Hi Edna, nice to see you.' Edna gets to her feet still holding the gun. On all of us."

Buck looked questioningly at the remaining Beignet and, not wanting to interrupt his narrative, Stella simply nodded in the affirmative. He finished off the beignet in a cloud of powdered sugar, which he washed down with a gulp of coffee.

"Where was I? Oh, yeah. Edna's holding the gun on us. "About this time Carmen starts to tear into Floyd. I swear that woman has a death wish … and Edna starts shooting. Luckily she doesn't have it in her to actually kill someone, so she fires into the ceiling."

"Of course, she could have killed us," said Sam.

"It didn't occur to her that anyone would be in the attic," said Buck. "A hell-bent woman does not think too clear, you know. The next thing we know, Stella's buddies show up."

"I can't believe all those people ended up there at the same time," said Stella.

Buck looked off across Decatur Street toward Jackson Square and shook his head. "I have to admit, I didn't see that cluster… uh, that dust-up coming. But I pegged Edna for the attempted murder of Finger after my first visit to the Fashion Emporium. I'd narrowed it down to either Carmen or her. It seemed too premeditated for the likes of Carmen.

"Why didn't you tell me, Buck?" said Stella.

"I had no proof. And you're so darned butt-headed, I thought you might get yourself more involved. Besides, my main objective was to keep you out of harm's way. I promised Sam, here."

"And you always keep your promises," said Stella.

"Right," said Buck. "That's one reason I couldn't accept payment from you. I was reporting to Sam. Wouldn't've been ethical in my book."

"So Sam knew what was going on the whole time?"

"Pretty much," said Buck. Might seem chauvinistic and all that, but we wanted to protect you. You were way over your head in this thing."

Buck took out his wallet, threw some bills on the table and said, "What do you say we walk off the sugar? Folks are waiting on this table."

They crossed Decatur and headed down St. Ann alongside the square where artists sat working at their easels or talking to potential customers. Buck took up his tale.

"Edna had managed the Paradise RV Park over in Pascagoula where she met Floyd. She knew the ins and outs of RV's and the propane tanks that run the appliances, hot water, and all that. She had the means, the opportunity and the motive. Floyd did her real bad. And let's face it, she's insecure and unstable." He shook his head. "Man, I've never seen a woman could cry that much."

"What about Carmen?" said Stella. "I thought for sure, with that temper of hers, she did it."

"She was a contender, all right," agreed Buck. "But like I said, it's not her style. If Carmen kills anybody, it's gonna be with her own two hands. In the heat of passion. She's a very passionate woman." He looked at Sam, and some kind of man-to-man signal passed between them.

The threesome was now halfway around the square, the center of which is the famed St. Louis Cathedral. They silently reflected on the outlandish details they'd heard as they followed Buck's lead into Pirate's Alley. At the end of the alley William Faulkner once called home, they turned left on Royal and headed up St. Peters back toward the river.

"Okay, we know Edna followed Carmen to Chartier House, but how did Carmen know to contact the street car conductor?" asked Sam.

"Like Edna, Carmen was obsessed with finding Finger. Carmen's crazy, but she's smart and she's cagey. She just hit all of Floyd's old haunts and kept her ear to the ground, same as me. I have to admit I underestimated her. During my... uh, undercover project with her, there was quite a lot of rum involved." He smiled at the memory, but had the decency to look somewhat apologetic. "I may have let a bit too much information slip."

"Good grief, Buck," said Sam.

"I know, I know. But let's move on. Carmen evidently tailed me here and scared the you-know-what out of sweet, little Amber who told her that Floyd and I were at Chartier House. Edna followed Carmen.

After the initial ruckus settles down, your friends show up, Marilee talks Edna off the ledge, so to speak, and you know the rest." Buck scratched his head. "What I didn't figure was that Edna didn't attempt a premeditated murder after all. She just walked away and let the faulty gas valve do its thing. And I have to admit, the idea of a trap door never entered my mind."

"Wow." Stella shook her head, digesting the strange facts surrounding Floyd Finger. "I just don't see how a man like Floyd can drive women to such … such insanity," she said.

"The guy's got a way with the ladies. I'll give him that," said Buck. "Of course, the women he chooses to involve himself with are near certifiable in the first place. That's part of it. And Finger … well, he's got a thing for adrenaline."

Stella sighed. "Do you think he'll change his ways?" she asked the men.

"I'd rather put my money on a rigged Roulette wheel," said Buck. "But who knows? Miracles happen every day. Now I hate to leave good company, but I've got an appointment." He smiled at Sam. "Seems Amber from the haunted bike tour has further need of my services."

"Wait, Buck," said Stella. "I don't know how to thank you. I want to reimburse you for …"

"Now don't start all that. Like I said before, I wouldn't feel right about a monetary compensation. But I will make you a deal. I won't take up decorating houses if you promise not to do any more detective work. Both could be dangerous."

Stella had to laugh. "You've got a deal," she said.

She and Sam spent the next couple of hours wandering. They drove to the National World War II Museum, then to Magazine Street to shop for thank-you gifts for Marilee, Helen and Paula. As she explained to Sam, it was the least she could do. After all, the brave threesome had dropped everything and come to her aid at great peril—not to mention they took a chance on losing the lease on the former Oh, Baby! boutique. Sam wasn't so sure about the boutique part, but he had to agree a show of gratitude in the form of mementoes from New Orleans was a good idea.

They found a parking space near Stella's preferred shops. He took her hand to help her navigate the root-cracked pavement and didn't let it go. They set off down the sunny sidewalk of Magazine Street. A case of wine, one small oil painting, four loaves of bread and three lovely linen scarves later they'd worked up an appetite and returned to the French Quarter.

They headed to Bourbon Street where they found themselves at that grand, old-line bistro, Galatoire's, where it is said that lunch is always a party. The restaurant's brass chandeliers, tiled floors, linen-covered tables and mirror-lined walls give it an ambience almost as marvelous as the food.

Sam and Stella began their long-awaited feast with a glass of good white wine and a toast to their good fortune. The waiter, a convivial Cajun who helped with their selections, soon arrived with turtle soup, fish meuniere amandine and, of course, lots of French bread. The outstanding meal was finished off with dessert of crepes maison and strong coffee.

"It will take me a month to run off this meal," laughed Stella.

"Aw, you gotta splurge once in a while," said Sam as he signed the check. "Besides, you deserve it. You solved the mysterious case of Floyd Finger." He pushed his chair back. "You ready to get back to reality?"

"I can't wait to get back to reality," said Stella. "But there are still a few questions."

Sam groaned. "Like what?" he asked as they left the restaurant.

"There is still the matter of the ghosts at Chartier House."

"And the mystery of whether you'll take the job," said Sam.

"That, too," agreed Stella.

But, as we know, Stella is quite the procrastinator. She decided she'd think about that tomorrow.

45.

Cheers, Y'all!

While their northern counterparts celebrate December in boots and sweaters with cocoa in front of the fire, coastal inhabitants spend much of the holiday season languishing in cloudy humidity. This warm, decidedly un-festive weather is interspersed with brief periods of dazzling, cold days that would be described as fall in cooler climes. Despite these hints of real winter, Stella grew up thinking that if it weren't for Christmas, December in Bayview would be remembered for little more than wet, brown leaves.

Visions of Washington all done up in white filled her head as she'd slogged through a week of sultry, sweaty weather. Families in shorts roamed Christmas tree lots. Attendants perspired as they heaved spruce and balsam and pine onto car roofs. In an attempt to boost her holiday spirits, Stella set the air-conditioning on low, turned on the carols and addressed Christmas cards.

But before you could say humbug, the jet stream had a change of heart, delivering a shot of polar air all the way to the Gulf of Mexico. Smoke began to curl from chimneys. Stella's neighbors threw on sweaters and headed outside, humming Christmas tunes with great enthusiasm. Though the air was downright frosty, Stella threw open her windows, welcoming the rush of cold with as much excitement as she'd once greeted D.C.'s first snowfalls.

As she stood at her kitchen sink, wearing her new boots and washing lettuce, the notes to Old MacDonald floated in through the window. It seemed that Sam and Elliot were also soaking up the seasonal air as they sang together on Sam's patio.

When it came time to name an animal Sam abruptly stopped strumming and singing, leaving it up to Elliot to fill in the musical blank. Elliot, high on Christmas and cold air, called out chicken or duck or whatever as loud as he could.

Every now and then he would yell, "giraffe" or "alligator," and Sam would stop playing. "What?" Sam would respond in feigned shock. "What kind of farm has alligators?"

"A alligator farm!" yelled Elliot, laughing so hard he could hardly speak.

Stella stuffed the prepared lettuce into a bag and realized she was laughing, too. She gathered green onions, just-picked satsumas and glazed pecans into containers and grabbed a jar of salad dressing made with Tutta's cider vinegar. Minutes later the doorbell rang.

Sam stood on her porch holding a bottle of wine. Elliot was crouched behind the boxwood.

"Where is Elliot?" said Stella, at which point he jumped up and yelled, "Boo!"

Stella feigned a fright, Sam shook his head, and the threesome set off to Tutta's house.

Though Andrew had accompanied her from Washington to Bayview only once, Stella rarely missed this annual event where she joined her sisters and their families to trim the Grays' tree, drink milk punch and laugh at a lifetime of homemade ornaments and holiday disaster stories—like the time Bo's lab jumped on the dining room table and ate Tutta's standing rib roast. All this was enjoyed to the background of Tutta's favorite holiday cd, the Johnny Mathis Christmas album.

"Merry Chrithmas, everybody!" Elliot called as they entered Tutta's living room.

"It looks like Elliot is getting his two front teeth for Christmas," Stella whispered to Sam.

"Yeah, and you were right. He's starting to lose the lisp."

Bo Gray took up his usual station on the patio where he grilled chicken. Whenever the kids or Johnny Mathis became more fun than he could stand, he'd take his bourbon and water out to "check the meat." Sam and Stella's brothers-in-law, Dave and Doc likewise wandered to and from the patio, talking football and tractors and other manly concerns with Stella's dad.

The men took an instant liking to Sam, though to be truthful, he owed much of their acceptance to Andrew who'd spent most of his one Christmas visit to Bayview smoothing his hair, checking his phone and looking at his Rolex. Sam, on the other hand, was into farm equipment (he had a vintage John Deere up at Sitaspel), hunting (he'd killed that twelve-point buck at the tender age of ten, remember) and football (huge Alabama fan, he could recall almost all of Bo's winning field goals).

Doc had a cabin just north of Scratch Ankle, so he and Sam got into the who do you know that I know up the country conversation. By the time that was exhausted, they'd discovered a dozen mutual acquaintances and one distant relative in common.

By the time the succulent chicken, crisp salad (compliments of Stella) and Ann Olive's rice and tomato casserole had been consumed, everyone was stuffed.

Bo took the littlest granddaughter on his lap and said, "I could take another bite, but I don't believe I could swallow it."

Alice made a liar out of him by passing Tutta's lemon squares, which were his favorite. He ate three.

Tutta looked at the tree and smiled at the children. "Beautiful! Just beautiful!" she exclaimed.

Actually, it looked terrible. All of the ornaments were bunched at the bottom. Icicles hung in shiny clumps. Garlands trailed the floor, lacking any sense of symmetry.

Over the next weeks, however, the tree would slowly transform from unsightly duckling to Christmas swan as Tutta straightened and rearranged a little each day. This way the grandchildren wouldn't notice she'd made improvements to their handiwork. Yet as Christmas grew closer the tree grew lovelier—before their very eyes, it seemed. It was the Gray family's version of a Christmas miracle.

Elliot passed out well before Sam turned into Whimsy Court. Once he was snug in his bed, his prized Spongebob figure in his fist, Sam built a fire. He handed Stella a glass of wine, and they settled into his leather sofa.

"I've got some news," said Stella.

"Good or bad?" asked Sam.

"Umm, a little of both, I guess. I talked to Ed Beche today. He's gotten to the bottom of the ghosties at Chartier House."

"No kidding. So what is it? Swamp gas? Air in the pipes? Bats in the rafters?"

"None of the above, believe it or not."

"Don't tell me it's really haunted."

Stella laughed. "No. We don't believe in ghosts, remember."

"Oh, yeah. Okay, so what is it?"

"It turns out that the owner of the Haunted Bike Tour is a very resourceful guy named Bobby Beaudreau whose old auntie lives next door to Chartier House. Auntie Beaudreau shared Bernard's and Elnora's sordid history of murder and mayhem with her nephew. The nephew…"

"Bobby Boudreau, who owns the Haunted Bike Tour," said Sam for clarification.

"Right. Bobby figured the story and the house were suitably spooky for the bike tour. He then simply slipped through his auntie's courtyard gate and entered Chartier House through an unlocked window.

"Every now and then … just enough to keep the rumors of sho-nuff hants going … he'd flash a picture of Elnora in an upstairs window and/or moan like the dying Bernard."

"I can't believe anyone would fall for that corny stuff."

"I know. But the tourists were paying to be scared, and Chartier House is pretty spooky after the sun goes down. Bobby also had lurid flyers depicting the grisly deaths of Bernard and Elnora, which he handed out to the cyclists. And they started and ended the tour with cocktails, remember.

"Anyway, once Beche had access to the house and chatted up Auntie Boudreau next door, he figured it out. He hid in the house for a couple of nights during the time of the tour, and sure enough eventually caught Bobby frauding his customers with the fake ghost act."

"So you're taking the job?"

"Well … no. That's the bad news."

"Because of de Campos?"

"Yes. I just don't trust him. I'm done with sketchy relationships of any kind."

"Including Andrew?"

"Yes. Andrew tops the list."

"You made the right decision." Sam shook his head. "You can't involve yourself with people you don't trust. Unfortunately, I speak from experience. Sorry about Beche, though. I know how much you wanted to work with him."

"I am working with him. That's the good news. He's bought a house in Seaside. It was one of the first ones built down there and has been on the rental market for years, so it's in need of a complete redo." She sighed. "It's not Chartier House, but it is Edgar Beche. And it is Seaside, which happens to be one of my favorite places. It'll be fun. And best of all, uncomplicated."

"No ghosts? No shady money men?"

"Not a one. Beche is drafting the plans and working on the landscape design, but wants my input. On everything. And he wants me to furnish it with a very generous budget."

"That's great. And Stella, you deserve every bit of it."

"Thanks. I feel good about it. You know what Beche said? He said, 'I like your style, kiddo.'" Stella wiped a tear away.

"He sounded just like Gris. Just like him." She hesitated, then added, "You know, for a second or two…"

"You thought maybe it was him?"

"It's silly, but yes. It was like Gris telling me I'm finally in the right place."

"He didn't happen to mention anything about your next door neighbor, did he?"

Stella looked at Sam expecting to see the teasing grin, but he wasn't smiling. He searched her eyes as if trying to read her thoughts there. She had never seen him look so earnest.

"I love you, Stella." He took her hand in his. "I love you very much. And in every way. I love you like a friend. I love how you are with Elliot. I love your honesty." Finally that heart-melting smile spread across his face. "And man, do I love making love with you. I guess what I'm trying to say is you're the one, Stella."

She threw her arms around his neck. "Oh, Sam, I love you, too!"

She pulled back and looked into his eyes. "Does this mean you want to …?"

"Yeah. It definitely does. I want to marry you, Stella. I want to grow old with you. I want to see your face the last thing at night and the first thing every morning.

"Oh, Sam …"

"What do you say, Stella? Will you marry me?"

"Yes! Yes, of course, I want to marry you!"

"Good. Because I got this just in case."

He took a small box from his pocket, opened it and took out a square-cut diamond set in platinum. He slipped it on Stella's finger. It was so beautiful, that Stella couldn't speak.

"I hope those are tears of joy," said Sam.

"They are. Because it's perfect," she said. "Absolutely the most perfectly beautiful thing I've ever seen."

She wasn't looking at the diamond sparkling away on her finger, however. She was looking at Sam Poole.

46.

A New Chapter

When people in their forties and fifties fall in love, it's rarely a simple thing. The fact that they're available implies prior relationships that didn't pan out—sometimes quite spectacularly. This naturally results in a level of weariness and wariness young people don't even recognize. Some think they do, but they don't.

In addition to the instability brought on by falling in love, the more mature among us are also grappling with that stage of life known as middle age. Which is second only to puberty in its ability to create chaos. Most of these seasoned life vets think they know what to expect, but like the younger versions of themselves, they really don't.

To further complicate things, by this time in their lives, they have narrowed their career choices, put down roots and most likely procreated. There is nothing short of true love that would induce a pair of good, rational people to attempt to sort through this pile of mismatched baggage.

Between them, Sam and Stella owned two rather small houses on Whimsy Court and a half-renovated duplex on Park Boulevard in Bayview, a condo in Washington, D.C., one ex-wife, one little boy and an English spaniel. Stella had grown to love Elliot, didn't care where she lived as long as it was with Sam and had resigned herself to having Sam's ex (who in the spectrum of exes wasn't half-bad) in her life forever. She was also settling, more or less, into the limbo-esque state of step-parenting.

Sam loved Elliot and Stella more each day and didn't care where he lived as long as Stella and Elliot were happy. He had long ago reconciled himself to having Jennifer in his life forever. He had to admit she was a good mom, and that, after all, was the main thing.

Elliot had grown to love Stella. He could even say her name since his front teeth were coming in nicely. Stella's big family had coaxed him out of his shell, and he and Thomas already referred to one another as cousins. He loved Whimsy Court, and wanted to stay there. His main concern was some sort of water feature for the SpongeBob crowd.

By accepting the realities of their situation, Stella and Sam had made impressive strides in handling the baggage. However, the question remained: Where to put it?

The answer came one warmish January evening as they were having drinks with Ruth and Al Brinkly at number thirteen. The Brinklys announced that they were moving to Birmingham to be near their daughter.

"So many emotions!" said Ruth. "We hate to leave Whimsy. And the thought of strangers living in number thirteen …"

"But the house is getting to be too much for us," said Al.

"And we'll be near our children and grandchildren in Birmingham," said Ruth.

"Moving is a pain in the patootie," said Al.

"All those prospective buyers tromping through our home," said Ruth. "We're not looking forward to that."

Sam and Stella looked at one another.

"Are you thinking what I'm thinking," said Sam.

"I think so," said Stella.

Al winked at Ruth. Ruth smiled and nodded knowingly.

And so it was that Sam and Stella sold numbers two and four and bought number thirteen. It was the perfect size. There was an ideal spot in the large back garden for a water feature just like the one Stella left behind at number two. The SpongeBob crew would love it. Nearby, a low branch was just right for a set of romantic wind chimes. A lovely brick wall encompassed the entire back yard. This was a plus for Babe, Sam's English Spaniel and Toots, Stella's new labradoodle pup who were slowly but surely learning to coexist.

Toward the end of April, Stella and Sam were married. Stella was resplendent in a fitted, lace gown and Ann Olive's veil (Ann Olive insisted). Bo Gray walked his favorite daughter down the aisle and was so overcome with emotion that a couple of tears trickled down his face. On top of that, he was so happy he didn't care who witnessed this rare display. Elliot and Stella's nephew, Thomas sat on either side of Bo and were very well-behaved. Ann Olive and Alice wore pale green silk and served their sister as matrons of honor.

Buck served as best man and was downright dapper in a new seersucker suit. Unfortunately, he wore his signature belt buckle. You know—the one with his nickname spelled out in little deer antlers.

Kitty and Pup were there in matching outfits. Surprisingly they each sported one of Pup's "voodoo" scarves. Kitty was hesitant at first, but she looked so darn good in the thing she just had to wear it.

Marilee and her family were all in attendance (even though the guys had tickets to the wrestling championships in Oklahoma City). Edgar Beche and Paula G, whose business venture with Marilee was still going strong, attended even though they didn't know most of the crowd. Thanks to their outgoing personalities, they quickly made friends with everyone. Helen and her husband, Sandy were there, of course. Due to her continued exercise and sensible eating regimens, Helen looked particularly svelte in a size twelve navy ensemble.

As the sun set on Bayview, Alabama, a small, but exquisite reception followed in the back garden of number thirteen. Tutta baked the wedding cake—five layers of vanilla cake filled with lemon curd and smothered in lemon buttercreme. The Bayview Register even ran a picture of Tutta next to her creation in its Bayview Life section. The caption above the color photo read, Tutta Gray's tower of confection perfection.

Helen, who, if you remember, is the director of Bayview's botanical gardens oversaw the flowers.

Varying shades of white and green with touches of the palest yellow turned number thirteen's back yard from good to glorious. Bayview brides are still copying those arrangements.

Ruth and Al Brinkly teared up when they saw it. Mostly because they were finally free of its maintenance, but no one knew this.

The newlyweds spent the first two weeks of their married life in Italy where the weather was good, the atmosphere molto romantico and the architecture … Well, what can I say? It was Italy.

By the time Stella was through with Beche's house in Seaside, the place was breathtaking. The interior and exterior flowed together as seamlessly as the expanse of turquoise gulf beyond its porches. A bit of D.C. sophistication rescued it from over-beachiness.

One article mentioned that it evoked the romanticism of an Italian villa. And of course it possessed that indefinable something—Stella Gray's magical touch. Beche named his house Sea la Vie which everybody thought was quite catchy. Sea la Vie graced all the good magazines and cemented not only the working relationship but the friendship between Stella and Sam Poole and Edgar Beche.

On a particularly lovely summer evening as the sun made its spectacular descent, turning the gulf silver and pink, Edgar handed Sam and Stella a drink. He looked around him and smiled at the beauty.

"Stella, I can't thank you enough," he said for the millionth time. "It's not at all what I expected. Yet I love it!"

Sam turned to his wife. "And I never expected to be married again." He kissed Stella's cheek. "But you know what, I love it." A slow smile spread across his face. Ms. Poole, I believe I have figured out the key to your success."

"And what might that be, Mr. Poole?"

"You've managed to give us all what we never knew we wanted."

• • •

Margaret P. Cunningham

Author photo by Chelsea Francis Photography.
ChelseaFrancisPhotography.com

Margaret P. Cunningham's short
stories have won several national
contests and appeared in magazines
and anthologies including eight
Chicken Soup for the Soul books. She
grew up on her father's nursery in
Mobile, Alabama, where she lives with

her husband,
Tom. She enjoys
writing, reading,
gardening and
"beaching it"
with her friends
and family. Also
by this author: